"Are you flirting with me, my lord?"

Duncan's countenance took on a hunger she could not misinterpret.

"After what has transpired between us, I am not flirting."

Jenna dropped her gaze and increased the movement of her fan. "You are bold."

"I am entranced."

She did not know what to say. She had agonized that he would ignore her completely. Now she worried that what he spoke would lead them into something they would both regret. But regardless of what lay between them, she wanted to be with him....

* * *

Her Rebel Lord
Harlequin® Historical #225—December 2007

GEORGINA DEVON

has a bachelor of arts degree in social sciences with a concentration in history. Her interest in England began when she lived in East Anglia as a child and later as an adult. She met her husband in England, and her wedding ring set is from Bath. She has many romantic and happy memories of the land. Today she lives in Tucson, Arizona, with her husband, two dogs, an inherited cat and a cockatiel. Her daughter has left the nest and does Web site design, including Georgina's. Contact her at www.georginadevon.com.

Her Rebel Lord
GEORGINA DEVON

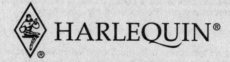

HARLEQUIN®

TORONTO • NEW YORK • LONDON
AMSTERDAM • PARIS • SYDNEY • HAMBURG
STOCKHOLM • ATHENS • TOKYO • MILAN • MADRID
PRAGUE • WARSAW • BUDAPEST • AUCKLAND

ISBN-13: 978-0-373-30534-6
ISBN-10:   0-373-30534-6

HER REBEL LORD

www.eHarlequin.com

Printed in U.S.A.

Chapter One

1746 De Warre Castle, near Carlisle and the Scottish Border

Crash!

Jenna de Warre jumped back from the glass bottle that had just violently hit the floor of her stillroom. One second the pieces of glass were in focus and the next they blurred. She was so nearsighted. 'Twas that which had caused the accident in the first place. She had been reaching for a different bottle and her arm had brushed the one that fell. She took a deep breath and put the frustration from her.

She blinked rapidly and pushed her spectacles up the bridge of her nose. The glass shards came into focus. Irritated with her clumsiness, she bent and whisked the pieces into a dustpan and tossed them into the bin under the work bench.

She stood up and knuckled her lower back. The day had been long and promised to be longer still. Mistress James was due to deliver her fifth child at any time. And she had still to prepare the draught for the mother-to-be that would help ease the birthing pains.

She took a deep breath of the cold air. Winter was the worst time of year to work in her stillroom. Even with a roaring fire and her fingerless wool gloves, her hands were clumsy from cold. Normally she didn't come here at night, but she had been fretful from idleness and this occupied her. She doubted the babe would come tonight.

The creak of door hinges startled her, although she felt no real fear. They were too far from town for anyone to be here who did not belong or know their way. Still, it was late for someone to be seeking her. Eyes wide, peering over the rim of her spectacles, she wondered who was using the only door that opened onto the outside at this time of night.

'Jenna?' a male voice whispered, a strong Scottish burr making her name nearly unrecognisable.

'Gavin?' Her cousin stepped into the room, and joy widened her full mouth into a grin. 'Is that truly you?' She set down the pestle and rushed around the table, arms wide to hug him.

'Shh,' he said, slipping inside with a furtive glance behind. 'No one should know I'm here.'

Puzzled, she fell back. He shot the bolt in the door before moving to the entrance that led into the castle and locking that as well.

'What is wrong?' Apprehension crawled down her back. 'You look awful.'

He smiled wryly. 'Leave it to you to point out the obvious.' The smile died, leaving his long, narrow face haggard and pale. 'I've been better.'

He sank with heavy relief on to the only stool. His

thick grey cape pooled on the floor, the hem wet and laced with mud. His scuffed and filthy riding boots left prints on the stone pavers. He looked like he was travelling fast and without comforts.

Her disquiet intensified. To keep herself from blurting out questions before he was ready, she poured out a generous portion of whisky, which she kept for medicinal purposes, and took it to him. He downed the liquor in one long swallow as she knelt before him.

'Thank you. I needed that.'

She smiled up at him, took the empty glass and set it on the floor. She caught his heavily gloved hands in hers, but said nothing, waiting patiently for him to explain. She had learned as a child that Gavin could sometimes be led, but he could never be pushed.

He was tall and as lean as a sapling. Hair the colour of mahogany waved around high cheekbones, so much like her own but without the freckles that were the bane of her existence. There were days she refused to look in the mirror because she did not want to see the dirt-red spots. His nose was a long hook, while hers was just short of one.

Bright green eyes, dulled by exhaustion and a narrow-lipped mouth drained of colour told her he was on the last dregs of his energy. Her heart ached for him.

If only he hadn't fought for Bonnie Prince Charlie.

His ruddy complexion returned slowly as the whisky burned its way through his body. 'I need yer help, Jen.'

The haunted look in his eyes reminded her of the day he'd fled to her from the bloody field of Culloden. He had been lucky to escape. Many Scots who had fought for the Stuart Prince had not been so fortunate. Her stomach knotted.

'You know I will do everything I can.'

'Aye, that you will.' He swallowed hard, the action bobbing his Adam's apple and accentuating his thinness. His gaze skittered away from hers, only to return. 'I need money, Jen. Lots of it.'

Now it was her turn to gulp as she shook her head helplessly. 'I have none, Gavin. Only my jewellery.'

'That will do,' he said. 'Have ye any more drink?'

Her gaze narrowed as she looked him over. Rare among his peers, Gavin was not a drinker. 'Some.'

He smiled, but she could tell it was an effort. 'Will ye no' give me more?' His burr was pronounced, a habit he had when things were not going well.

She rose and poured another generous portion. 'What is wrong?'

He took the full glass and downed the contents before answering. 'The redcoats caught me two weeks ago. I managed to escape their filthy prison. I am fleeing to France.'

Worry and fear made her stomach cramp. 'You are lucky. Why did you not send word? Father would have tried to get you released.'

His mouth twisted. 'Aye, that would have been ironic. Bloody Ayre asking that a Scottish Jacobite be freed.'

She paled at Gavin's use of the name given to her father by the Scottish. Her sense of desolation was made worse by knowing that the name was earned, and Papa would never be free of the stain it cast.

During the first Jacobite uprising, Papa had been a young army lieutenant, eager for promotion and confident in his support of George I. At the orders of his commanding officer, he had led his troops in the massacre of an entire Highland village. Her mother, the youngest daughter of a Scottish laird, had fallen in love with the young English soldier the year before. Against her parents' orders, she had married Julian de Warre, who was later made Viscount Ayre by the English king for his actions.

Jenna's mother had died ten years later, worn out by grief over what her husband had done. To this day, Papa regretted his actions and regretted even more the loss of his wife because of what he had done.

'They might have let you go because of Papa,' Jenna finally said.

'Aye, I know, Jen. But I could not do it.' Silently he held out the glass, a wince drawing a line between his brows.

Frowning, she filled the glass and handed it back. 'Are you hurt?'

His eyes met hers over the glass rim. 'Only a wee bit. Nothing to fash yourself aboot.'

Her lips pursed in irritation. 'You were ever one to be evasive, Gavin James Steuart, when the truth did not suit you. How badly hurt are you?'

'I told you. Not much.' His gaze slid away from hers.

'Liar.' She stood and studied every inch of him, although most of him was hidden. 'Take off your cape so I can get a good look at you.'

His mouth turned down as he prepared to defy her.

'No, do not be taking that stand with me, Gavin.' Her tone softened. 'You know I love you and want to help. If you are injured, you will have trouble. 'Tis not likely you will find other aid when you must remain in hiding.'

He sighed and the tightness around his mouth eased. 'You always could manage me when you had a mind to.' He undid the clasp at his throat and let the cape fall to the floor.

Jenna gasped and sank back to her knees in front of him. His jacket was stained black with blood over his right shoulder. 'We must get this off so I can see how bad the damage is.' She plucked at his coat.

Long, painful minutes later, Gavin's pale flesh was exposed. The wound was jagged and deep. A musket hole.

'Is the bullet still in?' she asked, probing gently and wincing with each involuntary flinch of his body.

'I do no' ken.' A weak smile curved his lips. 'It felt like my entire shoulder exploded. Surely the ball went out the back.'

She examined him, front and back. 'Yes. An exit wound.'

He blanched. 'Ah, good, then. I'm fleein' for me life. Tonight, I meet The Ferguson, who will smuggle me out o' England.'

Jenna's brows raised in appreciation. Even she had heard of The Ferguson, the scourge of the English army. Tales said the man had single-handedly defeated a whole platoon of redcoats. Some said that if he had been in charge of the Scots during Culloden the battle would have ended differently. She did not think anyone could have bested the English army. There had been too many of them.

Momentarily diverted, she said, 'You know The Ferguson? You move in exalted ranks. I have always thought he sounded romantic.'

Gavin grunted. 'Leave it to a woman to think Duncan is romantic. He is not. You can not be a fighter and be romantic.' He shook his head. 'Duncan and I were at Eton together. Then he went to Cambridge and I went to Edinburgh.' Gavin grimaced. 'I could no longer stand being in England, but Duncan said going to school with the English helped him understand them better. Made him better at besting them.'

'And it seems to.' She pushed to the back of her mind her foolish fascination over a man she had never met. 'Let me clean the wound and bandage it properly. Otherwise the skin will fester.'

Stubbornness moved over his face once again. She poured him more whisky and handed it to him before laying a hand gently on his good shoulder.

'Aye, I know, Jen. You are a healer, just as your mother was.' He gritted his teeth. 'Get on with it, then.' He gulped the liquor down.

She worked as quickly as possible. 'It appears clean, but you have lost a lot of blood. I will need to sew it shut, poultice it and wrap it tightly.'

He nodded. 'More whisky, if you please.'

'Are you going on tonight?' she asked, knowing the answer, but wanting him to understand why she was going to refuse him.

'I moost.'

'Then, 'twould be best for you to have no more.' She took the empty glass and set it on the table, well away from him. 'Otherwise, you will not be able to stay on your horse.'

'You are sensible as always, but 'twould be nice. Still, I've a ways to go, and I mustn't be late. The tide will wait for no man, not even The Ferguson.'

Jenna took the hint and quickly bandaged him. When she had finished, he rested his head on her worktable.

'I would give you something else for the pain, Gavin, but laudanum would only cloud your wits more. Wait here and relax as much as you can while I fetch my jewellery.'

Minutes later, she returned and handed him a small velvet sack. ''Tis all I have. I wish 'twere more.'

Gavin poured out the meagre contents: a loose ruby and one sapphire, a single-strand pearl necklace, such as a young girl would wear, an amethyst brooch and a thistle leaf done in emeralds. He handed the thistle leaf to her.

'I cannot take this, Jen. 'Twas your mother's.'

She shook her head. 'No, Gavin. She would want you to have it. Mother never cared for jewels, only people, and you are the only son of her only sister. Take it. 'Tis the most valuable.'

'I will repay you, Jen. That I promise.' He slipped the brooch back into the bag and secured the packet in the pocket of his jacket. 'I must be going.'

He rose and swayed slightly before catching himself with one hand on the edge of the table. Jenna rushed to him and put an arm around his waist.

'Are you sure you can travel?'

'I moost. If I miss tonight, the next chance is a month away. Not many ships, even smugglers, will carry convicted Jacobites. And no one will hide one.' His mouth twisted bitterly.

Worried, Jenna watched him go to the outside entrance. She could not let him go alone. 'I will go with you.'

He turned, irritation etching lines along his mouth. 'That you will not do.'

'How will you stop me? Besides, you will be safer if I'm with you. You cannot tell me the redcoats are not hunting for you, Gavin Steuart. 'Twould be a lie. And if your wound continues to bleed, I will be able to treat it.'

She did not say what she thought—that if his wound continued to bleed he would not have the strength to escape without help. Or that he might not even live. If he stayed in England, his chance of living to an old age was even less than that.

'True,' he muttered in the tone of voice he always used when he saw himself losing an argument with her.

'They won't be looking for a couple.'

'Aye,' he said, resignation moving over his face.

'I can ride as well as you and will not slow you down.' That, too, was true. Many times as children she had outraced him. And she jumped better. 'I also put on riding boots when I fetched the jewels.'

He put up one last fight. 'I am going to the Whore's Eye, a raunchy tavern near the coast.'

She grimaced. 'I have heard of the place. Nothing good, either.'

''Tis not the place for a woman, let alone a lady.'

'I can take care of myself, Gavin.'

He sighed, the lines of pain around his eyes deepening. 'I will let you accompany me part of the way. No matter how much help you will be, I canna let you go all the way.'

Seeing the determination in his eyes and knowing he could only be pushed so far before he became intractable, she concurred. When they reached the point where Gavin ordered her to turn around, she would refuse. He was not the only stubborn person in this room.

'A deal,' she said.

Before he could think of another argument or condition, she grabbed her woollen cape and two blankets. The night was bitterly cold and storm clouds rode the sky like hounds after a fox. Better to be prepared.

He tried one last tack. 'But you stand out like a rowan berry in green leaves. That hair sparks even in this dim room.'

Her first reaction was to bristle at his reference to her hair. 'Twas the second bane of her existence, after the freckles. But she knew he was only trying to keep her from accompanying him. She might make light of the situation, but she was following him into mortal danger. The English would do whatever it took to recapture an escaped Jacobite. Even now, months after Culloden, they rode the Scottish hills, killing and imprisoning any man who might even remotely have fought for Bonnie Prince Charlie. They would think nothing of killing Gavin—and her with him—if they found them.

She swallowed the whimper of fear that threatened to escape her throat. If Gavin saw her weakness, he would use it to start another argument and they did not have time.

'I will keep the hood over my head, Gavin. Now, we'd best be going.' She moved to the door and pushed him out into the damp, blustery night.

He shivered. ''Twill snow before we reach our destination.'

''Tis why I have brought two blankets.' A soft whicker caught her ear. 'Why did you not put your horse in the stable?'

'Do not be daft. The last thing I need is for some stable boy to know I've been here and then to tell a redcoat.'

A chill chased down her spine. 'I am not used to subterfuge. Sorry.'

'Just see that you get your own mount without them knowing why.'

She had not thought of that. 'Wait a minute.' She rushed back to her stillroom and picked up the bag she took when calling on a sick person, adding what was left of the whisky to the pack. Returning to Gavin, she said, 'I will say I am going to deliver Mistress James's baby. We had word earlier she was due soon.'

She was well down the lane and through the gate that guarded the entry to de Warre Castle before she met up with Gavin. He emerged from the shelter of brush and tree. She would swear he wavered in the saddle. She held her tongue.

The speed of their passing flipped the hood off her head. Icy pellets of water hit her face like miniature musket balls. Jenna hunched her shoulders up. Melting hail blotched her eyeglasses, blurring her vision. She took the spectacles off and secured them in her bag of medicinals.

She pulled even with Gavin and asked, 'Why leave from here? 'Twould be easier and quicker to cross to France from the eastern coast.'

'And better watched, I'd warrant.' Gavin spurred his mount on. ''Tis colder than a witch's—' He caught himself. 'My pardon, Jen.'

'No pardon needed. I've heard worse.'

She kept her attention on their path and her companion. The moon peeked fitfully out from the canopy of clouds, silvering the bare tree limbs. She loved these cold, stark nights. They were harshly beautiful. But tonight, she wished it were warmer.

A glance showed Gavin slumped over, his hands clutching the pommel. He rode with an awkwardness that was not normal. She had hoped her assessment of his wound was too severe. She was afraid she had been right. Anxiety tightened her chest as a premonition of trouble twisted her stomach, that part of her that was most susceptible to nerves.

Off to one side, as though coming through one of the bordering fields, she heard the sound of horse's hooves in sucking mud. The glow of a storm lantern pierced the night's darkness, flickering through the surrounding trees like fairy light.

Gavin caught the bridle of her horse and pulled them to a stop. 'Hush,' he whispered, his voice nearly lost in the sough of the rising wind.

A troop of six men rode not thirty feet from them, their mounts following the trail she and Gavin skirted. Crimson flashed in the lantern's illumination.

Redcoats.

English.

Jenna's hands turned clammy. She could not have spoken if her life depended on it.

The sounds of hooves plopping in mud and men muttering among themselves reached her as they passed. The storm lantern cast a baleful yellow glare on the dirt track and disappeared into the distance.

Jenna released her breath, only then realising that she'd been holding it. Blood rushed to her head and for moments she was dizzy.

'That was close,' she whispered, the scare making her breathy.

She glanced at Gavin for his signal to go forward. He sat as one frozen. He must have been even more frightened than she. After all, he had just escaped the redcoats and then to have them nearly discover him…

Uncomfortable speaking so soon after their close call, she reached out to him, intending to comfort with her touch. As though moving slowly through heavy water, he slid to one side. Jenna watched in shocked

denial as he tumbled to the wet ground and lay in a motionless heap.

She jumped down and knelt beside him, heedless of
the mud weighting down her skirts. She bent her lips to
his ear. 'Gavin,' she whispered, putting as much
command into her voice as possible without raising it.
She could not take the chance that a stray brush of wind
would carry his name to listening ears.

He did not move.

She shook him. Nothing. Her left hand grasped his
right shoulder just as the metallic tang of fresh blood
met her nostrils. The wound must have reopened. Apprehension chewed her insides.

There was no time to change the bandage. 'Gavin,'
she ordered, 'you have to get up.' She stooped above
him with her hands under his shoulders and pulled with
all her might.

He tried, but his body was like a sack of corn, flaccid
and heavy, too cumbersome for her to lift without his
help. He sprawled back down.

Tears of frustration and fright sprang to her eyes. She
swiped them away, determined to save him, no matter
what. But how? He had lost so much blood and more
seeped from him as he lay here in the cold. She took
deep calming breaths until the fear threatening to devour
her eased. If he could not get up and ride, then he could
not leave for France and safety. She had to get help.

She would have to leave him here, under the shelter
of a hedgerow. She tugged at him, managing to slide
him along the slick ground. He groaned, but she kept
pulling. There was nothing else she could do.

Gasping for breath, she sank once more to her knees
beside his head. 'Gavin, I must leave you here. Go on

without you.' She sucked in air and willed herself to speak calmly, even though her entire body shook. 'Gavin, I am going for help.'

He gazed up at her, his eyes glassy from pain. 'The Ferguson,' he said, his voice a bare thread. 'Go to Duncan.'

Even now he would not give up his goal of escape. ''Twould be better to take you home and hide you in one of the priest holes.'

He shook his head. 'No. Duncan. Not safe anywhere but France.' He coughed and shivers racked his body.

The ground was so cold. She jumped up and fetched the two blankets. Returning, she rolled him up in them. Her mind raced the entire time. Much as she hated to think it, he was right. The only person she could trust to help her with Gavin was The Ferguson. Anyone else might betray him or be tricked into doing so.

'How will I recognise The Ferguson?'

His eyes opened, shining like glass in the silver moonlight. 'Silver cross. At his neck.' His lids drifted lower. 'Always wears it. Do no' know why.'

'What colour is his hair? His eyes?'

'Do no' know. Changes. Eyes are hazel.' His eyes shut completely.

Her chest clenched painfully. She swore softly, words a lady should not know, words she only heard in the stables. If she did not hurry, it would be too late. She jumped up and made for her mare, pausing long enough to tether Gavin's horse to a bush. Tears blurred her vision as she mounted.

Glancing back at her cousin, she whispered, 'Do not die on me, Gavin Steuart. Do not ye dare. I will haunt you in hell if you are not here when I return.'

Swallowing the anger created by her fear, she turned the horse away. The Whore's Eye was not too much further. Many's the time she had overheard servants talking about the lawlessness of the seamen and worse who frequented the place.

She had no choice.

Only another Jacobite could be trusted with Gavin's life. She prayed she would reach The Ferguson in time.

Chapter Two

Jenna halted at the door to the Whore's Eye, her boots sinking into a muddy puddle. Three feet above her head a battered sign with a large blue eye painted on it dropped large drops of water on her head. Her soaked cape clung to her like a woollen mitten, and her hair fell in a limp rope down her back. The spectacles she had put back on, after tying her horse to a tree some distance away, were blurred.

Fingers numb from the cold, she pulled the hood of her cape over her hair, then fumbled with the handle until the heavy oak door swung inwards on protesting rusted hinges. Jenna stepped into the opening. The odours of unwashed bodies, onions too long cooked and rancid ale hit her nose like a slap. Cheap tallow candles flickered from some of the plank tables, adding their acrid scent. After the bitter clean of the storm, the smells were nauseating. The fireplace, where a large kettle hung full of what promised to be mutton, provided a minimum of light and an eye-stinging haze.

Gavin had said this place was the haunt of scallywags and highwaymen. A quick glance around told her Gavin had been kind.

She would not choose to come here with an armed escort, let alone by herself. But 'twas a risk she had to take. Gavin's life depended on her.

The men here looked rough and more than reprehensible, pursuing their pleasure in groups or alone, as the mood took them. All drank. A lone buxom wench worked the tables, her charms spilling out of a tight bodice and her arms large enough from hefting ale-filled tankards to floor any male who might take advantage.

Jenna's mouth twisted in a reluctant glimmer of admiration. The woman probably welcomed the extra bit of change a randy man provided. Jenna had long ago lost count of the number of illegitimate children she had helped bring into the world.

Someone yelled, 'Close the bloody door, yer bloody fagget!'

Jenna winced as she closed the door and slid to the side, keeping her back to the wall. The last thing she had intended to do was draw attention. No matter that she was in one of her working dresses and her cape was plain black, she obviously did not belong here.

Her clothing started to steam in the smoke-infested warmth and the stench of wet wool added itself to the other odours. Her nose wrinkled at the assault before she remembered to make her features placid. No one in this room would be bothered by these smells and to show that she was would only offend anyone who might look at her.

She took a moment and removed her spectacles and wiped them on her soaked sleeve. She needed to be able to see the silver cross. She put them back on and they instantly fogged. She sighed and waited. Patience was a virtue. The steam soon evaporated and the figures closer to her came into harsh focus.

The skin at the nape of her neck crawled and in a nervous twist, she looked to her left—and nearly fainted. Four redcoats sat at a table not twenty feet from her. One of the soldiers watched her with heavy-lidded intensity. Could he be the officer who had passed Gavin and her? If so, did he recognise her? Surely not. She had kept the hood of her cloak over her hair, hiding her face.

Instinctively, she bit her lower lip.

Why were they here? This was a tavern not normally frequented by their like. Were they here because of Gavin? Did they know he was to meet The Ferguson, who would smuggle him out of England and over to France? Was that why they had been travelling the same road? It could not be. She had to believe that or all was lost.

Jenna gulped down hard on the fright swelling in her throat. Her bottom lip was raw from her teeth. She edged along the wall away from the man's regard, trying desperately to ease the thundering of her heart. Perhaps if she ignored the redcoat he would go back to his drinking. Still, the muscles in her neck tensed.

She had to find The Ferguson.

Her gaze darted around, searching for a tall man wearing a silver cross. She would wager no one but The Ferguson would wear such a thing in this place. The ruffians here did not have the wealth. Hopefully he wore it. He had to. There was no other way she could recognise him.

How often this past year had she heard wondrous

tales of The Ferguson's exploits? She could not count them, let alone remember them all. There was the time he had single-handedly held up ten English soldiers and robbed them, leaving them with nothing but their small clothes. Gavin said The Ferguson had taken the uniforms to be used by Jacobites trying to infiltrate the English ranks to learn military secrets. That was before the Battle of Culloden. A more recent time, The Ferguson had saved a Highland crofter's family from being burnt out of their home. The man was a figure of almost mythic proportion.

A flurry of noise came from the back door, deep laughter and the rumble of conversation punctuated by a woman's seductive tones and a man's husky voice. A couple coming back from enjoying a tryst. 'Twas not unexpected in a place such as this. Jenna glanced their way, even though she knew The Ferguson was not one of the pair. He was here to rescue Gavin, not dally with a wench.

The two moved deeper into the room. Jenna squinted. Her spectacles allowed her to see many things better, but they could not bring everything into perfect focus.

Still, she saw enough. The man was tall, with hair so dark it seemed to absorb the meagre light. His shoulders were broad, emphasising the leanness of his hips, which the woman in his arms was too appreciative of. One of her hands lingered on his thigh, speaking plainly of what they had been about. Her face was turned up to his, her brown hair tumbling down.

They were a striking pair.

Someone scraped a chair leg across the rough floor. Someone else grunted. Jenna looked back the way she had come. The redcoat with the heavy-lidded eyes was moving her way. She told herself he was going to the privy, but her heart insisted on hammering at her ribs.

She gripped the neck of her cape tighter to secure the hood over her red hair as she moved out of the redcoat's path, inching between chairs until she was closer to the couple. A glint of silver flashed. It came from the man with the woman. From his throat. It could not be what she thought.

But what if it was?

She dared not ignore it. She cast another glance over her shoulder, only to see the soldier nearly on her. He was not going outside. Her heart increased its panicked beating.

Even if the dark-haired man had not worn the cross, she would have gone to him now. He was not an English soldier and he was already with a woman, so he would not be interested in her that way. No man ever was. But she could act as though she were here to meet him. With luck, he would be too surprised to naysay her immediately and his presence might be enough to deter the redcoat from his pursuit of her.

The serving wench winked at the man and moved to the tap area. This was her chance. Jenna scuttled forward and sat awkwardly on the hard wooden bench across the table from the man. Leaning forward, she started to speak and stopped. The glint of silver that had first drawn her was a cross.

She looked at the man again. Long and lean, with cheekbones like chiselled granite, he looked back. Hair, black as the darkest night, absorbed what little light there was and fell thickly to his shoulders. His jaw was strong and smooth. She glanced at his hands where they cupped around a tankard of ale. His fingers were elegant and strong, the nails short and free of dirt. If his hair were snagged into a queue, his grooming would be that of a gentleman.

However, his clothing was anything but fashionable. A loosely fitting brown coat that looked twenty years out of mode and a threadbare muslin shirt covered his broad shoulders.

He was a mass of contradictions. Yet he wore the silver cross she was to look for.

She had to take the risk. Gavin was dying. She inhaled sharply, taking in with the air courage and determination.

He watched her with eyes as yellow and hard and sparkling as citrines. Hazel eyes.

He looked feral and dangerous—a wild animal caught in a moment of near civilisation. He blinked and the image disappeared. He was only a man who had been fondling a tavern wench minutes ago.

Still…he wore the cross.

His blatant study of her set her nerves on edge. She spoke harsher than she had intended. 'I've need of your help.'

His sensual mouth twisted up, and his gaze lingered where the cape clung to her breast before lifting to meet her eyes. 'You'd best speak little and softly. No woman of your station could have reason for being here.'

Jenna looked furtively around the room, her attention lingering briefly on the table where the three redcoats sat. She did not look behind to where the other soldier still stood. Her shoulders hunched before straightening again.

'Have I spoken loudly?' she asked, her brows rose in a haughty challenge. 'Or to anyone but you?'

He shrugged. 'I don't know. I just came in.'

Her scowl intensified. 'You are an infuriating man.'

'I doubt I've anything you would want, mistress,' he said, assuming a humble expression.

Jenna wondered if her lips were blue. They did not want to move. 'Are you here to meet someone?' she whispered.

His eyes narrowed, glinting dangerously. Like a caged lion she had once seen in a book.

'Aye,' he muttered. 'Nelly.' He angled his head in the direction the serving wench had gone and grinned rakishly.

Jenna blushed from the roots of her red hair to the top of her black cloak. She watched his fine, sensual mouth twist in amusement and wished for at least the hundredth time that she did not flush at the slightest provocation. It was the curse of her hair.

'What impertinence,' she said before thinking. Chagrinned at her uncontrolled response, she bit her lip to keep anything else from spilling out.

His eyes flashed wickedly. 'And your question was not?'

She turned away, trying to ease her temper. He was right. But she dared not ask him outright if he was here to meet Gavin. There was no way of telling who might overhear, and not just Gavin's life was at stake. The English soldiers would willingly kill The Ferguson and anyone found with him. And she did not even know if this man was the Jacobite hero she sought.

She glanced quickly back at him, intending to look away as though he were of no import, but his tawny eyes caught and held hers. Unable to tear her gaze away, she lost herself in the amber pools with their brown striations and black, black pupils. His eyes narrowed, the full, short blond lashes casting shadows on his cheeks.

With a part of her mind, she registered that his lashes should be ebony to match his hair. Then the thought flitted away.

Jenna took a deep breath and forced herself to break the hold this man had on her. He was more vital and more handsome than any man she had ever met. He would be arresting if he passed her on a crowded street. But she was here for Gavin, not to fall under some strange man's spell.

'I…I have a friend,' she murmured after what seemed an eternity.

Somehow, in spite of his attraction for her, she remembered to look around and make sure no one was any closer than they had been. Particularly not the English soldier who seemed to be following her around the room and still stood some distance away, his shoulders propped against the wall.

The man across from her raised one brow when she did not continue. ''Tis glad I am, mistress, that you have at least one friend.'

She scowled at him. 'This is not a jesting matter,' she said.

'No,' he said, his voice deep and mocking. 'It never is.'

A double meaning? She took a deep breath and started again. 'I have a friend. I think he was supposed to meet you, but he is wounded.'

There, it was out. Thank goodness she had not mentioned names.

Something dangerous flitted across the man's face. 'His name?'

She chewed her lip harder until the metallic tang of blood told her she had bitten through the skin. If he was the wrong man, she and Gavin were dead.

'What is your name?' she mumbled, staring determinedly into his eyes, searching for something she could not explain.

Exasperation and a hint of impatience tightened his mouth. 'No games. My name is Duncan. And your friend's?'

She closed her eyes in relief. How many Duncans could there be in this tavern? More than one this close to the Scottish border, but surely not more than one wearing a silver Celtic cross.

She opened her eyes to see his reaction. 'Gavin. His name is Gavin and he's badly hurt.'

Worry flitted across his face. Jenna let out the breath she had been holding. He would not be upset unless he was The Ferguson. She had made the right decision. Now they had to get back to Gavin before it was too late.

'We must leave,' she said. 'He is…' She told herself not to cry. 'He is lying in the mud. Wounded. Badly.'

'Then there is no time to waste,' Duncan said.

Thank goodness he understood. Jenna stood and turned toward the front door.

'Not that way,' he said, grabbing her shoulder and stopping her. 'Through the kitchen.'

His hand slid around her waist and pulled her tight to his side. The hard sinews of his flank pressed intimately against her hip. The musky scent of his maleness surrounded her. Her stomach clenched into a roiling knot.

She tried to pull away, needing the safety of the entire room between them, but willing to settle for inches. Anything that kept him from touching her so intimately.

His embrace tightened. 'We are a couple, leaving to do what couples always do.'

His words and what they implied jolted her, brought back the picture of him entering the room with Nelly, the tavern wench. 'Two women in one night?' she said before thinking.

He cast her a sly look just instants before his mouth descended. Against her lips, he murmured, 'Pretend you're Nelly.'

Then he kissed her.

Her first kiss. It was not chaste. It made her mind twirl and her gut twist. It was incredibly arousing. It scared her as nothing else had.

He drew abruptly away. Jenna's senses swirled.

A commotion at the entrance drew her attention, and she belatedly realised the noise was what had made him stop. He had not been immersed in their kiss as she had. He had been playing a skilful game with her and anyone else in the room who had wanted to watch. Pain constricted her chest. She ignored it as best she could.

Another soldier entered. A groan of despair escaped her. Too many redcoats. But this one was different from the four already here. From the braid on his epaulettes to the arrogant tilt of his head, he was obviously the leader of the group already here. He took off his cockaded hat and shook off the water, exposing his silver-blond hair and pale blue eyes.

She gasped. The newcomer was Captain Lord Johnathan Albert Seller, a man who had visited her father a few months ago. Though they had not met formally, there was the very real possibility he would recognise her, even in this environ.

The fingers on her side dug into her ribs. The

Ferguson dragged her through the door into the kitchen. If she did not know better, she would think he also recognised Captain Seller. But that could not be. A Jacobite and an English army officer did not know each other. Ever.

The Ferguson released her and she stumbled. She felt cold and bereft with his warmth gone. She was demented to feel thus.

Noise and cooking smells engulfed her. Warmth wafted from the fire where a mutton roast turned on the spit, propelled by the efforts of a tiny urchin. The proprietor, identifiable by the none-too-clean white apron around his skinny waist, nodded briefly at Jenna's companion, then ignored them.

Nelly slid in the door behind them. Duncan made a nearly imperceptible nod to the woman. She acknowledged it with a wink. Then he strode across the room and into the night.

Jenna followed him through the outside door and a blast of wind hit her. The sleet had turned to rain, and clouds obscured the full moon. At least it was not freezing—yet. Desperation twisted her stomach.

She caught up with The Ferguson. 'Gavin's hurt. We must hurry. My horse is this way.' The nearly incoherent words spilled from her mouth as rain ran in rivulets down her face.

His hand wrapped around her wrist and jerked her to him. He was wet as she, although they had only been outside for scant minutes. She stared up at him, his action and the harshness of it taking her by surprise. He was a darker shadow in the black night so she could not make out his features. But she felt his heart beating steadily and strongly against her breasts.

Abruptly, she became aware of the warmth radiating from his body and the way it sheltered her from the worst of the wind that pounded at his back. He was an inferno in his heat and a rock in his strength.

'Not so fast.' His voice was a deadly growl. 'Who are you? And why should I believe a word you say? You could as easily be an agent of that German bastard's, sent to trap me with information forced from Gavin by torture. You wouldn't be the first,' he added in an undertone.

Jenna blinked away water and looked up at him. He made sense, even if her immediate thought was to kick him in the shin and gain her freedom from his disturbing hold.

'Jenna. I am Jenna de Warre.' She felt him stiffen and his hold on her wrist turned painful, causing her to flinch. 'You are hurting me.'

His grip did not ease. 'What does Bloody Ayre's daughter have to do with a Jacobite?'

She should have known he would recognise her father's name. But it was too late now.

'Answer me.' His voice colder than the night, he radiated tension.

For the first time, Jenna felt fear of the man who held her close as a lover, yet harshly as a gaolor. She should have dissembled, used a different name. Anything. But she had not thought beyond getting help for Gavin.

She groped for words and nothing came. She stared up at him, his face in shadow, telling her nothing of what he thought.

He shook her. 'Answer me, woman. Your life depends on it.'

Fresh fear stole her breath away. She had been so unprepared. Finally, she realised what she should have known all along. Duncan would not—could not—let anyone live he could not trust with the secret of what he looked like. She was more a danger than most, or so he must think.

The man holding her thought she would betray him at the first opportunity. Somehow she had to convince him otherwise. Gavin's life depended on that.

She had to choose her words carefully. 'My father has regretted what he did for his entire life. My mother died from grief when I was young because of what my father did. She was Scottish.' She paused to lick lips that were cold and stiff. It did not help. 'Gavin is my cousin. Could be my brother, we are that close. His mother came to live with us and raised me along with her own child. Our mothers are—were—sisters. I would do anything to save Gavin.'

Long minutes dragged by. Jenna squinted in the darkness, wanting to read his thoughts by the expression on his face, but was unable to see his features. Despair began to creep up on her. She forced back a tear of frustration and shattered hope.

If he would not come with her, then she would escape from him and go back to Gavin on her own. Somehow she would get her cousin on his horse. If she had to, she would ride home and bring someone from her father's castle. She would bring her father. She should have done that at the beginning. It would be dangerous for Gavin, but no more so than leaving him in the cold and wet. There were no other choices.

The kitchen door opened and a beam of yellow light split the dark. Duncan yanked her back with him into the shadow of a large oak where the glow did not penetrate.

A redcoat stood in the entry, a storm lantern in his right hand. Seller.

Could things get any worse? Jenna wondered, her hands breaking into cold sweat. She felt the man holding her stiffen until he seemed ready to explode from the tension he suppressed.

Seller stepped into the rain just as a female form materialised beside him. Nelly. She said something to him that Jenna could not hear and pulled on his arm that held the lantern. He looked down at her and spoke. Nelly nodded and her hand slid from his arm to his chest. Seller stepped away from her and further into the dark.

A gust of wind ripped through the tree sheltering Jenna and Duncan, bringing cold stinging rain with it. It hit Seller and Jenna saw him sway. Nelly appeared by his side once more, urging him back inside with her body pressed to his. This time he went.

The air whooshed out of Jenna. 'So close,' she muttered.

'Too close,' Duncan said. ''Tis time to go.'

Hope flared in her. 'Are you going with me to Gavin?'

He held her for another second before pushing her away. She took a shaky step back, bracing herself against the tree trunk.

His voice harsh, he said, 'Understand this. I do not trust you, and I will not think twice about killing you if you're lying.'

She shivered, but anger and determination stiffened her spine. 'And I you, if you do anything to harm my cousin.'

Chapter Three

'Fair enough.' The Ferguson motioned Jenna toward her tethered horse. 'I will meet you at the bend in the track.'

Teeth chattering, she nodded before realising he could not see her. 'At the bend. In five minutes or so.'

'Close enough.'

She shivered and looked around for something to use to mount her mare. A hand gripped her shoulder and she jumped. It took all her control not to squeak.

'What?' She twisted around to find The Ferguson so close his breath was a warm caress on her chilled face.

'I just realised you rode side saddle.' Disgust dripped from his words.

She bristled. 'Of course.'

'And your teeth chatter enough to draw attention from a deaf man.'

She tried to pull away from his hold. 'I am cold.'

'I will bring you another cloak or a blanket.'

'I do not need anything—'

He cut her short by grabbing her waist and lifting her onto the saddle. Even after he let her go, she would insist he still touched her. It was a sensation she had never experienced before and it was not comfortable.

The fact that his hold on her waist had felt exciting and illicit was something she pushed to the back of her mind. No man should make her respond like this. Particularly no Jacobite.

She had been so jumbled that he had turned his back to her and made his way to the stables before she realised it. It was too late to tell him not to bring her anything unless she yelled, and she had no intention of doing that. The last thing either of them needed was to draw attention and have Seller come back outside because her voice carried.

She settled her leg over the saddle horn and turned her mount, Rosebud, in the direction they were to rendezvous. All the while her mind worked.

The Ferguson must be known here and the workers must approve of what he did, particularly Nelly, or he would not move so openly. Even in her sheltered life, she had heard about secrets told to bed partners and imagined that could be deadly to a man of his ilk. But that was none of her business.

She and Rosebud made their way through the mud and rain.

She was determined to rid her stomach of the strange sensation that had plagued that part of her body since her first sight of the Jacobite. The unease was because she knew he was the only person who could help her save Gavin. Nothing more.

She would not let it be anything else. He was a Jacobite, the opposite of everything Papa stood for.

Yet, her mother had been Scottish. She was half-Scottish. Her beloved cousin was all Scottish.

She pulled up at the bend in the road and squinted into the darkness behind her. Her glasses were once more in her saddlebag because they were no help in this weather. She heard the soft suck of his horse's hooves pulling out of the muddy track before she saw the dark outline of his body.

'Here.' He held out a wad of cloth. 'A blanket. Belongs to the stable lad, but 'tis better than nothing.'

She scowled. 'Kindness from the man who will kill me if I endanger him?'

'Better to die warm than cold.'

Her first inclination was to refuse the offer, but she was more practical than that. The weather was beastly, and the last thing her cousin needed was for her to get too sick to care for him. With as much grace as she was capable of, and knowing he could not see her scowl in the darkness, she took the blanket and swung it around her shoulders. The damp wool smelled of hay and horses and less pleasant things. Soon it would be soaked as everything else she wore, but for the moment it warmed her.

'We had best hurry,' she said. 'Gavin has not much time, I fear.'

She urged Rosebud on, wishing she could hurry, but knowing she should not for safety's sake. The footing was precarious and the moon a poor substitute for a lantern. One moment the muddy track shone with a silver sheen. The next it nearly disappeared as the clouds scudded across the sky in time to the rising wind.

Jenna prayed Gavin would survive. He had a strong constitution and had survived a wound at Culloden and later internment in an English prison. Surely he could live through this. He had to.

In spite of her worry about her cousin, she was intensely and uncomfortably aware of the man riding behind her. When the wind let up for a moment, she could just hear the creaking of his leather saddle and the soft whickering of his horse. At times she thought she heard The Ferguson swearing under his breath, but neither of them dared talk. Sound would carry on the wind for some distance.

For all she knew, the redcoats had left the inn and were behind them. Reacting to that thought, she turned her mount left and on to a narrow trail that went through the fields. This route would not be travelled by someone unfamiliar with the area.

She had only gone several steps when her companion's hand clamped down hard on her wrist. She had sensed him moving abreast with her, but had not thought he would stop her.

'Where are we going now?' His words were a hoarse, angry whisper.

'A way that is unknown to the English.' Her reply was swept away by the wind. 'A shortcut.'

'How do you know that?'

She swallowed a sigh of irritation. Every minute they argued was another minute longer in their journey, another minute Gavin lay on the cold, wet ground.

'Because I have lived here most of my life. Because I have been out on worse nights than this, going to a birthing or tending to someone so sick the family fears they might not make it until morning. Because I know what I am doing.'

She could feel his gaze on her even as his fingers tightened momentarily before relaxing and leaving her. The breath she had not realised she held sighed from her lips.

'If this is—'

'I know,' she said with a weary sigh, 'you will kill me. And I believe you. Now can we go?'

In reply, he moved ahead of her so she had to urge Rosebud forwards in order to regain the lead. Jenna hunched into the stable boy's blanket and clenched her jaw.

She knew he followed by the soft whickering of his horse. She hoped he was scanning the area for redcoats as she was. The last thing they needed was to be stopped. The soldiers might let her go, but they would arrest him and likely hang him without a trial.

She urged Rosebud on, glad of the meagre glow from the moon to see by. It was a risk. A passing soldier might see them, but likely would not go out of his way to stop them, thinking them locals returning home.

She needed to reach Gavin. As it was, her cousin would not be crossing to France tonight. And if they were not lucky and prompt, he might not be leaving for a long time.

They entered a copse of trees and instantly what light there had been disappeared. Jenna slowed even more.

'Are you sure we are saving time?' he asked, doubt lacing his words. His voice floated on the cold, wet wind.

Exasperation was an emotion Jenna did not often feel. This man seemed to make the worst come out in her. 'Yes. I have trod this path many a night. Gavin is just the other side of this copse.'

'I hope so.'

The urge to turn in her saddle and berate him for his doubt was strong, but she knew it would accomplish nothing. And someone might overhear them. She gritted her teeth and kept going.

Minutes later, they exited the trees into a clearing. She stopped and slid from her horse. Squinting, Jenna could barely discern a darker spot on the ground that was her cousin. Heart pounding, she rushed to his side. She squatted down.

Gavin's face was a pale glimmer in the returning moonlight, with his mouth pinched down and his jaw clenched. In spite of the cold, his high cheeks were washed in scarlet. A fever.

She heard The Ferguson take a deep breath. 'We must get him to shelter.'

Without bothering to look at him, she said, 'I know. I cannot move him myself. Otherwise I would have taken him home and hidden him instead of fetching you. He cannot cross the channel as he is no matter what he wants.' She turned to face him. 'I need you to help me lift him to his horse and tie him to the pommel. Then I need you at the end of the journey to help me get him into a priest's hole where he will be safe. After that, you can go.'

His eyes narrowed in irritation. 'I am not yours to order as you please.'

She bit her lower lip. 'No, you are not. I forgot myself in my concern for my cousin. I need your help. Gavin will die without it.'

He nodded. 'Where is the wound?'

'His right shoulder.' She lifted his cape and the blankets to show where the bandage bulged.

'Fetch his horse closer while I get him up.'

Not waiting for her, he pulled the coverings from Gavin and grabbed her cousin's good shoulder. With a grunt, he lifted Gavin enough to get his arm around his friend's waist. Duncan stood, Gavin in his arms. The

men wavered and she knew her cousin's dead weight
threatened to topple both of them on to the ground.
Jenna winced and hurried the animal, but knew there
was no easy or nice way to do this.

'Hold the horse steady,' The Ferguson ordered when
she reached them.

He half-carried, half-dragged Gavin to the horse's
side and draped the unconscious man's hands and arms
over the saddle. Duncan pushed until Gavin's body
hung face down over the saddle.

Gavin moaned in pain. Instantly Jenna moved to the
other side of the horse where Gavin's face and shoulders were. She was glad the animal was well trained
enough to remain motionless.

'Gavin, 'tis me, Jenna.'

'Jenna? What the…? Ah, I passed out. It hurts.' His
voice was hoarse and his words nearly incoherent. 'My
head is…I'm upside down.'

'Gavin,' Duncan said, 'I'm here and, if you will help,
I'll get you sitting in the saddle.'

'Duncan?'

'Yes, my friend. We are going to get you to safety,
but I need your help.'

With a struggle that Jenna knew caused Gavin
more discomfort, they got the wounded man strad-
dling the horse. The animal stood its ground until
they were done.

'Much better,' Gavin whispered.

Jenna held out a vial. 'Drink this.'

Gavin gasped as he swallowed. 'What is this?'

She smiled. 'Whisky and laudanum. You will feel
better for it.'

'I'd best tie you to the saddle, then,' Duncan said.

'The last thing I want is for you to fall again and for me to have to get you back up on the horse.'

'I'm fine,' Gavin protested.

'Then why are you shaking like a leaf in a storm?' The Ferguson asked. 'Better to be safe than to be regretful.'

Knowing she had done her best for Gavin, Jenna found a log and mounted. When she was settled, she studied the man who still stood close enough to catch her cousin if he slipped. His clothing clung in soaked folds to his body. Likely they would all be sick from this night's work.

Without a word, she took the reins of Gavin's horse and headed in the direction they had been travelling before coming upon her cousin. She didn't wait for The Ferguson to follow. After watching him with Gavin, she didn't doubt he would be close. It was obvious he cared for her cousin. She was thankful for that.

She sensed him moving behind them.

Jenna felt as though the weight of the world sat on her shoulders. Shivers racked her body and each gust of wind cut through her clothing like knives through butter. She knew Gavin felt worse. Her heart ached for her cousin.

Worse would be when he realised he had not made his escape across the water. Then there was his companion— The Ferguson. Hopefully the man would leave as soon as he helped her get Gavin safely into the priest hole.

Even as she thought that, she knew she didn't really want him to go so quickly. He was the Scottish hero of Culloden. Tales of his derring-do circulated even amongst the English.

And she was not immune to him.

She should be. Even though she sympathised with

the Scots, she had not supported Prince Charles Edward Stuart's claim to the English throne. But neither did she believe the surviving Jacobites should be hunted like animals.

She sighed and wiped water from her brow and eyes and squinted into the murky distance. Being near-sighted, she thought she could just discern the hunch-back outline of de Warre Castle against the night sky. Goodness knew it seemed they had been travelling long enough to cross the breadth of Cumbria, so they should be home.

A dark line of trees marked the road leading to the castle. Gravel crunched under the horses' hooves. Soon.

'Now the rain stops,' she muttered, realising that for the first time this night water didn't run in rivulets down her face. She heard The Ferguson chuckle, a deep, rich sound that made her entire body tingle.

'Lucky for us it didn't stop sooner. No one will even know we passed. The water will wash away any trace.'

'Ahh, I had not thought of that.'

'Subterfuge is not a way of life to you.'

The derision in his voice hurt, but she forced it aside. He was right.

But how to get Gavin into hiding without someone seeing? She didn't worry about being seen out here. At this time of night no one would be looking outside. But when they went to the priest's hole, they would be moving through the house. How much could she trust the servants?

And The Ferguson. He would not like being seen. He had made it clear he would kill to protect himself.

She edged closer to the man and whispered, 'Follow me.'

Carefully picking their way by the sporadic light of

the moon and stars, she went to the outside entrance of her stillroom. This was not the first time she was thankful she had had this door put in.

Stopping her mare, she lifted one leg over the saddle and slid to the ground, ignoring her skirts rucking high enough to show her boots and stockings. She pulled the heavy key from her pocket and opened the door.

The Ferguson followed her, Gavin in his arms. She made her way by the light from the banked fire to the tinder and candle she kept on the sill. It took several times before she had the candle lit.

She motioned to the same chair her cousin had sat in earlier. With more gentleness than she would have thought possible, the man laid Gavin down.

'We must get him into dry clothes and warm. The priest hole is hollowed out of stone and cold. No place for a sick man, but 'tis the safest.'

He turned his head to look at her. 'Fetch clothing while I undress him.'

She bit her lower lip. 'He is unconscious now, but likely will rouse when you start moving him around.' She took a deep breath to calm the apprehension she felt for Gavin. 'He will be in great pain.' For a moment she thought she saw tenderness move over the man's rugged features.

'There is nothing for it. Nor will it be the first time he has hurt.'

She nodded. 'You fought with him, did you not?'

He stared at her, and she wondered what he saw in her face. 'Aye. Side by side, like brothers.'

She realised he was telling her that her cousin would be safe with him although he could not keep Gavin from discomfort or worse. 'I will be back shortly.'

She turned and fled from Gavin's critical condition

and from an emotion she did not want to examine. She was the daughter of Viscount Ayre, not a Jacobite sympathiser no matter that her mother had been Scottish and her beloved cousin was a convicted Jacobite. She would not side against her father no matter how she might sympathise with the Jacobites and secretly admire the daring of this man. She would not be attracted to a man who personified rebellion against the Crown.

The chill of the castle walls intensified her cold from the outdoors and the sopping clothes she still wore doubled her discomfort. She hurried on. She would change later. She had to fetch Papa's old clothes, packed away in the trunks on the third floor. In his youth Papa had been Gavin's size.

She did not want Papa to know what she did. He was a man of honour and loyal to the Hanoverian king. Much as Papa loved Gavin, it would torment him to know he sheltered a Jacobite—even a beloved Jacobite.

The race for the dry clothing helped her teeth stop chattering. She was partially warmed by her exertion by the time she returned to her stillroom.

A fire burned, its ruddy flames making Gavin look hot. He was wrapped in the shawl and a blanket she kept to ward off the cold, his modesty barely covered. His drenched clothes were a dark puddle on the floor.

She shut the door and locked it. They had got this far; the last thing they needed was to be discovered because it was in the small hours of the night and she had thought them safe and they were not.

'At last.' Irritation was a burr in The Ferguson's voice. 'I began to think something had happened to you.'

She looked at him. The light cast his face into angles

and shadows. His mouth was a sensual curve, his eyes dark hollows. She realised anew how attractive he was.

'I had to go to the top floor to find clothes so as not to waken anyone.'

He scowled. 'He is worse.'

Her hands clenched, her nails going through the cloth she held. Kneeling down, she dropped the material and reached for Gavin. His forehead radiated heat.

'He has a fever.'

'I was afraid so.' Worry made his voice harsh.

She spared a glance for the man. 'I will not let anything happen to my cousin.'

'So you are a miracle worker and would undo what the English have done.' Bitter derision laced each word. 'You, the daughter of Bloody Ayre. What if Gavin were not your cousin? Would you have saved him then or turned him over to the redcoats in the tavern?'

Her shoulders tensed at his name for her father, but she knew better than to argue. She could not win and Gavin needed help—now.

'I have not the time for this.' Rising, she moved to her work table. 'Get him dressed.' Without seeing if her order was being followed, she rummaged in her vials. She pulled the stopper from one. 'This is laudanum. Added to what he has already had, it will keep him unconscious while I remove the bandage and clean his wound.'

She held it out. The Ferguson rose with a fluid grace that was more like that of a wild animal than of a man. She wondered if he had gained such power from fighting the English he hated so.

He had removed his gloves as she had, and when he took the glass from her their fingers touched. Tingles raced up her arm and she started. He pulled his hand back as though he had been stung. He turned his back on her.

Dazed, she spent a precious moment watching him. With his overcoat and jacket off, it was easy to see that his back was broad and his hips narrow. He was a fine figure of a man. Belatedly, she noted there was a black stain on his white shirt, as though mud had dripped from his wet hair.

Unwilling to continue pondering the man who had sparked her admiration for his bravery and daring from the first time she had heard of his exploits, she focused on her work. Gavin needed her.

She picked up the pot she kept ready and flung tea leaves into it. She filled it with water from a nearby bucket and hung the pot on an iron rail which she swung into the flames. In Gavin's mug she put ground willow bark. It would be bitter, but it would help with the fever.

'We can all use something hot. Gavin particularly. We need to warm him so he does not catch an inflammation. I see you found the blankets.'

He wrapped the woollen covers all around Gavin in spite of the heat from the fire. She noted that he had saved none for himself.

She fetched clean cloths and several herbs to make a poultice. After she laid everything down, she got a brace of candles, which she handed to The Ferguson.

'I will need the extra light from these to see what I must do.'

He grunted as he took the brass holder. Wax dripped down the sides, but he managed to keep the candles angled so the hot material did not fall on Gavin.

Her cousin moaned as she wrestled with the soaked bandages.

'It would be easier if you cut those off.'

'You are right. I should have thought of that.' Chagrin at her failure made her voice skip. She had been too self-conscious at his nearness. This was not like her.

'No one is perfect,' The Ferguson said softly. 'Even you.'

Not knowing how to answer, she ignored his comment. All her life she had striven to be the best she was capable of. Nothing else was acceptable. That was Papa's motto, and she had taken it as her own.

'A knife is on my work table—will you get it, please?'

She sensed him standing and leaving. The fire still heated the side of her closest to it, but there was an emptiness on her other side, a coldness not born of temperature. More like loss.

She took several deep breaths and willed her fingers to be still. She was not normally fanciful.

'Here.' He held the knife, handle first, to her.

She took the sharp instrument from his hand, careful not to touch his fingers. She didn't want to know if she would experience the same *frisson* of awareness that she had before when their skin had met.

Gingerly, she cut away the blood-and-water-soaked bandage. She could not smell rot in the wound, but knew it was too early. She must ensure that it stayed this way.

'Please pour the tea,' she said. 'Mugs are on the shelf above.'

She was grateful that he did as directed without protest. Her mug he set on the fireplace grate. Gavin's he gave to her.

She shook her head. 'I need you to get it down him.'

Without waiting to see how effective he would be,

she took one of the clean cloths and dipped it in the nearby bucket of water. Gently she cleansed the wound. Even sedated, Gavin began to move and groan. Some of the tea dribbled down his chin. The Ferguson stopped.

'He needs it all. The warmth and the willow bark I put in it will help him.'

The Ferguson nodded and continued dripping the hot fluid into Gavin, wiping up what spilled.

She found the small knife where she had laid it near the fire. Using the tongs used to put coal on the fire, she picked up the knife handle and held the blade in the flames. She felt rather than saw The Ferguson tense, but he said nothing.

He had been in many battles and seen many men wounded. He knew what she intended. She would cauterise the flesh. Better pain now than lingering death from rot.

'Please hold his shoulder.'

She pulled the knife from the fire and grasped it with a wad of cloth to protect her fingers from the heat. She took a deep breath to steady her hands and pressed the hot metal to Gavin's skin.

The hot sizzle of burning flesh filled the room. Gavin's eyes started open, and his body jerked beneath The Ferguson's hold.

'Hold still, Gavin,' The Ferguson ordered, his deep baritone a soothing rumble that even Jenna started to obey before catching herself. 'She needs to make sure there is no dead flesh to fester later.'

Moisture filled Gavin's eyes, and his jaw clenched into harsh angles. But he stopped fighting.

Jenna finished as quickly as possible. The bleeding

had also slowed with the burning. 'Good.' Her murmur was barely audible. 'I am sorry, Gavin.'

He looked at her. 'I know, Jen. I know.' Exhaustion dragged his eyelids down, and his entire body relaxed.

She took another deep breath, this one shuddering as tears threatened. It was hard enough causing pain to someone she did not know or knew slightly, but to cause her beloved cousin such agony was hard to bear. But she knew it had been necessary.

'I am going to bind you back up, Gavin, but first I want you to finish the tea.' She nodded for The Ferguson to put the mug to Gavin's lips. 'You need the warmth. Then I am going to finish with you, and we are going to get you into hiding.'

Gavin drank greedily now that he was awake. Still some dribbled on to the blankets.

Over her cousin's body, The Ferguson watched her. She felt uncomfortable at his intense scrutiny.

'Have I blood somewhere?' She wiped at her chin, then her cheek.

He shook his head. 'I am trying to figure out how a woman who looks as though a stiff wind will blow her over has the strength you have shown tonight.'

She flushed, wishing she had a smudge instead of having him compliment her. 'I only did what was necessary. Anyone would have.'

He shook his head again. 'No, they would not. I have seen battle-hardened men balk at what you have done tonight.'

Heat engulfed her at his continued praise. 'You exaggerate.'

He stared at her, his eyes first hazel, then tawny, de-

pending on how the firelight reflected from them. Unable
to continue under such study, she turned her head.

'I will make sure none of the servants are about.' She
started to stand, only to have her legs refuse to cooper-
ate. She was exhausted.

The Ferguson carefully laid Gavin back down
before surging to his feet. He held his hand to Jenna.
'Let me help you.'

She stared at his outstretched hand, not wanting to
touch it. The last thing she needed in her current state was
to have his help. She was too susceptible to him when
he was threatening to kill her. How much more so would
she be when he was being sympathetic? Too much.

'Thank you,' she muttered, 'but I am fine.'

She reached for the stone-set fire surround and
gripped one of the protruding rocks, intending to pull
herself up. She didn't realise he had moved with her
until she felt his hands on her waist. His fingers felt like
bands of iron as they closed over her softness.

'You don't wear stays,' he said, his voice gruff as he
lifted her as though she weighed nothing.

Her flush became a full-fledged blush. 'That is none
of your business.'

She turned to face him, only to find her nose level
with his loosely tied and dirty neckcloth. Musk filled
her senses. His scent. She shivered, but not with cold.

He released her and stood back. 'Of course it is not
the business of a gentleman, but I am no gentleman. I
thought we had established that.'

She tilted her head and tried to stare down her nose
at him. Papa did it so well. All she accomplished was
to make him grin.

'So we did. Now I must make sure it is safe to move

Gavin.' She paused and thought. 'If I am not back by
the time the clock strikes the half-hour, you must try to
hide him here.' She looked around. There was no place
large enough to secrete him. 'But I do not know where.'

'We will manage if it comes to that.'

The gentleness in his voice caught her. She looked
back at him. Something about the way he held himself,
the look in his eye, as though nothing were impossible,
gave her confidence in him. Likely it was this same
quality that made him such a redoubtable commander
and smuggler of hunted men. People would trust him
and follow him.

She nodded. 'Yes, yes, I am sure you will.'

She paused long enough to light another candle
before bolting.

Chapter Four

❧❧❧❧❧

Outside her stillroom it was quiet and chill. The priest's hole was on the third floor, back in one of the oldest portions of the building. It would be dank and unhealthy, but for Gavin safer than a warm bed.

She paused at her room and gathered up coverlets and pillows and a chamber pot before continuing on her way. 'Twas hard to navigate with all the bedding and keep her candle flame from the material, but she managed. Need gave her strength.

She said a silent thank-you when no one was about. The priest's hole was just off the staircase that led to the servants' quarters. She paused, but heard nothing from above. There should be several hours before anyone stirred.

She put the bedding into the small area, closed the door that looked like another panel in a fully panelled room that had once been the lord's bedchamber, and headed back. Her clothing was still damp and uncomfortable, made more so when she had put the bedding down and the cold air had hit her anew. She shivered and told herself to ignore her own discomfort.

Both men were where she had left them. Gavin even had some colour back in his cheeks, although she thought it was more from fever. Worry about his weakened state gnawed at her. She wanted to put him in a warm room with a comfortable bed and feed him hot tea and broth, but she could not do that. Everyone knew him and everyone knew what he had done.

She beckoned to The Ferguson. He picked up Gavin as though her cousin weighed nothing and followed. She hoped he could carry her cousin for the three flights of stairs, each one narrower than the one before.

Ten minutes later, seeing no one, they deposited Gavin on the makeshift bed. Gavin was unconscious. She set a bottle of laudanum beside him and a pitcher of water that she had laced with willow bark. Unless something untoward happened, she would not be able to return until tomorrow night after the family and servants had gone to bed.

With a worried frown, she pushed the damp russet hair from Gavin's brow. He felt clammy, but there was nothing more she could do.

She stood and faced The Ferguson. Skirting around him, she told herself the warmth she felt was from her clothes finally starting to dry, not from his nearness. Safely past him, she motioned him out of the small chamber that had been crowded with just Gavin and heart-thumpingly so with the three of them.

She chided herself for being so susceptible to this man. It wasn't even as though he did anything to entice her. If anything, it was the opposite. No woman in her right mind should be this attracted to a man who would kill her in a second without compunction if he felt she threatened his safety.

She spun on her heel and hurried back the way they had come.

He silently followed her.

She locked the stillroom door and turned to him. 'Thank you. He would have died if you had not come with me.'

Now that the immediate work was done, reaction set in. Tears of relief and anxiety threatened to spill over. Somehow she held them at bay.

He was still as a pond on a summer evening. Still as she could never be. And yet, raw energy came off him in waves.

He reached out and touched her cheek. She felt moisture. Surely she had not cried. She was not the type. Yet when he pulled his hand away his finger sparkled in the warm glow of the fire.

'I'm sorry,' she muttered, more embarrassed. 'I never cry.'

The excitement and fear of the night seemed to have seeped into her bones. She slumped, only to catch and draw herself up.

'You have had a trying day. And he is not out of danger yet.'

'I know.' Her answer was a small sound, not at all like her normal assured tones. She had to do better than this. 'He will get better. I know it.'

The Ferguson's full, beautifully shaped mouth quirked up at one corner. He was the most devastatingly handsome man she had ever seen. Even if she had not known he was The Ferguson, she would have paused to look at him twice—once she got past the filth of his clothing, she reminded herself. It was a futile attempt to ease the attraction he exerted on her.

'If you have any say, he will be mended by the morrow,' he murmured. He crooked one finger under her chin and tipped her head up. His heavy lids were slumberous and his eyes were dark.

Anticipation began to curl in her stomach like the first tentative wisp of smoke in a new fire. He leaned down, and she knew he meant to kiss her. Again. She let him.

His mouth touched hers. This was not the harsh, conquering touch from the tavern, but an exploratory overture. She delighted in his touch.

His lips moved against her skin, inviting her to respond to him. She did not know what to do. He was the only man who had kissed her on the lips.

'Open for me,' he murmured, his voice husky.

She did and his tongue slipped in, then pulled out. His teeth nipped the inner corner of her lower lip, sending wisps of feeling coursing down to her stomach. The urge to touch him was nearly overpowering, but she was too inexperienced and instead locked her hands into fists at her side.

When he finally pulled away, she felt bereft. The warmth that had comforted her while he kissed her fled. Goosebumps broke out on her arms.

It was an effort to open her desire-weighted eyes, but she managed. He smiled down at her.

'Thank you,' he said, moving back and making her a formal leg that would have been the envy of any dandy.

She marvelled at his skills. 'I… Will you be back to check on Gavin?'

His wonderful mouth twisted. 'You must think me braver or more stupid than I am to come again into Bloody Ayre's domain.'

She blanched. In her response to him, she had forgotten everything else. He had not. 'No, I am the stupid one. It would be too dangerous. How will I get word to you when Gavin is well enough to leave?'

'I will know.' He did not elaborate. 'But for now I'll take his horse with me. That will be one less clue for the English soldiers when they come to pay their respects to your father.'

She nodded, prodding herself to move and follow him to the outside door in spite of the pain twisting in her stomach from his hard words. She should have remembered how he felt about Papa.

She still had to take her mare to the stable. Hopefully the horses had not taken any harm from the cold. When she went out, she saw he had covered all of them with extra blankets.

She stood for long moments, watching him as he mounted and rode into the still-dark morning. It would not be sunrise for some time. Feeling the bite of the weather that had turned to snow, she headed for the stables, her horse whickering in relief behind her.

Even though she was not adequately clothed, she barely felt the cold. It scared her to know that his kiss was the reason.

Jenna groaned and rolled on to her side. Her entire body ached and damp seemed permanently embedded in her bones in spite of the feather comforters piled on her bed like mounds of snow. Her head hurt, too.

The only good thing was that at least the warmth

from his kiss had not lasted through her sleep. That would be too unnerving.

'Miss Jenna, 'tis time ye was up.' The sound of china and crystal added emphasis to the words. 'There be a guest—unwelcome, but a guest nonetheless, and your father requests your presence. An English officer.'

Jenna recognised her maid's voice. Lizzie Smith had been with her all her life, first as nanny and now as personal maid. The other woman had grown old in service.

'An English officer?'

'Aye.'

Surely it was not the redcoat from the Whore's Eye. 'Twould be too great a coincidence. And yet, why not? Papa was retired from the King's Army. But if it was the same man, he might recognise her. But she had kept the hood of her cape up. Hadn't she? She could not remember. And there were precious few redheads around.

What a muddle. Perhaps she would have Lizzie powder her hair, even though it was usually done only for formal occasions. The man might not have seen her clearly enough. And she had been drenched and bedraggled. Nor would he expect to see the woman of last night here. It might be enough disguise.

Jenna levered herself up, wincing at the stiffness in her muscles. She had done too much lifting last night with Gavin, but there had been no acceptable alternative. She hoped her cousin was comfortable until she could get to him.

'What time is it, Lizzie?' The clock was on the bed table beside her, too close for her to see clearly without her glasses. She had left them on her work table.

The older woman turned her ruddy, lined face to Jenna. Frizzed white hair framed her round cheeks. 'Past eleven.'

'What?' Jenna bolted upright, ignoring the insistent twinge of her abused body. 'Eleven! I never sleep past eight, even in the winter.'

'Not normally, no.' Lizzie moved to plump the pillows behind Jenna. 'But Joshua says you were out late last night with a birthing. It must have been a difficult one.'

The maid lifted one eyebrow, waiting for Jenna to explain where she had been. Joshua was the stable boy who must have seen her horse gone.

Jenna took a breath and told her lie, unable to meet Lizzie's eyes. 'It was a premature call. The babe is near and the father got overexcited.' She smiled as though the falsehood was truth.

Lizzie snickered. 'Ever like a man to rush things.'

Jenna flushed. No stranger to what happened between a man and a woman, she understood her maid's underlying meaning. More times than she could count, she had heard women whispering how a man wanted his pleasure with no regard for the woman. And then look where it landed her, and with none of the delights to make up for the pain and danger.

And yet…she felt the phantom touch of The Ferguson's mouth on hers. Her toes curled and her breath caught.

To cover her reaction, she pushed back the covers and swung her feet off the bed. Chill air hit her. She grabbed for her nearby woollen robe and hustled into it before going to the fire. She extended her hands and turned slow circles, hoping the warmth would wipe out the tingle she still felt from the memory of Duncan's kiss.

'What have you laid out for me to wear?' Better to think of something different.

Lizzie picked up a teal-satin *pet-en-l'air* jacket trimmed with heavy lace. There was a quilted cream-satin petticoat and lace-edged kerchief lying on a nearby chair. A matching round-eared muslin cap completed the outfit. Jenna smiled her approval. Simple as she liked, yet warm enough for the winter day after she layered her chemise and another petticoat under it all.

'That should be perfect.'

'I should say so.' Lizzie sniffed. 'I might not be French trained or spend months in London, miss, but I know what's proper.' She cast a look at Jenna. 'And what becomes you.'

'True. You have a good eye.' Not everything looked equally well with Jenna's ginger hair and freckles.

Ah, freckles. She crossed the room to her mirror and wash basin and peered at her reflection. Muddy brown splotches marched across her nose. She reached for the milk wash and set about scrubbing her face.

Lizzie harrumphed. 'No matter how you rub, those won't come off, Miss Jen. I doan care what the advertisement says.'

Jenna rinsed with ice-cold water, her teeth chattering. Her complexion glowed like polished glass, but the freckles remained. She groaned. Now she looked like a milkmaid.

'Best I dress.' She did not try to hide her disappointment. Lizzie knew how she hated the brown spots. 'Papa is likely getting impatient.'

'Hah! He was impatient when he sent me to waken you.' Lizzie picked up the freshly cleaned and ironed chemise as Jenna stepped out of her nightdress.

'Oh, dear.' Jenna hated upsetting Papa. He was so

loving that she did everything she could to ease his day. Keeping him waiting was not what she normally did.

'Here, now.' Lizzie held out the stays.

Jenna groaned. She preferred to go without as The Ferguson had discovered last night. But when she couldn't…

She sucked in her breath and held it. It was her little rebellion. Lizzie pulled the stays tight and secured them. Only when she was sure the maid was done did Jenna let her breath out. This way her stays were always a little looser than they would otherwise be. She might not have the smallest waist, but she was more comfortable than most women and she did not believe that having a tiny waist was worth not being able to breathe properly.

Except… The memory of The Ferguson lifting her last night and commenting on her lack of stays brought heat to her already rosy cheeks. She had felt so vulnerable, actually feeling the print of each of his fingers along her waist. Stays kept a woman from feeling much when touched. But last night, she had felt everything. She shivered.

'I'll have you dressed in just another moment, and you'll be much warmer.'

Jenna grinned at Lizzie's mistaken understanding. 'Thank you.'

Once she was dressed, Jenna sat for Lizzie to style her hair. The maid wound Jenna's curls close to the head as fashion dictated.

In her best, nonchalant tone, Jenna drawled, 'I believe I would like it powdered this morning.'

Lizzie's eyes opened wide. 'I must have heard you wrong, miss.'

Jenna resisted the urge to grit her teeth. 'No, you did not. I want it powdered this morning.'

Lizzie shook her head. 'Even I know that isn't done.' She raised one grey brow. 'And even when it should be done, you refuse.'

Jenna lifted her chin. 'I can and will do exactly as I please, thank you.'

Lizzie met Jenna's eyes in the mirror. 'You always were stubborn when you set your mind to something.'

Jenna forced a tight smile. 'Yes. And I intend to do as I please, not as fashion dictates.'

With a sigh of resignation, Lizzie fetched the flour and the cape to put around Jenna's shoulders to protect her clothing. Several breath-holding, eyes-squeezed-shut minutes later, it was done. Lizzie pinned the muslin cap with teal ribbons on Jenna's now-white hair. Her *toilette* was finished, except for teal stockings and plain black leather shoes that were both comfortable and practical.

'You'll do,' Lizzie said proudly. 'In spite of the hair,' she added in an affronted undertone.

Jenna ignored the last comment. A glance in the mirror told her she looked as well as could be expected, even if she was slightly outrageous with the powdered hair. She would never be a beauty, but she was clean and well groomed in a casual way that suited her. And the powdered hair suited her complexion.

More importantly, she did not look like the drenched rat from the Whore's Eye last night.

She stood and smoothed down her skirt. 'Then I will be on my way.'

Unwilling to let her charge go without gilding, Lizzie stopped her. 'You should wear that strand of pearls your mama left you.' She gave her a sly look. 'They would go very nicely with the hair.'

Jenna froze. She dared not let Lizzie—or anyone—see that her jewellery was missing. The pieces should be with Gavin's horse, which was with The Ferguson. What a tangle the disguise of the hair had created.

She waved her hand in a dismissive way. 'Oh, that would be too much. I am not dressing for Papa's guest.'

Lizzie arched one greying eyebrow. 'What if he's an eligible bachelor?'

'I am not looking for a marriage partner, Lizzie, and you know that. Papa needs me.'

Lizzie sniffed. 'Iff'n you ask me, 'twould be the best thing for both of you.'

'Well, I am not asking you.'

Until meeting The Ferguson, Jenna had never been interested in men except as patients and friends. And after last night, the last man she would find intriguing was an English soldier. While she had never considered herself a Jacobite, in spite of knowing her cousin was one, seeing how the English tracked down men like Gavin, she began to have more sympathy for the hunted fugitives and less for the English.

This was still uppermost in her mind when Jenna paused at the heavy oak door to the parlour. Surely the English officer from last night was not here, and she had sat through the torture of powdering her hair for naught. Her luck could not be that horrible for he would recognise her even with her hair powdered. Surely.

Burke, the butler, had followed her once she entered the foyer. He bowed his wig-covered head, the wrinkles at his eyes and mouth pronounced, and opened the door. 'Miss de Warre.'

Jenna gave him a small smile as she swept into the room, her voluminous skirt swishing before her and falling behind her like a wave of cream. From the corner of her eye she caught a glimpse of crimson. Tension engulfed her. She kept her gaze on her parent and her chin up.

'Papa, I hope I have not kept you waiting.'

Viscount Ayre stood. He was a tall man, slim and straight with just a hint of a stomach. His eyes were a deep, kindly brown. His skin was swarthy and his hair dark. She had inherited her colouring from her mother.

Papa held out both hands. She put her fingers in her father's warm palms, barely managing not to grasp at the security he always made her feel.

She sensed the other man rise, and only then did she turn to face him. Seller. Her smile felt frozen on her face, and she would swear the blood drained from her cheeks. Somewhere she found the strength to pull her fingers from Papa's safe clasp.

'Jenna,' Papa said, 'I would like to present Captain Lord Seller. He is here in command of a garrison.'

She made the other man a shallow curtsy. 'My lord.'

He bowed to her, his fashionable bag wig, so popular with military men, and well-fitted red uniform lending him an air of distinction. 'Miss de Warre, my pleasure to finally meet you in person.'

She kept the smile on her face, wondering when he would denounce her and demand to know what she had been doing at the Whore's Eye last night. When he continued to gaze at her, one dark brow raised as though he wondered at her perusal, she turned away and sank into a chair that was thankfully close enough so she did not have to move. Her legs would not hold her long enough to go elsewhere.

'How delightful to have the English army here, Captain Lord Seller.' She finally managed the words, glad she had not had her stays laced tightly. The room seemed closed and tight enough without having the added difficulty of breathing.

It was all she could do to keep her fingers from shaking. If he suspected her of anything, he would demand to search the house. She was not sure the priest hole would go undetected. Nor did she want Papa implicated in the treason she perpetrated with Gavin.

Seller waited until Papa sat back down before sitting himself. His manners were impeccable. 'Twas too bad he was the enemy.

His bearing was much like Papa's, which was to be expected, both having a career in the military. From there they diverged. Seller was shorter and slighter, yet with an air of wiry strength that she felt sure stood him in good stead when using a sword. His eyes were a piercing blue and his brows black as night. His mouth was thin and his jaw straight. He was the epitome of an English soldier.

'No one can be more delighted than I am, Miss de Warre, now that I see what the country has to offer,' he murmured, his tenor voice smooth and pleasant.

And still he did not denounce her. Perhaps he had not seen her clearly last night. Perhaps she was safe.

Jenna narrowed her eyes at his comment, which could be taken many ways. She chose to take it literally. 'Twas easier. 'Ah, then you must have been here for some time and had the opportunity to see how beautiful Cumbria can be even as winter closes in on us.'

'Unfortunately, no. I only returned yesterday.' A sly smile tugged at his well-shaped lips.

She tensed, but when he said nothing more she focused on his lips, which she thought too thin. Not like The Ferguson's sensual mouth. She blinked at her erratic thought. Never in her life had she thought of a man's lips before. What was happening to her?

Papa drew her attention back to the moment. 'Captain Lord Seller is here because rumours have reached London that Jacobites are fleeing here before seeking transport to France. He is not here for pleasure, Jenna.'

She concentrated on keeping her hands relaxed in her lap even though her tendency was to twist the fringe of the shawl around her shoulders. Did Seller know about Gavin? Was that why he was visiting them? Surely not, or he would not be here on what appeared to be a social visit, but would be scouring the countryside or turning their home inside out.

It was an effort to act as though she cared nothing about the man's mission. A woman of her position would only be concerned if she felt threatened, and there was no reason for her to feel that.

So she played the social role. 'That is too bad, my lord. You will be too busy to participate in the round of festivities the winter season brings. With Christmas just past, we must find other *divertissements*.'

Seller looked at her papa before returning his attention to her. 'I will be occupied, but not to the point that I won't be able to accept invitations. Just not as many as I might like.'

Burke entered with a silver platter that held a cream-coloured card. He gave it to Papa, who read it quickly.

'It seems we have more company. I had not expected them today, but no matter.' Papa turned to the butler. 'Please show them in.'

Burke bowed and left. Jenna raised a brow, wondering who was here. They rarely had guests this early in the day and now more visitors within an hour of each other.

The butler returned and announced, 'Mrs McNabb and Lord Byrne.'

A lady glided into the room followed by a gentleman. Jenna's gaze passed over the woman to stare at Lord Byrne.

Even though it was early in the day and in the country where clothing was casual and practical, he wore a peacock-blue velvet coat over a silver silk waistcoat that was embroidered with metallic threads in the shape and colours of the bird he resembled. Black pantaloons and silk stockings completed his *toilette*. Diamanté buckles secured his shoes. He would fit perfectly into a crowded London ballroom.

Were it a sunny day, he would have blinded her—and she was used to dandies. One of their neighbours had a son who thought himself the epitome of the London man about town. But Lord Byrne had an air about him that argued against the effete stance of one well-shod foot in front of the other as he made his bow, an elaborate fan flicking as though the room were too hot when it was really very cool.

Instead of a wig, his hair was curled and powdered until it was the colour of storm clouds. A black ribbon held the queue and wrapped back around and tied over the stock and ruffle at his neck.

A heart patch, perched on the corner of his full, well-shaped mouth, drew her attention to that attractive attribute. It was disconcerting to find that Lord Byrne's lips reminded her of The Ferguson's.

Once again, she remembered last night's second kiss.

Just the thought made her flush; the room suddenly too warm for comfort. She closed her eyes and willed herself to stop this foolishness. It had been a kiss. Nothing more.

When she looked again, Lord Byrne was studying her with an intensity that belied his costume. Thick sable-coloured brows and lashes gave him a sultry look in keeping with his full sensual mouth. His eyes were hazel.

Except for the colour of his hair and his clothing, he reminded her of The Ferguson. She frowned.

'Viscount Ayre,' a woman's low voice said, interrupting Jenna's thought.

Jenna forced herself to look away from the man who she was sure was much more than the dandy he played and looked at the woman who accompanied him. She had forgotten Mrs McNabb in her reaction to Lord Byrne.

The woman was older, yet still beautiful. Tall and willowy, she carried herself with grace. Her skin was porcelain fair with a small tracing of lines around her eyes and lips.

She was very similar to Lord Byrne in colouring and features, likely his mother. There the similarity ended. Her dress was more conservative. Her clothing was much like Jenna's, only in golds and browns. Her blond hair was not powdered under the muslin cap.

She was a distinguished woman, who also looked tired and worn. Jenna wondered what tragedy had aged her early, but doubted she would ever know. Jenna rose to meet Mrs McNabb, mindful of her manners.

Papa stood. 'Mrs McNabb, welcome to de Warre Castle.'

She nodded regally. 'Thank you for receiving us on such short notice.'

Papa smiled. 'My pleasure, madam. May I introduce you to Captain Lord Seller? The Captain is here to protect us.'

Jenna started at what she thought was a hint of sarcasm in Papa's voice. Surely not. He of all people would believe that Captain Seller truly would protect them.

'Seller, I had not thought to find you this far away from London.' Lord Byrne's melodious baritone seemed to float across the room as he made his languid way to the soldier. 'The last time I saw you, you were in his Majesty's private guard.'

'Ah, Byrne.' Seller's tone was a sneer. 'I see you have not changed.'

Lord Byrne stopped and drew himself up. 'Of course not. Why should I?' He snapped his fan shut, but the look in his eyes was cold. 'I am happy with the person I am.'

Seller lifted one black brow. 'I see. What brings you to the wilds of Cumbria? I had thought you never likely to leave London.'

Lord Byrne yawned behind his fan. 'We are rusticating. Mother had a penchant for the country, so I bought a hunting lodge. Nothing major.'

'Captain Seller,' Mrs McNabb intervened, 'how nice to see you again. It has been a long time.'

The Captain turned to her. 'Madam.' He bowed. 'The pleasure is mine.'

The butler re-entered with a tea tray and cakes. There was stronger drink for the men. This far north, they observed the niceties when it pleased them and ignored them when it did not.

Mrs McNabb and Lord Byrne sat in chairs opposite Jenna and her father. Burke built up the fire.

'Viscount Ayre and Miss de Warre,' Mrs McNabb said, 'we would like to invite you to a dinner in a fort-night.' She pulled a gilt-edged envelope from her muff and handed it to Jenna's father. 'A house warming.' With a gracious smile, she turned to Seller. 'Captain Seller, you are also invited, although, since I did not know you were here, I don't have an invitation. If you give me your direction, I will send one.'

There was silence for long minutes while Seller watched Viscount Ayre. Something was about. Jenna's stomach started to twist.

Finally, when Jenna thought she would tear her shawl with her nervous twisting, her father said, 'Captain Seller will be staying here.'

Jenna was thankful she already sat, otherwise she might have made a spectacle of herself. As it was, shock gave her fingers added impetus and the sound of her nails ripping through the fabric of her shawl seemed very loud to her ears in the silence following his announcement.

Her father turned an apologetic smile to her. 'I meant to tell you later, my dear.'

She nodded. 'I will notify Mrs Joiner, Papa.'

She hoped the unease she felt about the English soldier being billeted with them did not show in her voice. This would make it doubly hard to care for Gavin. It was now too dangerous for her cousin to stay here. She would find Seller a room as far from the priest hole as possible, but something must be done.

'That is easily settled, then,' Mrs McNabb said. 'I will have an invitation brought round for Captain Seller.'

Jenna forced a smile, thankful everyone was done with their tea, drink and cakes. Manners bade them leave shortly, even Seller, who was not yet billeted with them.

Something made her glance at Lord Byrne. He watched her with an intentness that belied the casual negligence of his pose. There was a coiled energy about him even though he seemed to lounge against his chair. When he realised she returned his attention, his mouth curled up faintly.

She blinked, taken aback by his attraction. Did he know how devastating he was? The knowing look in his eyes said he did. She flushed and looked away, feeling like a schoolroom miss caught in the grownups' circle and ignorant of how to go on.

It was a disconcerting feeling for a woman of five and twenty.

Thankfully, Mrs McNabb chose that moment to stand. 'We must be going, Lord Ayre.'

She held her hand out to the viscount, who took the delicate white fingers and raised them to his lips. A large blood-red ruby graced the third finger of her left hand.

'My pleasure,' he said, genuine pleasure in his tone. 'I look forward to dinner.'

Jenna gave him a piercing look. Her father was always polite. He was rarely as delighted as the smile on his face implied.

They were no sooner quit of the room than Seller rose. 'I too must take my leave.' He made a bow to Jenna. 'Miss de Warre, I am delighted to meet you again. I hope to further our acquaintance.' He turned to her father. 'My lord, thank you for your hospitality.'

Viscount Ayre stood easily. 'I am glad to be of service to the Crown.'

'Yes, sir. I will return later in the day with my belongings.' Captain Seller made a quick exit.

It took all Jenna's self-control not to rush from the room. She had to select a bedchamber for Seller, and she needed to check on Gavin. Even though it was day time and she had not planned to visit Gavin until night, her nerves were strung tight with knowing the soldier would soon live here.

She turned to her father. 'I must go make sure a room is prepared.'

He smiled kindly at her. 'I am sorry to discommode you, my dear. I wish he were not staying, but I will not—dare not—disobey a direct request from the king.'

She sighed. 'I know, Papa. I would never expect you to do so.'

'I hoped you would understand.'

There were so many unspoken emotions in his voice that Jenna longed to comfort him. She knew he was loyal to his king, even as the memory of what he had done as a young soldier haunted him. Papa had many regrets to live with. If only he could put them aside, but when Mama had died it seemed that Papa stopped trying to forget his past.

'It will be fine.' Her job was to reassure him, no matter that she was not so sure. Things had just become so much more difficult.

He sighed. 'There is more, my dear.'

Jenna's already churning stomach clenched. 'What, Papa?'

'As I said, Seller is here because of Jacobites.' He took a deep breath, regret in every line of his face. 'He tracked one to this area, only to lose him in the bad weather and rough terrain.'

It took every ounce of control Jenna had not to tear out of the room to Gavin, even knowing she could do nothing if he were discovered. 'Oh?'

Papa laid a warm hand on her arm. 'Jenna, the man will be desperate. A desperate man is a dangerous man.'

Her pulse pounded. For the first time in her life, she wanted to move away from Papa's reassuring touch. She did not want him to realise she was upset. He would start questioning her, and she was not good at dissembling.

She managed to smile, hoping it was reassuring. 'He is only one man, Papa, and likely not wanting to be discovered. I doubt he will cause any harm.'

Papa released her, but worry thinned his lips. 'I would ask you not to go out at night or alone on your healing…'

'But you know I will do what I must for others.'

He sighed. 'Yes. Just, please, remember what I have said and take precautions.'

She nodded.

Jenna did not think things could get worse. She had her beloved cousin hidden, wounded and fleeing for his life. An English officer was moving into their home, and his men were going to be billeted around the country. Papa was warning her about the dangers presented by Jacobites.

And she was halfway to being in love with the worst Jacobite of them all.

It was too much. She left in search of the housekeeper.

Chapter Five

Several hours later, Jenna carried a candelabra with three lit candles. Even during the day, the castle was dark in the winter months. It was also cold. She shivered and wished she had put a shawl over her *pet-en-l'air*. She also wished she could have brought several blankets for Gavin without anyone wondering why she had them.

Reaching the hallway that led to the stairs to the servants' quarters above and the room that opened to the priest's hole, Jenna stopped and looked and listened. When several minutes went by with nothing, she entered the small panelled room and rushed to the hidden door. She pushed the mechanism that opened the hidey-hole, wincing at the grating sound as she stepped into the small room, closing the entrance behind her.

It was like an ice house. Her worry for Gavin increased.

He lay on his good side, huddled like a babe. She went to him and laid the candelabra on the floor. She eased him to his back and wrapped the blankets about him as best she could. His body shook with cold, yet his forehead burned.

She noted he had not drunk any of the water she had left. It contained the tree bark that would fight the fever. There was a light cover of ice on the water that she broke. She moistened a nearby rag with the water and dribbled it into his mouth. It seemed she did this for ever until the small of her back hurt from bending.

In between drips, Gavin thrashed. He needed warm soup and better care than she could give him here, particularly when Seller arrived. She could not take a chance someone would see her enter here. Most did not know this priest hole existed. Papa did. He had shown it to her when they first came to live here.

'Jenna?' Gavin's raspy, weak voice held a rattle.

Her worry intensified. He could not get an inflammation of the lungs. 'Yes, Gavin.'

'I am so hot.'

'I know,' she murmured. 'You have a fever.'

He tried to wriggle out of the blankets, and it was all she could do to keep him snug. She was not strong enough for this. His wound smelled of blood, but not of putrefaction. It was a thing to be thankful for.

'Hot.'

'You must stay covered, Gavin.'

His fever-glazed eyes stared at her as he continued to struggle. She had brought a small covered mug of broth. Most of the heat would be gone, but it would give him strength none the less. It might also make him less delirious and better able to listen to her about staying in the blankets.

'Gavin, please, be still. I have some broth.'

He continued to look at her, then nodded.

She was a long time getting the broth in him. Then she had him drink from the medicated water. He calmed down. The water also contained laudanum. He lay back and closed his eyes.

'Gavin,' she said softly, 'I must go. Please stay in the blankets.'

His eyelids drifted up, and he gave her the smile he always had for her. 'Get The Ferguson, Jen. He will know what to do.'

She wondered if he was still confused before realising he was right. Gavin could not stay here, not in this condition and with Seller moving in.

'I will, Gavin. But promise me you will stay covered.'

He nodded, not bothering to look at her again as he fell into a laudanum-induced sleep. Worry gnawed at her. She brushed the copper-coloured hair from his cooling brow.

She must find The Ferguson again and had no place to go but back to the Whore's Eye. Tonight. Gavin could not stay here longer.

But what if…?

A picture of Lord Byrne formed in her mind. He was much like The Ferguson in facial characteristics. True, they had different hair. Nor could she imagine The Ferguson dressing as a fop. He was too vibrant, too masculine to dress like a peacock. She was delusional to even think there was a similarity. Enough of this fruitless conjecture. She had to do something for Gavin.

The cold in the room penetrated to her bones. There was no place to build a fire here even if she could have risked it. The warmth from the three candles was not enough, and she dared not leave them unattended for fear of fire. She sighed and rose, holding the light.

At the door, she pushed the panel open, once more wincing at the grating sound, and listened. Nothing.

She slipped into the corridor, only to see her father. She nearly dropped the candlestick, her fingers shaking like leaves in a gust of wind. She stilled her hand.

'Papa.' What was he doing here?

'Jenna,' he said evenly. 'I see you are using the priest's hole.'

She wanted to lie, but she had never done so to him. Besides, all he had to do was go into the small room to see Gavin.

She nodded. 'Please, Papa, pretend you did not see me.'

He raised one greyshot dark brow. 'If 'tis that bad, my dear, then perhaps I should look.'

She shook her head. ''Tis better if you do not.'

'Because I am a loyal subject of George II?'

She nodded again, her throat tight with apprehension. 'It would be best. For everyone.'

His steady grey eyes studied her. 'What about Seller?'

She bit her lower lip as she made herself meet his gaze. 'He has created a problem.'

'I thought he might, but he has a letter from the Duke of Cumberland asking me to billet him. I could not refuse, even if I would.' Sadness tinged his voice.

Jenna reached for him with her free hand, forgetting her own worry in her father's misery. 'I know that, Papa.'

He sighed. 'I suppose I have caused enough pain in the past for the followers of the king across the water. And my family,' he added so quietly that Jenna almost did not hear.

'Oh, Papa, please, do not blame yourself so.'

He looked past her to the door. 'Your mother died from sorrow at what I did to her people.'

Jenna shook her head violently. 'No, Papa. She died

in childbirth and the babe with her. Aunt Hortense was there. She told me.'

He sighed again and looked back at her. 'Hortense is a kind woman—as was your mother.'

'She is a practical woman. And Mama loved you. Aunt told me that. Mama loved you for the man you became, not the man who followed orders.'

He patted her hand, which still lay on his arm. 'You are as kind and generous as your mama, my dear.'

Caught in his pain, Jenna wrapped her arm around him and laid her head on his shoulder, careful to hold the lit candles away. 'I love you, Papa.'

He held her as he so often had when she had been younger, a motherless child. He had given up his army career to be with her and to raise her. Papa was the world to her.

'I love you, too, Jenna.' His voice broke.

Her heart ached for him. For long moments, she rested in the warmth and safety of his embrace. It had been a long time since she had turned to her father for solace, but he was always there for her. Now she had to be there for him.

'Then, please, Papa, forget you found me here.'

He stiffened before releasing her. His shrewd eyes studied her. 'Perhaps that is best. I owe your aunt a great deal. But best you find another place for him. Seller is no fool.'

He knew Gavin lay behind the door. She was not surprised. Papa was canny and smart or he would not have risen so high in King George's army and been trusted enough by the Duke of Cumberland to earn a viscountcy for his efforts against the Jacobites. Now he was giving her a chance to save her cousin. From love.

Relief washed over her. 'Thank you, Papa.' She rose on tiptoe to kiss his cheek. 'I will.'

'Please be careful, Jenna. Remember what I told you earlier.'

She nodded. 'I will, Papa. But there are some things that I must do, no matter what the consequences.'

'I know, my dear.' Sadness made his narrow face seem overly long. 'Seller said he would be back tomorrow afternoon with his gear.' He patted her hand before gently removing it from his arm and walking away.

She watched his proud, straight back until he turned the corner out of sight. She loved her father, and it hurt to see him have to go against his loyalties to his king when he already had so much to bear. His conscience was troubled enough without this betrayal. But Gavin was family.

She had to move her cousin tonight. She had to find The Ferguson.

Jenna returned to her room and rang for Lizzie.

'Miss, word just arrived from Mistress James. It seems she thinks her time is come again.'

Relief swamped Jenna. Here was her excuse to leave. Even if Mistress James was wrong, Jenna could safely leave the house. She would deliver the babe before going to the Whore's Eye. No one need be the wiser about her real motive.

The Ferguson was her only hope for Gavin. She had to have a safe place for her cousin.

'Miss Jenna?'

The maid's unspoken question jolted Jenna from the circle of her thoughts. 'I must change into riding clothes quickly.' She could not travel as she was. She did not want to repeat last night's physical discomfort any more than was needed.

The weather was too bad, and she would be on small roads where a carriage would easily become stuck in this weather. Better to ride, as was her norm. A carriage would draw even more attention and comment at the Whore's Eye than her second appearance. But she had no other way to contact The Ferguson, and contact him she would.

Once more the idea that the Jacobite hero was actually Lord Byrne flitted through her mind. Again, she denied it. The Ferguson was too strong, too magnetic to be a dilettante lord. Unless it was a disguise.

But she did not have the luxury of making a mistake. She would go to the Whore's Eye and try to contact the man she knew really was The Ferguson.

Soon she was dressed and hurrying to her stillroom. First things first.

She took the bag of medicinals she would need from the shelf where she kept her birthing supplies, knowing Lizzie had sent word ahead to the stables and ordered her mare prepared. Everyone in the castle knew the procedure after these past five years, and they all did their part flawlessly.

Jenna made her way to where her horse stood, ready to go. The stable boy gave her a gap-toothed grin. She smiled at him. 'Joshua, please remind Lizzie to tell my father that I am gone and will be home late.'

He nodded. 'Yes, mistress.'

A groom stood nearby. Jenna bit her lip. She dared not tell him her second errand. Nor did she dare go without him. She always took a groom—except last night, and then she had excused herself by the lateness of the hour. The man was here now and dressed to accompany her. She would think of something.

'We have not a moment to dawdle,' she finally said and motioned him to follow her.

He boosted her into the saddle. She pulled the collar of her cape tight around the jacket of her riding outfit and set the mare into a canter. The uncomfortable gait was jarring, but it covered distance quickly and was safer than a gallop. Her patient's child would not wait.

Still, it took longer than she liked to reach the small stone cottage where her work would begin.

Hours later than Jenna had anticipated, she eased the newborn from the mother's birth canal. Blood and mucous covered the mite. Jenna wiped the fluids from the child's face and swabbed out its mouth before giving it a light swat to make it scream and start breathing. The boy-child scrunched his eyes mightily and protested the change in his environ.

Jenna cradled the newborn to her breast, uncaring that he would ruin her gown. 'You have a lusty lad here, Jane.'

The tired mother smiled wanly. 'Bless you, miss, for coming.'

She smiled at the mother. ''Tis my pleasure to help in this miracle.'

Jenna picked up the nearby swaddling cloth and wrapped the babe herself, reluctant to give the small bundle up. It was thus every time for longer than she cared to ponder.

With a sigh of regret, she laid the squirming child on his mother's stomach and watched as Jane loosened the ties on her blouse and began to nurse. A piercing ache filled Jenna's breasts.

She rose and turned away from the disturbing scene. She had thought herself inured to the emotion elicited by the noisily sucking child. She should be, for it would never be her delight to hold a babe of her own.

Papa needed her too much.

She would never marry, even if someone braved her spinsterhood to ask. She could never leave Papa with his guilt and his melancholy. She was all he had. She knew there were more days than was good when Papa would not rise from his bed if it were not for her.

And the only man who had ever tempted her was a man who was forbidden. Not that The Ferguson was interested in her. It was just as well. She could never betray Papa with a Jacobite.

To keep herself busy, she washed her hands in the bucket of water she had prepared before starting the delivery. Turning back to the new mother, whose eyes were already closed from exhaustion, she wished there was someone else here to give instructions to, but there was not. The father was out. Bad for the mother, but good for her excuse to go to The Whore's Eye.

'Jane.' She waited until the woman opened her eyes. 'See that you take this if you have trouble breast feeding.' Jenna laid a packet of dried fennel seeds, vervain and stinging nettles near the pallet. 'Make a tea from it. It will stimulate your milk. Rest between feedings. You should sleep now and, hopefully, the babe with you.'

Tired and unaccountably melancholy, Jenna exited the cottage. She petted Rosebud and crooned to the mare, giving her an apple as reward for waiting so patiently. The horse daintily ate her treat, her brown eyes soulful, while Jenna secured her bag of supplies.

Sam, the groom, waited as patiently. He had stayed in the small shed where the family housed their farm animals. It was Jenna's experience that most men did not enjoy childbirth.

He came to her now and laced his hands to help her mount. 'Thank you, Sam.'

He smiled even though his lips were white from cold. 'It seems everything is fine?'

'Yes, just longer than I had thought.'

He nodded. 'That it was, miss.'

Contrition for his discomfort made her sorry she had to drag him still further afield. 'We have one more stop to make.' His face fell, but he said nothing. 'The father needs to be notified.'

His gaze shifted, and she knew he disagreed with her. Everyone knew Jane's husband did as he pleased and returned when he wanted. But this was Jenna's excuse.

'As you say, miss.' Still not looking at her, he asked, 'Does anyone know where he is?'

Jenna stiffened her determination as the lie tumbled from her lips. 'The Whore's Eye.'

'Wha—' He snapped his mouth shut, then realised he was her protector. 'But you can't go there, miss. No lady goes there.'

She took a firm grip on Rosebud's reins. 'I am. I will not leave a new mother alone when her husband's whereabouts is easy to locate.'

She urged her mare forward to stop any further protest the groom would have, and she knew he had plenty. But she was determined.

The sun had left long ago and the sky was clear and the night cold. It would be freezing soon. Jenna watched her breath form miniature clouds in the silver light of the full moon. Moonshadows danced on the frost-sparkled ground.

Exhausted as she was, she truly did not want to go to the inn, but she had to find The Ferguson. Gavin's life depended on it.

It was a cold thirty minutes on windy tracks to the place. She was thankful there was no rain.

Perched on a promontory overlooking the sea, the tavern was a favourite spot for the local smugglers. It was also an ideal spot to smuggle people out of the country. She had realised how perfect last night. It also helped that the Whore's Eye was on the road from Carlisle to the coast. No wonder Gavin had been directed to come here.

Her spirits lifted. Surely The Ferguson was here often since Gavin had indicated the man had a network. Likely the local smugglers. That could be a dangerous thing. Men who made their livings illegally did what they must to survive. Just as The Ferguson had made it clear that if she endangered him, she would not last.

A *frisson* of unease skated down her spine, which felt cold enough to be coated in ice. Even with more clothing than last night and no rain, she was uncomfortable. She would much rather be home in front of the fire. Poor Sam had to feel worse, but he had said no word of complaint after his first remonstrances.

Once more, she dismounted and handed Sam the reins. 'Both of you need to go inside the stable. I will not be long.'

The look of disappointment on Sam's face would have been comical if she did not feel so sorry for him.

He had hoped to go into the inn where it would be warm. But she did not want him to see her make contact with The Ferguson if the man was here. She had learned that much. Nor did she have to enter secretly because she was here looking for Jane's husband.

A lad looking the worse for wear came from a ramshackle building that Jenna decided was the stable. He scowled at her, his lank brown hair nearly hiding his wary eyes.

She smiled at him. 'Please see that my mare is kept warm and my groom is brought a hot drink. I will not be long.'

She dug into her pocket and pulled a copper out and handed it to him. He took the money, a look of surprise twisting his mouth.

Because she never knew when word would come that she was needed, she always carried small amounts of money with her. A small single-shot pistol nestled in the pocket on her other hip. She was not unaware of the danger her travels put her in, even with a sturdy footman for protection; she was just not willing to stop when what she did helped others.

Sam handed his horse's reins to the boy and followed her. She turned to him. 'No, I will go in alone. Stay and make sure nothing happens to our horses. They are in more danger of being stolen than I am of being accosted.'

She saw him struggle with her impropriety. They both knew she spoke only part of the truth. In a place like this, she might easily be raped while he waited outside. But she could not risk him seeing what she intended to do. Gavin's life was too precarious and what The Ferguson did too important. She would do what needed to be done to protect them, even though it endangered her.

Determined, she slipped inside the door. The familiar odours of mutton and onion assaulted her nostrils. The room was not as smoky as the night before, and the stink of wet wool was gone. Yeast from the ale was a familiar blanket of scent.

As before, she skirted the outside wall. She looked rapidly from side to side. It would be best for her story if Jane's husband, Caleb, truly was here.

Movement caught her eye. Red.

It took every ounce of control not to jerk in that direction. Instead she took a deep breath and increased her pace, moving crabwise.

A group of men diced near the fire. One stood out. A tall man with coal-dark hair and a raffish tilt to his head made her pulse speed. The Ferguson. She hoped. Her glasses were in her saddlebags.

A hand gripped her shoulder and squeezed painfully. Jenna jumped, taken by surprise because her focus had been on her quarry. Her peripheral vision showed red.

'Not so fast,' a cultured English voice said.

Her hands fisted and she forced them to relax as she turned to the man who held her prisoner. Even without her glasses, which were in her saddlebags, she recognised him. 'Captain Seller,' she managed to say around the constriction in her throat. 'Release me.'

He stared hard at her, his hand falling away. 'Miss de Warre?' His thin mouth thinned more. 'What are you doing here?'

She stepped back and hoped he could not see the pulse she felt pounding in her temple. It always happened when she was agitated. Or she shredded something with her fingernails. 'I might say the same of you.'

He scowled at her. 'I am a man and this is a place to drink.'

She snorted. 'You could do that in our drawing room.'

His eyes narrowed. 'I am also looking for someone, as you well know.'

She forced a flippancy to her tone that she was far from feeling. 'So am I. I am looking for the husband of a patient.'

'The husband of a patient?' he echoed her, disbelief raising his black brows.

She nodded, realising they formed a spectacle for the entertainment of the other people in the room. The rough and dangerous men here could be her protection from this man and his suspicions.

She raised her voice. 'Yes. Mistress James just birthed her fifth child. A boy at last. I think her husband will want to know.'

'You think a peasant will care about that?' Seller sneered. 'He is not even concerned enough to be home.'

She sneered back at him. She had to fend him off. Finding Jane's husband was nothing but an excuse. Still, Caleb James might reasonably be here. Nor did she like Seller's attitude toward these people.

'The boy will be valued. He will help work the land and will not cost a dower to marry off.'

'And you came to a place like this to find the father? I find that very interesting.' He watched her like a snake watches its prey. 'How conscientious of you.'

She heard disbelief mixed with condescension in his tone. She was a country mouse to him. It irked her, but better he think that than the truth.

Loud laughter followed by raised voices made her turn to the dicing table. The Ferguson stood and stared down the man across from him.

'Are you calling me a cheat?' His voice was deadly soft, and the hair stood up on Jenna's nape.

She wondered if he was causing a diversion for her. That was a dangerous game.

Without another look at Captain Seller, she started toward the table. The man could not be so daft as to intend to fight one of the men who frequented this place. She was sheltered, but she lived in this area. She knew what some of these men were capable of. She had treated the victims many times.

If The Ferguson were injured, there would be no-where safe for Gavin. His opponent had a vicious smile on his mouth as he lunged, a skinning knife in his hand. As she watched The Ferguson dodge the killing thrust, her heart seemed to lodge in her throat before starting a rapid, staccato beat that nearly choked her.

Surprise at the strength of her reaction caused her to stumble. She caught herself. She was worried because he was the only person who could save Gavin. She was not worried because she feared for his safety. She did not know the man.

She surged forward. She had to stop the fight. For Gavin.

Before she reached the circle of men who were now betting on the two fighters, a figure stood and blocked her way. She tried to move around, only to have someone grip her wrist. She was getting heartily tired of being handled.

'Let go of me.' She jerked her arm only to have the person—woman—who held her move forwards until they stood nose to nose.

'You doan belong here.' Vehemence leant the woman's words force. 'You will be the death of him.'

Surprise held Jenna stiff. The woman who had been sitting on The Ferguson's lap last night and fondling him in a too-familiar way faced her. Her black brows were a fierce bar across her forehead.

'I need his help.'

The woman forced Jenna backwards and to the side. A quick look at the fighters told Jenna The Ferguson was not only holding his own, but beating back his attacker. Thinking quickly that Seller was also watching her and likely wondering why she had sped toward a fight instead of running from it, the last thing she needed to do was make the redcoat more interested in the scuffle than he already was. Nor had Caleb James materialised.

She allowed herself to be manoeuvred away.

Chapter Six

The woman propelled Jenna through a door, and it was all Jenna could do to keep her footing as they stepped down. No one tried to stop them and no one followed. Everyone watched the fight.

They were in the back hallway and through it. The woman's grip shifted, and she pulled Jenna down some steps into a small room with one candle. There was no fire. Jenna could barely make out the woman's features, but knew her for the tavern wench Nelly.

'What are you doing here?' Nelly's grip tightened until Jenna thought her wrist would break.

'I told you to let…me…go.' Anger started in the pit of Jenna's stomach.

'So you can go back in and make him pick another worthless fight in order to protect you from the redcoat? I doan think so, *my lady*.'

Her term of courtesy was an insult. Jenna felt as though she had been slapped. She was strong from her work with sick people who needed to be lifted and turned as often as they needed medicating. Her fury at being ordered about increased that strength. Jenna wrenched her arm out of the woman's grasp. She would have a bruise or skin rash from the movement needed to free her wrist, but she did not care.

It felt good to know she could break the woman's hold. It gave her a sense of power. 'That is better,' she muttered, rubbing the bones where the woman had squeezed.

'You are a selfish bitch.' The woman's voice was a lash.

'I am desperate,' Jenna stated flatly. 'If that makes me selfish in your eyes, then so be it.'

'Leave before you cause him worse trouble.'

The urge to refuse was strong. There was something about this woman that rubbed Jenna wrong, like a cat whose fur is being pushed the wrong way.

'I need to speak to him.' She would not tell the woman about Gavin.

The Ferguson might bed this tavern wench, but that did not make her trustworthy. Men bedded women all the time and it meant nothing. She knew from the number of birthings she attended where there was no man.

And the twist in her stomach and the taste of sourness in her mouth meant nothing. So what if this woman was his lover? He meant nothing to her. Never could mean anything to her. He was a Jacobite through and through. She was not. Her father was Bloody Ayre.

There would never be anything between them except Gavin's rescue. That was enough. She would make it enough.

She heard footfalls and a sharp intake of breath. 'Foolish woman.' His cold tone cut like a northern wind as he closed the door behind himself.

Without thinking, she asked, 'Are you all right?' She moved toward him. 'Did his knife get you?'

Her attention focused on scanning him for blood; it took her several minutes to look at his face. One black brow was raised in sardonic amusement.

'Now you worry about my safety? 'Tis a little late.' Irony laced the words. 'But don't worry. I'm none the worse for your stupidity.'

Having reassured herself that he was unharmed, she noted the tightness in her chest was gone. But not for long as his words and tone sunk in. Jenna lifted her jaw and squinted to bring his face into better focus. She did not need to see fine details to know he was angry.

'I had to find you. Gav—' she cast a glance at the woman who still stood too close '—someone's safety depended on it.'

His full sensual mouth thinned. 'I know that.'

'What?' Anger seeped past her bravado. 'How?'

His gaze flicked to his doxy and back to her. 'Not here. You may be reckless, but I am not. Anyone might overhear.'

Jenna realised with a start that their entire conversation was taking place in harsh whispers. She had heard everything as though they yelled. 'As you say. But what is—'

He cut across her. 'Not here. I will come to you later. Be prepared.'

She closed her mouth on words she knew would be useless. He would do as he wished, and she must deal with her own reaction to him. A sharp glance at the woman and back to his inscrutable face and she pivoted on her booted heel. She headed back to the taproom.

Strong fingers closed on her shoulder for the second time this evening. Only her reaction was so different as to be unrecognisable to her. The hand holding her now belonged to The Ferguson.

Awareness radiated from his touch. Her face flushed and the warm kitchen seemed stifling. She rounded on him, embarrassment and unwelcome response fuelling her emotions. 'What now?'

One black brow rose. 'Best you leave by the back door that leads into the garden. Otherwise, Seller might insist on accompanying you. A lady alone and all that.' He paused as though considering. 'Are you alone?'

She gaped at him. With part of her mind she realised his hair was lamp-blacked because there was no sheen to it. She told herself to remember the detail for later, if she could remember anything but her body's reaction to his touch.

'I have a footman with me.'

'Good. This is no place to be unescorted.'

His concern penetrated the sense of pleasure his touch always generated in her. She met his gaze with a question in hers. He looked at her, concern darkening his eyes to warm amber. It took her aback to realise he truly cared about what happened to her. It also made her more vulnerable to him.

Her hand strayed to where he still held her. She made herself pry his fingers lose instead of twining hers with his. 'Do not touch me again,' she managed to say as his hand fell to his side, afraid that if he kept touching her she would finally lose what self-control she had. The last thing she wanted was to cling to him.

His lips curled sardonically. 'As the lady wishes.' He made her a mockery of a bow.

Her blush intensified even as she registered that he was very skilful at the courtly motion. Uncharacteristically so.

'Humph! I never knowed such carrying on.' The woman's full country accent and annoyed tone cut like a whip.

Jenna's discomfort became close to mortification as she realised the tavern wench had seen her response to The Ferguson. A lady did not wear her emotions on her sleeve, no matter how trying the situation.

It was all she could do not to run to the door and out into the cold night. Somehow she managed to square her shoulders and stride past both of them without a look at either. She even got through the exit without stumbling.

When the door closed behind her, Jenna felt wrung out and leaned back against the building. Nothing had gone as she had planned—except that she had made contact with The Ferguson and he would help her. She had to trust him to do that.

And she had not found Caleb James to tell him about his new son. Hopefully the man was home by now. Jane would need his help.

Jenna took deep gulps of the frozen air and watched the puffed clouds of her breath float away into the night sky. The heat of seconds before evaporated and cold threads wove through her clothing. She stepped away from the building and headed for the ramshackle stable where Sam waited with their horses. She turned the corner that put her in front of the tavern and yards from the stables.

'Miss de Warre.' Captain Lord Seller's voice stopped her in midstep. 'I began to worry that something had happened to you and came outside to search.'

A shiver that was neither desire nor cold skipped down her spine. 'I am perfectly capable of taking care of myself, Captain Seller.' Belatedly she heard the rudeness in her words. The last thing she needed to do was alienate him. He was too powerful a man to have him seeking retribution against her or hers. 'But I thank you for your concern.'

'I am glad to know that, Miss de Warre. But as a gentleman, it is my duty—and my pleasure—to offer you escort home.'

He watched her, waiting for her to make a mistake. No matter that he was a remarkably handsome man. All she saw was a threat.

'Thank you again, my lord, but I have a footman with me. He is more than enough protection for me here in my own country.'

'A lady never has enough protection.'

'I do. No one would knowingly harm me.'

'Ah,' he murmured. 'Because of your good works. Everyone speaks highly of you. But there are goings-on here that have nothing to do with the ordinary folk you help so unstintingly. And the men who perpetrate these activities will not think twice about hurting you or worse.'

She blanched at his blunt words before feeling her cheeks heat with embarrassment. Ire followed quickly. 'A gentleman would not speak thus to a lady.'

His smile turned cruel. 'A lady would not need such warning.'

'Then since I am not a lady, I do not need your company. A footman is more than satisfactory for the likes of me, Captain Seller.'

She brushed past him, hoping he would not insist. She had no desire for his company. The man was insidious and not to be trusted. His first loyalty was to the king. He would betray Gavin in a heartbeat. And he might linger when she did not know when The Ferguson planned on contacting her.

Sam, her footman, emerged from the smoky light of the stable door. He led their horses. Jenna rushed to him and accepted his folded hands in lieu of a mounting block. He boosted her into the side saddle from which she looked back to see Seller standing where she had left him. He made no move to follow. Nor did he tip his tricorn as a gentleman would to a lady.

She realised he did not trust or like her any more than she did him. So be it, as long as he did not hurt Gavin or Papa.

They were minutes into their ride when Jenna heard a twig snap. She twisted in her saddle. 'Was that you, Sam?'

He shook his head. 'No, miss. I've been thinking we're being followed.' He looked behind them. 'Might be that soldier.'

Or The Ferguson, she thought. 'Perhaps.'

'I have a pistol.' Sam drew a large two-barrelled pistol from the holder that attached to his saddle.

'Hopefully we will not need it.'

'Shall I ride back and see?'

Somehow, she did not think Seller followed them. He had no need of secrecy. She hoped it was not someone intending harm. And doubted that it was. She was well known here and knew not many would set out to hurt her. That left only The Ferguson. If their follower was him, he would not appreciate her stopping and challenging him.

'No,' she finally answered Sam. 'Let us continue. Whoever it is, if it is someone, will make themselves known or not.'

* * *

Hours later, safe at home, Jenna made herself concentrate on the tincture of willow bark she was decocting when she really wanted to pace the room. Who had followed them? She still did not think it had been Seller. But if it had been The Ferguson, why was he taking so long to make his presence known?

Perhaps he waited until all chance was past of the servants being awake. But that did not answer her curiosity or ease the impatience that rode her.

He might not even come tonight. She pushed that away. He had to.

She had left Gavin for the third time a short while ago, and he was still feverish. The lack of warmth, food and care were taking their toll on him. He needed more constant care than she could give him.

But what could The Ferguson do for him? The man was a fugitive. Yet, instinctively she had turned to him without a thought for how he might accomplish what Gavin needed. She was indeed the fool he had called her in the tavern kitchen.

Soon she would have to go back to Gavin. The last time he had refused to eat the broth she had smuggled from the kitchen. This time she would make him drink it along with the water she had dosed again with willow bark.

She finished pouring the tincture into a container and capped it. A cold breeze wrapped around her ankles. Startled, she twisted to see the outside door was opening.

The Ferguson slipped into the room. He had not knocked. He went to the fire and held his hands to the warmth.

Gladness flared in her. She squelched it. She was relieved he was here. Gavin needed him. And she wanted to know. 'Did you follow me home?'

He glanced over his shoulder. 'And if I did?'

'Then what took you so long to come here?'

He rolled his shoulders as though tension had frozen them. 'The servants. The last thing any of us needs is for me to be spotted.'

It was as she had thought. 'Thank you for coming,' she said to his back. 'And for following me.'

'I wouldn't be much of a man if I left you to travel alone, even with a servant.' He turned. 'And Gavin is the brother I never had. I could not leave him here when Seller is going to billet here.'

She moved closer, surprised he knew. 'How did you learn that? I did not know until this afternoon.'

He shrugged, his labourer's woollen coat shifting loosely on his broad shoulders. 'I have ways.'

'Spies?'

'If you wish. Too much is at stake, too many lives depend on me, for me not to know everything I can about what is happening here. Smuggling Jacobites out of England is not a picnic on a sunny day. It is a life-and-death pursuit in the blackest of nights.'

'Poetical for the ruffian you portray.'

He smiled, showing white teeth in a face that was smudged with smoke. 'We all have our masquerades.'

'Some more than others.'

A glint of hardness made his hazel eyes spark like fine citrines. 'Some of us have more need than others.'

He looked like a man who could and would kill if necessary, and for an instant her original wariness of him returned. 'Ruthlessness is an acquired trait.' She was glad her voice did not shake with the sudden unease he had caused her.

'A required trait for a man in my line of work.' He paced toward her, flexing his fingers in their thick woollen gloves. 'Is Gavin ready?'

She sighed, and decided not to confront him with her suspicion that he was Lord Byrne. It was not important right now. Her cousin was. And if her suspicion was correct, this dangerous man might decide she knew too much.

'He is as ready as I can make him without being able to lift him and dress him more warmly.' Distress tightened her throat. 'Or care for him as he needs.'

His wool-rough finger touched the corner of her mouth, making her still. Little darts of pleasure shot from the contact. She closed her eyes briefly, unable to meet his hooded gaze when her body's reaction to him was betraying her good sense.

He spoke in a gentler voice than she had thought possible. 'Don't fret so. I will take him where someone will be able to care for him most hours of the day and night without fear of being caught. The only bad side of the situation is that none has your skills. 'Twould be better if he could be where you can openly care for him, but, since that isn't possible, we will make do.'

She fretted. 'Seller has come at the worst possible time.'

His laugh was harsh and low. 'Do you not know why?'

She gave him a puzzled look. 'He is here looking for Jacobites, but that is not unusual. The English are scouring the countryside everywhere looking for them.'

'But why come here, where your father—with his reputation—holds sway?' His voice was hard once more, and the glint was back in his eyes.

'Because Papa regrets what he did in his youth.'

'You are more maudlin and foolish than I had thought.' He strode away from her, his harsh words hanging in the icy air. 'Your father has no conscience. He massacred dozens of men simply because he was told to. Men who had welcomed him into their homes. That is not the work of a just or caring man.' He turned back to her, his mouth a thin, contemptuous line. 'And then he accepted a viscountcy, wealth and property for his perfidy.'

The blood drained from her face, and all feeling seemed to leach from her limbs. She managed to put a hand on her worktable to keep herself from falling to the floor under the sharp beat of his words—words that had too much truth in them for comfort. But she had to defend her beloved papa.

'He has suffered for what he did.' Her voice sounded small and weak to her ears. 'Papa is a good man.'

'Hah!' He paced until he was beside her, his hip against the table she still used for support. 'So speaks the dutiful, loving daughter.'

Bewilderment and hurt held her. 'If you hate Papa so much, why do you help Gavin who is my cousin, Papa's nephew?'

'Because Gavin is a Jacobite like me. Because I am not so embittered as to visit the sins of your father on a man who is nothing like him. Gavin has honour and courage.'

'So does Papa.' It was a cry wrung from the pain his words caused. 'No man could regret what he has done like Papa does. He never forgets. He blames himself for so much.' She stopped the torrent of words and took a deep breath, hoping to still the raging in her heart. 'He always remembers. He even sent recompense to the families.'

The Ferguson's mouth twisted, and Jenna wondered how she could have ever found it beautiful or allowed herself to be seduced by its soft movement against her own. His lips were diamanté-hard.

'No amount of blood money can replace the men whose lives he took.'

'Papa knows about Gavin, yet he chose not to betray him. You cannot tell me that is the act of a heartless man. I know differently.' Fierceness lent her the strength to push away from the table—and him.

He advanced on her. 'Do you? Can you read a man's heart?'

She backed up, searching his face, realising something was changing, but not knowing what. 'No one can do that.' She whispered the words, continuing to inch away from him. 'But I know Papa.'

His eyes darkened. 'Do you? Or do you just think you do?'

She blanched, but held firm. 'I do.'

'Do you know me?'

Bewilderment made her pause. 'No,' she answered truthfully just as he reached her.

'Yet you trust me.' He was unrelenting.

She raised a hand to keep him from her, dropped it. The last thing she needed in this circumstance was to touch him and feel her barriers fall. 'I trust you to do what is best for Gavin.'

He nodded.

Confused at the change of topic and her emotions, she nearly cried, 'But this has nothing to do with your reason for being here. Gavin needs you. You will help him. We both know that. Nothing else matters.'

He studied her. 'Are you sure of that?' His voice was a beguiling whisper that twisted through her resistance.

She took a deep breath, watching him all the while. 'Nothing matters but that you will help my cousin.' The words sounded wrenched from her.

His mouth curled sardonically. 'Not your father?'

She shook her head.

'Not your response to my touch?'

She shook her head.

'You lie.'

His bald words were like a slap. She searched for something to retaliate with or at the very least turn the advance back on him. 'As do you. You lie about your identity, with your lamp-blacked hair and your masquerade as a cutthroat rogue.'

'You're more observant than I've given you credit for.'

She almost thought there was admiration in his eyes, but knew she must be imagining it. Yet she was not imagining the effect he had on her, even after the awful things he had said about her father. There was something about this man that breached all her barriers and went to the core of who she was.

He was more dangerous to her than a potential murderer. He could steal her heart.

She had to put emotional and physical distance between them. The last thing she wanted after their angry words was for him to seduce her—something she both feared and hoped he meant to do.

Somehow, she turned her back to him. Her flesh pricked as though he moved up on her. She made herself step firmly to the fireplace mantel where she picked up a brass candle holder and lit the candle's wick. Her hand shook with the emotions he had pulled from her, emotions it was too soon for her to even hope to calm. She left the room without looking to see if he followed.

Hopefully the servants would all be abed for she could wait no longer. Things between them were becoming too complicated, too volatile.

She moved silently as she made her way to the back areas of the castle where the older portion hid small, cold rooms and narrow, steep steps. The flame flickered against the windowless walls, casting shadows that wavered with each step she took. With her free hand, she pulled her shawl closer.

She could barely hear his footfalls. But she did not need to. A sense beyond her five knew he followed.

She entered the chamber where the secret door hid. Looking over her shoulder for the first time in the entire trip, she realised he was close. Too close. She could feel the warmth of his breath on her face. His chest was scant inches from her back. It was an effort to turn away when she was torn between wanting to burrow into the strength she knew he possessed and the urge to smack him for his denouncement of Papa.

She did neither. She opened the door to the priest hole and slipped inside. Gavin watched them with eyes that to her critical study seemed more aware than they had earlier. Her pulse jumped in relief that he was responding to her treatment. The move might not be as hard on him as she had feared.

Kneeling beside him, she set the candlestick on the stone floor. His forehead was moist. Hopefully the fever was breaking.

'How do you feel?'

He grimaced. 'I have felt better.' He looked beyond her. 'Duncan. Thank goodness you are here. I cannot stay here and endanger Jenna.'

'You—' She cut off her rebuttal of his words. She feared he would be discovered. But as always, he was more concerned with others. Her cousin was a man who deserved to live even if he were not her cousin.

'At least you are coherent tonight, my friend. That is much better than the last time I saw you. And you are right. We are going to move you. Captain Seller from the English king's army is here looking for you.'

Gavin's sharp intake of breath turned into a racking cough that made his face contort in pain. 'Blast the man. He is the one who shot me.'

Jenna gasped, an immediate urge to run Seller through with a sword making her hand tingle. 'How dare he seek shelter here after doing that?'

Gavin subsided back on to the pallet and closed his eyes, his cheeks sharp planes that resembled bone more than skin in the flickering light of the single candle. 'He does not know my real name, Jenna. To him I am just another Jacobite criminal to be tracked down and treated like an animal.' He coughed again.

She shushed him. 'Enough. You are not strong enough for this and we must move you tonight.' She looked into the water pitcher. There was some left. 'Drink this. It has willow bark to help with your fever and the pain.'

He laughed weakly. 'The only thing strong enough to blunt this pain is a good Scotch whisky.'

'That can be arranged, but not until you are safely moved,' The Ferguson said. 'Are you able to walk if I help you?'

'Aye.'

'No!' Jenna pushed in. 'It will break open his wound.'

Both men looked at her.

'Shall I carry him?' The Ferguson asked sardonically.

'No!' Gavin said. 'I can walk aided.'

Chagrin made her colour as her gaze went from one to the other. 'Then I will check the bandage and wound in my stillroom.'

'I would expect nothing less.' The Ferguson stood and turned his back to her, effectively blocking her view of Gavin's face. 'Come along, old man.'

He reached down and helped her cousin to the side of the cot where Gavin sat for long moments taking deep breaths. The urge to help moved Jenna's feet before she realised it.

'Some laudanum.' She dug the wax-stoppered vial from her pocket.

Gavin shook his head. 'No, Jen. Better that I retain my wits for what is ahead.'

The Ferguson nodded. 'You always were a canny one. That's what made you so invaluable.'

Both men grinned at something they shared, but neither spoke. Jenna marvelled that men could find something to bind them in the act of war. In her experience it brought only death, pain and sorrow.

What seemed an eternity later to Jenna, they had Gavin in the corridors and headed toward her stillroom. They passed her father's room and Jenna thought she heard a noise. The two men stopped, and she saw Gavin bite his lower lip. He was in such pain. When the noise did not repeat, they moved again.

Jenna looked behind to see his father's door quietly close. He had been watching them. She knew better than to tell the others. Even though she knew he would never betray them, the men would not believe her. Knowing what they thought of her father was like a stab to her heart, but there was nothing she could do to change their minds. Only time and seeing him the way he really was could do that.

Finally they reached her stillroom. They had travelled faster the night before when The Ferguson had carried Gavin. Now he lowered her cousin on to the chair by the fire. Jenna changed the bandage, thankful the wound was clean.

'If nothing else happens, you should heal quickly.' She glanced at The Ferguson. 'As long as this trip does not overly tire him or give him the ague.'

He looked at her. 'I will do my best.'

'I know,' she said quietly.

Gavin sat with his eyes closed. 'Best we do this. I am not as strong as I would like.'

'How are you going to transport him?' Jenna asked. 'He will be hard pressed to stay mounted.'

'He must ride a short way. I have a wagon just off the gravel road that leads here. You will need to come with us to bring back his horse.'

'I will go with you to the destination.'

His mouth thinned. 'I think not. The less you know the better—for all of us.'

'Because you do not trust me.' Hurt pricked her.

'What you do not know you cannot be made to tell. 'Tis better this way.' He turned his back to her and started wrapping the blankets Gavin would need.

Her hands fisted as she fought the urge to cry. His lack of confidence in her was more painful than she would have thought. Particularly since she was nearly certain about who he was. But perhaps he would not take Gavin to his hunting lodge.

'Jenna—' Gavin's raspy voice penetrated her hurt '—he is right. You cannot be coerced to reveal what you do not know. Or tricked into some indiscretion when you have no secret. 'Tis bad enough you know I am here, but I trust you with my life.' His mouth, so like hers, twisted. 'Have I not already proven that by coming to you?'

She smiled at him, but they both knew it was a feeble effort. Fortunately for her pride, the moisture in her eyes did not fall. 'I will do as I'm told.' She was less able to keep the bitterness from her voice.

She wrapped Gavin in one of her father's old greatcoats and then draped a spare blanket over his shoulders. He groused, but she only tucked the wool closer.

It was her job to fetch two horses from the stables. Neither of the men could risk being seen. Fortunately she often helped herself when there was an emergency that needed her skills.

She led the two horses back to where the men stood. 'Where is your mount?' she asked The Ferguson—Duncan.

'I walked from where the wagon is hitched. A man dressed as I am would not have a horse and a wagon.' He grimaced. 'Likely he would have neither, but that can't be helped.' He helped Gavin on to the larger gelding. 'I will ride behind Gavin and help him keep his seat. 'Tis not far.'

After hoisting Gavin on to the horse, he came to her and grabbed her around the waist. With no ceremony, he swung her up so she plopped on to the sidesaddle. She gasped in surprise.

His mouth split into a wicked grin that showed a slash of white. 'Tonight you wear stays.' His voice was pitched only for her.

Jenna blushed scarlet, thankful no one could see in the night. She wished for a retort, but none came. All she could do was twist forwards in her seat and stare ahead, ignoring him and the amusement he did nothing to hide.

She only looked back at him when she heard Gavin groan. Her heart wrenched at the pain she knew her cousin was going through. If only he had dared to take the laudanum. Well, when they reached the wagon and Gavin was settled on the back bed, she would order him to take it.

With a release of breath, she watched The Ferguson swing up behind Gavin and wrap one arm around her cousin's waist. It was short work to the wagon, where the process of getting Gavin down and on to the wagon was no less disturbing.

Jenna sighed in relief when it was finished. Coming to the edge of the wagon, she pulled the blankets over Gavin's chest and held out the vial of opiate. 'Take all of this. You no longer need to be aware.'

He shook his head. 'I do, Jen. I must get from the wagon to the next hidey-hole.'

She clenched her teeth. In her need to ease his discomfort, she had not thought about the next phase of his journey. 'Then keep it for afterwards.' She turned and handed the vial to the other man.

The Ferguson took it without a word before getting into the driver's seat. He doffed his cap to her as he flicked the reins for the old donkey to move.

Jenna stood watching them until they were nothing

but a darker blot in the dark night. Not even the cold penetrated her relief at knowing Gavin would be safer now. But there was still a selfish kernel that wanted her cousin with her where she could provide his care.

She willed herself to release the emotion. This was better for Gavin. Better for her, too.

She would not have to see so much of The Ferguson.

Unless he was who she was beginning to think he might be…

Chapter Seven

J enna looked up at the night sky. It was clear with a full moon, the best type of weather to travel home after dinner on a winter's night. But Lizzie had said her bones ached, and they always ached before a storm. There was a good chance the evening would not continue this pleasant.

'If it stays this way, we shall have a delightful trip home,' Papa said. 'There is nothing like a cold, crisp night with the moon so bright you don't need a lantern to light the way.'

Jenna smiled. 'Let us hope the company is as good.'

He smiled down at her as Lord Byrne's footman opened the door of their carriage. 'It will be, my dear. You are here.'

'Oh, Papa.' Jenna's heart swelled with the love she felt for her father. After her mother's death he had cared unstintingly for her, showing her more affection than many children got from two parents.

After exiting the carriage, Jenna examined Lord Byrne's home. He had a hunting box, but, being one of the aristocracy's playthings, it was much larger than most of the local gentry's only homes in this part of the country. Still, it was built within the last fifty years and Jenna anticipated being warm inside its modern walls.

The wind picked up the hem of her black wool cape and sent tendrils of cold up her legs. It seemed she was never warm lately. Even her hands, in gloves and the warmth of her muff, were stiff from the chill.

The double-front doors opened to let a spill of candlelight on to the marble steps. A butler in green and silver bowed them in, and a line of liveried footmen took their wraps and her father's hat and cane. They were led to the salon where Mrs McNabb sat with the Reverend and Mrs Kingston. Lord Byrne stood by the fire talking to Captain Lord Seller and another English officer whom Jenna did not know.

She took the moment to look around. The room was very cosy, with fine damask and carved wooden panels on the walls. Mahogany, a very expensive wood imported from the New World, comprised most of the furniture. Their host and hostess were fashionable as well as wealthy.

Her gaze went to Lord Byrne. His burnished hair was pulled into a neat queue with the black velvet ribbon tied back around his neck. Another very fashionable statement. His coat and waistcoat were pine green velvet with silver embroidery along every edge and inches deep at the hems. His matching breeches fit his lean hips as tightly as the white hose on his well-shaped calves fit his lower legs. He wore black pumps. Pristine lace fell from his throat and wrists like a cascade of water down a mountainside.

He smiled and laughed at something the English

officer said, but there was a tautness about him that belied his easy manners. Jenna glanced at her hostess, Mrs McNabb.

That lady's silver hair was dressed close to her head on which perched a lace cap. She wore a peach satin sac dress with folds falling from her shoulders to the floor where they puddled on the fine Turkey carpet. Her stomacher was worked in gold threads, which the fingers of her right hand picked at.

She held herself erect. She was a lady from her head to the tips of her matching satin slippers with pointed toes and high heels that peaked from the folds of her gown.

Her eyes, so like her son's, scanned the room as though she looked for something to happen. It seemed to Jenna as though Lord Byrne's mother was tense. But surely not. She was merely concerned that her guests enjoy themselves.

Jenna suddenly felt gauche in her simple purple gown that was several years old and had not been à la mode when she'd had it made by the local modiste. Normally she was comfortable everywhere. This was an unusual feeling and one she did not like.

Nor was there any reason for it. She was here to enjoy the company, not to impress anyone.

Mrs McNabb rose and excused herself to the Reverend and Mrs Kingston when the footman announced Jenna and her father. 'Viscount Ayers and Miss de Warre, I am so glad you could come.' She held out her hand and smiled. The viscount kissed the tips of her gloved fingers like a London gentleman and she blushed. 'I am sure you know our other guests.'

He looked around. 'Of course. Kingston's living is

from me and Seller is currently our guest. Although…'
his eyes narrowed '…I do not recognise the officer
with Seller.'

Jenna thought Mrs McNabb's mouth tightened, but
it was gone so quickly she had to be mistaken. 'That is
Lieutenant Bering. He arrived today.' She gave the
viscount an inquiring look. 'I believe he expects to stay
with you as Captain Seller is doing.'

Jenna clamped her mouth shut on an automatic
refusal. It was bad enough having Seller. But this was
not her decision to make.

The viscount frowned. ''Twould have been better
for the lieutenant to call on me and ask himself instead
of my meeting him here.'

Mrs McNabb nodded. 'I wondered about his manners, but it is not my place to say.'

Jenna watched her father struggle with his instant
dislike of the lieutenant. 'Well, I won't refuse him.'

'I thought not,' Mrs McNabb said. 'Come and I will
introduce you.'

They had no choice but to follow their hostess. Jenna
smiled at the Reverend and Mrs Kingston. 'I shall return
to sit with you.'

They beamed at her. Their living might come from
her father, but they were also friends.

'Duncan, dear,' Mrs McNabb said, addressing her
son, 'please introduce our newest guest.'

Duncan? Jenna tried not to look surprised. So Lord
Byrne was called Duncan. Was it too much of a coincidence? Lord Byrne must be The Ferguson. Automatically trying to ease some of the tension she felt, Jenna
dropped into a curtsy. 'Lord Byrne. Captain Seller.'

Lord Byrne looked at her, his golden eyes gleaming.

He seemed to be enjoying the situation. 'Ah, Miss de Warre.' He made her a bow. 'And Lord Ayre.'

A tiny black star patch accentuated the curve of his mouth. A sensation of pleasure that Jenna was beginning to dread threaded its way up her spine. She found this dilettante of a man more interesting than she liked, perhaps because she thought him more than he pretended.

Captain Lord Seller and his companion bowed.

'May I present Lieutenant Bering?' Lord Byrne said without looking at the other man. 'He is arrived from London just today.'

Lieutenant Bering said, 'I am delighted to meet you, Miss de Warre.' Turning to her father, he added, 'And a celebrated hero like yourself, Viscount Ayre.'

'Lieutenant,' the viscount said, the voice that Jenna always thought of as warm and loving cold, 'I understand that you expect to billet with me.'

Both Lord Byrne and Captain Seller cocked an eyebrow. Jenna nearly laughed at their identical reaction. She doubted either man knew the other had done the exact thing. She had not thought them similar at all, but perhaps she was mistaken.

Lieutenant Bering paled under her father's scrutiny. 'Yes, sir. I would have called on you myself, but by the time I arrived, Captain Seller said you would be busy preparing for this evening.' His smile was an ingratiating show of teeth. 'I knew I could speak with you here.'

The viscount said nothing.

'What brings you to Cumbria at this time of year?' Jenna asked, trying once more to ease the tension that seemed to be increasing with each moment.

Lieutenant Bering smiled, his thin lips looking more

skeletal than reassuring. Even his frame was tall and thin. Fortunately the striking red wool of his dress uniform with all the ribbons and trim added weight. Sandy hair and brown eyes added warmth to his otherwise washed-out appearance.

'I am here to assist Captain Seller, Miss de Warre. Fortunately for me, I arrived in time to enjoy this social gathering and to meet the more important people in the area.'

A toady, she thought, keeping her expression pleasant with an effort. 'How unfortunate for you. This is the worst part of the year. No hunting and the weather, I'm sure, is much colder than you are used to, coming from London.'

His smile faltered a second only. 'I am here doing my duty.'

'Really,' Lord Byrne drawled. 'And what might that be—besides helping Captain Seller?'

The lieutenant's brown eyes flicked to Captain Seller, whose face gave nothing away. Bering cleared his throat. 'As I'm sure you have already been told, there are rumours that Jacobites are escaping from here.' He paused and his chest puffed up. 'Someone is smuggling them out, or so we believe.'

Jenna forced herself not to flinch even as she sensed her father stiffen. She knew this. This was the reason Captain Seller was here—but why another officer? 'Captain Seller and his troops are not enough?'

Bering's pale skin mottled. 'Ahem, nothing of the sort, Miss de Warre. Just that he might be understaffed.'

She sensed there was much left unsaid, but there was no polite way to interrogate the young officer. And to do so would make her look suspicious. The last thing she needed was another English officer watching her. Thank goodness Gavin was some place warm and safe known by no one in this room—unless it was her host. With luck, her cousin would soon be in France and safe.

'How fortunate for us,' Lord Byrne drawled. ''Tis too bad that a pleasant place in the country can be spoiled by Jacobites.' He flicked his wrist at a piece of lint on his sleeve. 'I, for one, hope you catch them quickly.'

Before anyone could comment, the butler announced dinner. Lord Byrne held his arm out for Jenna at the same time that his mother took her Papa's arm. The others followed them into the dining room.

Jenna was glad the walk was short. She found Lord Byrne's nearness unsettling. Beneath her fingers, his forearm was surprisingly muscled. A hint of musk and patchouli wafted from him.

When he guided her to her seat, she was glad to sink on to the embroidered green-and-silver chair. He was a very disturbing man, and he played a deep and dangerous game.

She murmured, 'Thank you,' only too aware of the knowing look in his hazel eyes. Were she imaginative, she might think him a predator studying his next meal.

Belatedly, she realised she was on his right. Across the table sat Mrs Kingston. Mrs McNabb sat at the other end with the viscount on her right. Beside Papa sat Captain Seller. On Mrs McNabb's left was the Reverend Kingston.

Jenna glanced to her right and saw Lieutenant Bering flip out the tails of his coat before sitting. She swallowed a sigh of chagrin. The man was stuffy and his job was not to her liking. Still…perhaps she could glean information that might be helpful to The Ferguson.

The dinner wound leisurely through the first course with light talk about the past hunting season. Jenna had never cared for hunting, although she acknowledged that it put meat on the table.

She glanced at Lord Byrne, only to see him watching her. 'Is my nose suddenly crooked or have my freckles turned a shocking shade of red?' she asked, wishing her tone was light hearted, but knowing she sounded acerbic. She was very sensitive about her freckles.

He smiled, the star patch catching her eye and making her attention linger on his too-sensual mouth. 'Your nose is perfectly straight and pert. Your freckles are enchanting.' He raised his wine glass. 'A toast to Miss de Warre's bewitching freckles.'

There was a startled moment of silence, and Jenna felt heat move from the point where her stomacher pushed up her bosom to the top of her forehead. The urge to cool herself was so strong, she found her fingers groping for the intricate ebony fan that lay on the table. She turned the movement into picking up her own wine glass.

'And a toast to our host for his wittiness.' This time she was glad of the acerbity in her tone.

She raised her glass and drank deeply without waiting for the others. Nor did she look around. The last thing she wanted was to see the pity and speculation in the faces of the other guests because of Lord Byrne's blatant mockery.

For Jenna, the dinner deteriorated from that point. Not even the prospect of subtly questioning Lieutenant Bering could save the evening.

As though he sensed her anger and thought it amusing, Lord Byrne leaned toward her and spoke softly.

'You are delightful when you blush, Miss de Warre. It brings out the porcelain pinkness of your complexion.'

She glared at him, her fingers clenched in the folds of her napkin. 'You look like a dandified fop, Lord Byrne, but your manners and words are those of a rapscallion. I do not appreciate your comments on my features.'

His eyes gleamed. 'You are the one who brought up your freckles, as I recall. I merely responded.'

It did not help her composure or mitigate her anger at him that he was right. Unreasonably, his observation infuriated her further. Which was even more out of character for her. She was rarely angry with anyone. Her inclination was always to help others.

She edged away from the man. 'You are, of course, correct, my lord. My sensitivities got the best of me.' She took another sip of wine. 'However, a gentleman would not have taken advantage of the situation.'

Something dark moved across his handsome features. 'I am never a gentleman, Miss de Warre. Best you remember that.'

A chill of foreboding moved across her bare shoulders, even though the room was delightfully warm. Goosebumps rose on the skin covered by her gloves.

'Miss de Warre,' Lieutenant Bering said in his nasal voice, 'I understand you are a healer.'

She took a deep breath and forced her gaze from her host to the man on her other side. 'Yes, Lieutenant, I am.'

His thin nose pinched. 'That is unusual in a woman of your position.'

'Not at all. Women of all ranks have been preparing tinctures and herbs for hundreds of years. My mother used to take food and calf's foot jelly to anyone who needed them.'

He gave her a weak smile and turned his attention to the Reverend Kingston. Jenna found her irritation with her host was nothing compared to how Bering made her feel with his unspoken criticism of her life's calling. She burned to give the impertinent man a dressing down he would not soon forget.

She heard Lord Byrne say something to Mrs McNabb, which drew her attention back to him. He finished speaking and, as though sensing Jenna's gaze on him, turned to her, a smile playing on his finely formed lips.

His smile turned mocking. 'Is something the matter, Miss de Warre? Is my patch askew?'

She pleated the napkin still in her lap. Stopped and folded her hands on her lap. 'No, nothing of the kind, Lord Byrne.'

'Ladies.' Mrs McNabb stood, giving the signal that the women were leaving for the drawing room. 'Duncan, please do not spend all evening in here.' Her tone was loving, but there was a haunted look around her eyes and the fine lines were more pronounced than earlier in the evening.

Jenna looked from one to the other and wondered if the mother knew what the son was about. She rose and followed her hostess from the room.

Jenna wanted to sit by the warmth of the fire, but knew Mrs Kingston suffered from the winter weather. 'Please, Maria, sit here.' She indicated the other woman should take the chair nearest the warmth.

'Thank you, Jenna, dear.' Mrs Kingston sank gratefully on to the well-upholstered seat. 'As usual, my fingers ache and the heat is most welcome.'

Jenna smiled, more than glad that she had forgone her own comfort for the other woman. 'I am sure I have something for that. I will be by tomorrow if that is acceptable.'

Mrs Kingston smiled, her homely features lightening. 'Of course.'

Jenna smiled back.

'Healing is a gift,' Mrs McNabb said.

Jenna looked at her hostess, who had just sat across from the vicar's wife. 'Yes, ma'am. My mother was a healer before me.'

'Ahh. You must get great satisfaction from helping others.' Mrs McNabb's eyes were warm with approval.

Jenna paused before answering, both surprised and pleased that the other woman understood. 'Yes, I do. My mother taught me before her death and then my aunt finished my training.'

'Commendable.' Mrs McNabb adjusted the fire screen between her face and the flames. 'People with means should help those less fortunate than themselves.'

Before Jenna could reply, the gentlemen joined them.

'Thank you, Duncan,' Mrs McNabb said. 'It is always nice to have the gentlemen present for cards or music.'

He made his mother an elegant leg. 'I always try to take your wishes into consideration, ma'am.'

'I know you do, dear.'

The smile she gave him was filled with love and pride. Just seeing it made Jenna's heart warm toward both of them. She still felt very charitable toward him when he approached her.

'Miss de Warre, I understand from your father that you have an interest in family history.'

Jenna had no such interest. She glanced at her father, who looked bland but winked. He was trying to match-make. No matter that she had told him repeatedly that she did not miss having a family of her own, he occasionally did these things. She could not gainsay him.

'Sometimes,' she murmured. It was not exactly a lie. 'I do like looking at portraits from previous times.' Which she did. The fashions were so different and she often wondered what the people's lives were like. Although she doubted they were much different from her own.

'Then, would you care to accompany me on a tour of our family portraits?' A mischievous glint turned his hazel eyes golden. 'Not everyone is here, as this is not our principal seat, but we did bring some with us. We plan to spend much time here, you see.'

Some of her former harmony with him and his mother remained. And she did not want to make her father look like a schemer even though she was certain everyone else knew exactly what he had intended.

She stood and brushed down her skirt. 'I would be delighted.'

He extended his arm and she placed her fingertips there. To her chagrin, awareness flowed from him to her. It seemed it did not matter what guise he wore, she reacted to him.

With a nod and smile around, but not another invitation, he led her from the room. She flushed as she noted everyone watching them with undisguised speculation. Particularly Captain Lord Seller.

They were in the gallery before either of them spoke. Jenna felt strange to be alone with him and curious as to why he was so public about it.

'Tell me, Lord Byrne, why did you really ask me to join you here?'

He stopped, and the sound of his heels on the wooden floor stopped with him. The area was eerily quiet. 'Because I could see the wheels turning in your head and did not want you to say something around the others that would have repercussions.'

She pulled her fingers from his arm. 'Really? And what might I be thinking that could have such repercussions?'

He looked down at her. 'You know exactly what I am talking about.'

She arched an eyebrow, undecided whether he was flirting with her or insulting her. She decided that believing he insulted her was safest for her peace of mind. 'And if I do, you must think I am very stupid to say anything around others.'

'No, but I think you are impulsive. Often that is worse than stupidity.' He replaced her hand on his arm and resumed walking.

Indignation simmered in her stomach, making it churn. Yet, she knew he was right. Acting on the spur of the moment had got her in trouble as a child. As an adult she controlled it better, but where Gavin was concerned...

'I admit I was impulsive to come to the Whore's Eye the other night,' she conceded. 'However, I was worried about my cousin.'

'You jeopardised more than your cousin.' His voice was hard, as were the muscles under her fingers.

Her pulse jolted. 'Your words are tantamount to an admission.'

He shrugged and guided her around the room. His voice dropped into a Scottish burr. 'You already ken the truth, even if you have no real proof. 'Twas in your eyes at dinner.'

Gooseflesh rose on her arms. At last he admitted to

being The Ferguson. 'So you openly admit your identity to me? I had thought no one was to know it at risk of death.'

He looked down at her, his face inscrutable. 'Is that why you have said nothing?'

She licked suddenly dry lips, and the hand not on his arm fiddled with the folds of her skirt. 'Yes. You have been very plain that if you feel your disguise is in jeopardy you will do whatever is necessary to protect yourself.' She made her fingers stop twisting the heavy satin material. 'I have no wish to enter an early grave.'

'No one does.' Brittle hardness took any allure from his voice.

Her stomach twisted. The danger felt palpable. But she was not one to shy away from possible harm. 'So, have I risked my life by agreeing that I know your identity?'

He stopped walking, forcing her to stop. 'You are the only person who has seen me in both guises. And even if someone else did, likely they would not realise the deception.' He started walking again. 'Most people do not see what they do not expect to see.'

'True,' she murmured, glad they were moving again.

'Then how did you do so?' He looked ahead, as though his question was nothing. But the twitch she felt in his forearm told her he was very interested in her answer.

Jenna wondered herself how she had realised. ''Tis hard to explain.' She could not tell him all the clues, such as the stalking grace of his movements that he was unable to hide, or the full, erotic curves of his lips that kissed her so well.

'Try,' he said, his tone an order.

She sighed. 'You lamp black your hair, but you did

not do the same to your brows or lashes.' That was a safe difference.

'Just from that you guessed?' Disbelief dripped from the words.

Embarrassment heated her cold face. 'There were other things.'

'Such as?' Now his tone held impatience.

She looked anywhere but at him. 'Well, your features are the same no matter what you wear.'

'Yes…'

'And your body is the same.'

'Ah…' This time his tone was far from cold.

'Yes, well, I am very observant. It comes from being a healer.' The words tumbled from Jenna's lips as she tried to stop her unnerving realisation that his voice was now anything but cold and dangerous. More like it was hot and enticing.

She had to change the subject before she said more than any lady should, such as how broad his shoulders were and how narrow and intriguing his hips were, or how well shaped his legs were.

Her stomach twisted, a sensation she dared not study. He was not for her. He was a Jacobite. Her father supported the Crown.

What's more, The Ferguson risked his life constantly for his belief. If she were foolish enough to love him, she would be in constant misery, fearing for his safety.

'Does your mother know?' she asked, wondering how that woman lived with the knowledge.

He sighed. 'Much to her dismay, yes.'

Jenna nodded. 'I can understand that. She fears for you and rightfully so. Particularly now with so many

English officers in the area—one billeted in our home. You could be caught and hanged or killed outright.' Her chest tightened painfully. Thankfully she did not care for him.

Another thought intruded. 'Is Gavin here?' Her voice rose in worry.

'Shh.' He put a finger to his mouth. 'We are alone, but never think you are safe. Speak softly as we have been doing.'

Chagrin curdled her pleasure in learning his secret. And disappointment at herself. She had just confirmed his assertion that she was impulsive. 'I am not used to the life of a fugitive.'

'Most of us are not. But we learn or we die.'

The flatness of his voice left her in no doubt that he was a master at what he did and had learned the hard way. 'I am sorry for what you have been through.'

He stopped again and used his free hand to lift her chin. He studied her face for moments that seemed an eternity to Jenna. Instinctively she knew he looked for something in her soul, and she held herself still and met his eyes openly.

'I believe you are, and not just because of your cousin.'

His words broke the spell that held her. 'Because I know you have suffered over him.'

He released her chin and she turned away from him, thankful he had not kissed her this time—or so she told herself. They had more serious issues than the way he made her feel.

'Is he in danger here now?' she asked. 'And why is Bering here? I thought Seller would be enough.'

He chuckled, but it did not sound truly humourous. 'Seller's superiors worry that he will be lenient.'

It was her turn to stop. 'Lenient? Why should he be and on whom? Surely they do not suspect you?'

He looked away from her toward the far wall where the light from a lone lit candle in a sconce sent shadows flickering against the wood panelling. 'Seller and I were once very close. We went to Cambridge together and roomed together. Those ties are hard to ignore. And he knows your cousin.'

The lull in apprehension gave way to full-blown worry. 'He does? And he still pursued him as though he was an animal? Shot him.'

His voice fell to a barely audible murmur. 'Seller is loyal to the Hanoverians. I don't blame him, and I don't think Gavin does either. We are Jacobites. We are enemies of everything Seller values.'

He started walking again, and Jenna reluctantly followed when all she wanted was to sink on to a chair and bury her face in her hands from fear for her cousin—and now for this man. This man who played a life-and-death game. She shivered.

'I thought my home was warm to you?' he chided.

She frowned. 'What?'

'You are shivering from cold.'

She shook her head slowly. 'No, I am shivering from fear. This is no parlour game you play.'

'I know.'

'Then why do you do it?'

'Because if I do not, these men will die as so many already have.' His voice darkened. 'You were not at Culloden. You did not see the slaughter. I will do everything I can to help those who survived. Most, when they reach me, are already wounded or sick. I shelter them until they can travel and then I get them out of

England.' Even though he spoke barely above a whisper, his dedication and conviction seemed to fill the room. His commitment was like a beacon.

'I can help you with the wounded ones.'

She spoke before thinking of the consequences. But she did not regret them. She spoke from the heart. The men he helped often needed medical care. And if they were caught, they were as good as dead. The healer in her longed to help them.

'You don't know what you are saying.' His arm tensed under her fingers and his tone was harsh.

'I am not naïve.'

'You are not Scottish, and your father is loyal to the man I am defying.'

Again, there was something in his tone that hinted of things unsaid, dark, dangerous passions. His jaw clenched and there was a twitch in his cheek. He was a man driven by demons.

'I am half-Scottish, but more than that, I do not believe that continued killing solves anything. I would help you no matter what.' She planted her feet, pulled her fingers from his arm and faced him. 'And what of you? *You* are an English lord.'

He planted his fists on his lean hips, brushing aside his dress sword. 'I am half-Scottish, as you are. My father was a Scotsman. My mother is English aristocracy. My title and lands came to me from her father. I was Lord Byrne before I was in leading strings. 'Tis an old and distinguished title.'

She snorted. 'And you turn it to such a use.'

Rare amusement lit his hazel eyes, making them seem like molten gold in the occasional flicker of candlelight that reached them. 'I am sure Mother's ancestors are spinning in their graves.'

'So what of your father's people?'

His countenance cleared of all emotion. His entire body stilled, as though he did not even breathe. 'McNabbs. A minor branch.'

'And the origins of the name you are known by. Why "The Ferguson"?'

His mouth twisted. 'My father's mother's people were named Ferguson. I chose the name to honour them, as well as hide my identity.'

'But what if it became known you fought at Culloden?'

His face twisted. 'I would lose my title, my property and my life. So far, I have managed to keep the Crown from learning things that would not be good for me.'

'Kept it secret? That could not have been easy.'

He shrugged. ''Twas not, but I am an influential man. As was my maternal grandfather. And very wealthy.' He smiled for the first time since they had started on this topic.

Her intuition told her not to ask, but her impulsivity blurted the words. 'And your father? What happened to him?'

He looked at her, then away. An emotion she did not want to decipher moved over his face, then was gone. 'He died while Mother and I visited my English grandfather who was on his deathbed.'

Compassion for the small boy he had once been filled her heart. She laid her hand on his chest, felt it rise and fall. 'I am so sorry. That must have been an awful time for you and your mother.'

He shook his head as though to clear it of pictures and memories. He looked down at her. 'It was.'

There was a hardness in his voice that told her the events might be in the past, but they were not forgotten. Trouble gnawed at the edge of her mind. She ignored it.

'That must make it even more difficult for your mother to know what you do.'

He removed her hand from his body and released her. 'It does.' Coldness leached from him, a coldness she had not felt from him before.

'Was your father a Jacobite?'

'Yes. My maternal grandfather managed to keep secret my father's true allegiance. Otherwise, the Crown would have never allowed me to inherit my grandfather's title. We did not return to where my father had been killed.'

She heard his pain even though his voice was cold. The urge to comfort rose again. This time she suppressed it. He had made it clear that her touch was not welcome.

'Shall we return to the others?' If possible his tone was colder. 'They will begin to wonder what we are doing.'

She shivered as her treacherous blush moved over her skin. She forced a laugh, but it was a weak thing. 'No one will think anything. I am a spinster and known to be too occupied in my healing and my papa for dalliance.' She had forgotten her previous mortification that everyone would know her father was trying to play matchmaker.

His gaze narrowed. 'Then they are fools.'

Without another word, he strode to the door. She had to scurry to keep up with him, all the while wondering what had happened to change him from the warm, engaging man who had brought her here to the frigid stranger who looked at her with unfathomable emotions playing in the depths of his eyes.

Chapter Eight

They arrived back in the drawing room in time for her to see her father smile at Mrs McNabb, a widow of long standing. Jenna now realised that Mrs McNabb was a very attractive woman who seemed to have the ability to make her father enjoy things.

'Ah, there you are, child.' Viscount Ayre rose and bowed to his hostess. ''Tis past time we were gone. Particularly as I have offered a ride to the Reverend and Mrs Kingston. The night is too cold for them to travel in their gig. The same for Captain Seller and Lieutenant Bering on their horses.'

Fortunately their coach was large and comfortable. But Jenna still wished they would not have company. She wanted to think about what she had learned this evening.

'Best you hurry, then,' Lord Byrne said, returning from the hallway. 'The butler tells me the weather is changing.'

Jenna shivered. 'It seems Lizzie is right as usual. She said her bones ached and a storm would move in before the night was gone.'

Papa grimaced. 'She is never wrong, much as I wish she were.'

'Especially tonight,' Jenna added. It seemed they were to leave before she could make arrangements to come back and see Gavin. She would just have to pay an afternoon call.

They were less than a half mile from Huntingdale, Lord Byrne's lodge, when the carriage stopped. Rain pounded on the roof like drums. Everyone exchanged looks. No smuggler or highwayman would hold them up. They had outriders and the carriage was well known and the occupants well liked.

'My lord—' one of the outriders opened the door '—there is a huge tree across the road and water is dammed behind it. The road is washed out. My horse can cross, but Hobbs says he cannot manoeuvre the carriage around the blockage. Nor is there enough light. And we don't have enough horses to clear the road.'

The viscount groaned, but levered himself out of the well-cushioned seat and into the cold and wet night. The chill, damp wind whipped in through the open door.

'Mercy, but 'tis a miserable night,' Mrs Kingston said. 'We are so lucky you and the viscount were the other guests, Jenna. When we left in our gig, the sky was clear.'

Captain Lord Seller shifted. 'The weather here is very changeable.'

'That it is,' the Reverend replied. 'The clouds could blow away as easily as they moved in. If it had been snowing instead of raining, we would make it home. As it is, we are likely stopped for the night. Fortunately, people who live here understand.'

Viscount Ayre returned and climbed inside, closing

the door with a resounding bang. 'We must go back and impose on our host's further hospitality.' He hugged his cape closer. 'It has been a long time since this road washed out, according to Hobbs. Of course this situation is caused by the wind blowing down the tree.'

'But then it has been raining more than normal and the wind is worse than I can remember it being in quite a while,' the Reverend added. 'Before your time, actually, Lord Ayre.'

The carriage rocked and rolled until it turned around. The rain pounded on the roof like a thousand gunshots and echoed in the silence. Thankfully the return trip was short.

Several hours later, Jenna shivered in her nightdress borrowed from Mrs McNabb. The older woman had been gracious when they had returned, quickly assigning everyone a bedchamber without a moment's hesitation.

Jenna also had her hostess's thick wool robe that helped against the cold, but like the nightgown was not long enough. Still, they were clean and she was thankful for them, otherwise she would be in her chemise, which would be worse. Mrs McNabb's slippers were a good fit.

Determined to make the best of the situation despite the fact that she had been unable to talk privately with Lord Byrne about seeing Gavin, Jenna sank on to a plain upholstered chair. She was close to the roaring fire and thankful for its warmth. Now all she needed was to figure a way to contact her host.

A knock made her start. Everyone should be in bed. Perhaps…

A spurt of energy set her on her feet and to the heavy oak door. Cracking it open, she saw Duncan McNabb, Lord Byrne. He was still in his evening clothes, but the light of his lone candle showed that the star patch at the corner of his mouth was gone.

'What are you—?'

'Shh.' He held one finger to his lips. 'Let me in.'

She blinked. A lady never had a man in her bedchamber. Her boudoir was acceptable, but even then the lady was in carefully arranged dishabille. This was not a situation like that. She shook her head.

He frowned and whispered. 'Do you want to see someone?'

Understanding made her nod.

He pushed at the door, and she allowed him to open it enough to slide inside. He shut it quietly. 'Everyone else is in their rooms. This is the perfect time, unless you want to go in several hours when it is closer to morning.'

'Are you sure no one is about?' The last thing she wanted was to lead someone to her cousin.

'As best as I can be. I thought of waiting until later, but doubt much will change. Guests normally stay in their own rooms—for a while at least.' He grinned at her.

She raised her eyebrows. 'And why would someone wander your halls at all?'

'Because Seller and Bering are looking for any clue that will lead them to the person or persons smuggling out Jacobites. The opportunity to search my home will be one they won't resist. Just as they won't hesitate to go over every last inch of your father's castle and grounds. They will have no honour.' His jaw clenched on the last word. 'That is why Gavin is safer with me.'

'Gavin is here, then? I had hoped, but the danger…
'Tis much safer than de Warre Castle. But you do not
have a priest hole.'

He shrugged, the candle flame wavering. 'You are
right, but we have something much better. And all my
servants are loyal to me.' He grinned and Jenna realised
he did not need the patch to make her attention focus
on the curve of his lips.

'What if they are not?'

'An assignation with one of my guests?' His good
humour fled. 'I do not condone that behaviour from my
servants or from guests toward my servants.'

Surprised, she took a step back as a blush rushed over
her cheeks. 'I did not mean that. I did not even think…that
is, I was thinking they might be prowling around.'

'Good guests stay in their rooms unless they are
meeting someone in secret, and then usually everyone
knows what is going on. To the best of my knowledge,
nothing of that sort is happening.' The scowl eased from
his face. 'And as I said, I will not countenance the other.'

'You are here.' She stated the obvious only to berate
herself silently the second the words were out. 'That is,
not that we have an…' She frowned when his smile
turned sardonic. 'Shall we go and see my cousin?'

It was what he had come for and what she wanted
more than anything. She worried about Gavin. If there was
a hollow sense of disappointment in her stomach, it was
because she was hungry or some such. It had nothing to
do with the fact that this man, whom she admired so much
and half hero-worshipped, was only here from duty to
Gavin, not from any desire of his own. Duncan McNabb
knew how much she cared for Gavin and Gavin for her.

He glanced down at her clothing and an arrested

look moved over his face. When he spoke his voice was rougher than normal. 'You should wear something over those. 'Tis chilly in the halls.'

Her blush returned along with an unfamiliar sense of helplessness. 'I do not have anything else.'

His gaze lingered where her ankles showed below the hems of her clothing before travelling slowly up, pausing where the robe gaped at her bosom. She was more amply endowed than his mother, a fact that had not mattered until this moment.

Then his eyes met hers. 'The cape you wore here.'

She had forgotten it in the play of emotions caused by his perusal. Her face felt like she had been standing directly in front of the fire for some time, and the last thing on her mind was being cold. But he was right. She needed the cape for decency if nothing else.

'Of course.' She pivoted and rushed to the wardrobe, which she opened and then whipped out the clothing. In one practised motion, she swirled the heavy black folds around her shoulders. She clutched the collar around her neck. Now she was decent.

'Very quick.'

'Sometimes more than others,' she muttered, thinking how long it had taken her to realise just how revealing his mother's nightwear was. 'Can we go now?' She wanted to escape this awkward situation.

He made her a mocking bow before going to the entrance where he held a finger to his mouth. Slowly, he inched open the door and listened. Then he peered out. After long moments, he held the door open wide enough for her to slip by.

She glided by him, her back to him so that her shoulder brushed his chest and her hip grazed his upper thigh. Now she knew the cold in the halls would be no problem, just the slight touches of forbidden body part to equally forbidden body part had ignited a fire she had never truly understood until him. Not even his previous kisses had torched her as the illicit touches did.

She felt him move behind her as he followed. She did not think they touched, but she felt as though his body pressed against hers. She heard the soft exhale of his breath and felt the warmth against her cheek. His musky scent engulfed her.

She took a deep breath. This arousal could not be happening to her. He was not doing anything to entice her. He was merely taking her to see Gavin. And their situation— regardless of what he had said earlier—was dangerous.

Determined to get beyond this aberration of emotions, she strode to her left. His fingers caught her shoulder through the heavy folds of her cloak and held. Tingles went down her arm and into her chest. It was as though he held her intimately in two places and all from one grip on her shoulder.

The knowledge of his power over her body was unsettling.

She clenched and unclenched her hands inside the cover of her cloak. Thankfully he could not see her reaction. Lifting her head, she raised her brows in silent inquiry.

Amusement lit his eyes, making him more disturbing to her sang-froid. He jerked his head in the direction opposite from the one in which she was heading. She nodded, wanting to shake his hand off her shoulder for self-preservation, but refusing to be so obvious.

He released her, and she swayed toward him without meaning to. She jerked back and nearly lost her balance.

Sardonic appraisal flashed over his face before he turned and moved away at a rapid pace. She closed her eyes for a moment and tried to still the rapid thudding of her heart. When she looked, he was nearly at a turn in the hallway. She rushed after him, hoping nothing else would happen to make her seem even more foolish.

She needed to concentrate on Gavin, not the handsome, virile man taking her to her cousin. She was nothing to this man. She needed to remember that.

They moved through the halls and down several flights of stairs. Jenna recognised the working area of the house. He led her through the kitchen and to a small door that opened to a pantry. Inside and hidden behind several kegs of ale was another door. He moved the barrels and opened it. Stooping, he passed through, the light from his candle flickering and casting his shadow back on her. She followed.

Straightening up, she looked around. Gavin lay on a pallet against the wall that backed the kitchen fireplace. The room was toasty. A sigh of relief escaped her as she rushed to her cousin.

She knelt and stroked the damp hair from his forehead. He stirred and his eyes opened.

'Jenna?' His voice was hoarse, but his face was no longer flushed as it had been when The Ferguson had spirited him away.

'How do you feel?' she whispered, afraid a loud noise might echo somewhere it should not. She began to feel a part of this secret, deadly game they played, where one side seemed to hold all the cards.

'Could be worse,' he muttered. 'Thirsty.'

She looked around. Nearby was a small table with an unlit candle and a pitcher and glass. She poured him some water and put the rim of the mug to his mouth. He drank greedily. When he was finished, he lay back down and closed his eyes.

She glanced at Duncan. He watched her with an intensity that unnerved her. 'What?'

He shrugged. 'Nothing.'

'Jenna,' Gavin said, drawing her attention away from the disturbing man, 'why are you here? What are you doing in Duncan's house? 'Tis not done.'

She snorted. 'Nor is it the thing to be a Jacobite right now, but you are.'

He chuckled, but it turned to a cough that made him wince in pain. She grabbed a nearby pillow and held it to his chest to stop his motion and ease the pain of his jolting.

'Yes, but that will only get me hung. It will not ruin my reputation.'

She shook her head. 'You always worry about the wrong things, Gavin.'

He looked past her for a long moment. 'Sometimes.' He took a deep breath. 'Still, why are you here?'

She told him about the dinner party and the situation. He listened with more patience than was his wont. That alone told her that while he talked as though he was much better, he was still very sick.

At the end of her tale, he said, 'Your dinner party makes me hungry for something besides gruel. I doan suppose there is anything left?'

'Gruel?' She laughed. 'They have been feeding you gruel?'

He grimaced. 'And laudanum and willow bark.'

She looked over her shoulder at her host. 'It seems you know how to care for the wounded.'

He met her gaze levelly. 'I've had a lot of practice.'

She sobered immediately. 'I imagine you have.'

'Yes.' He turned away. 'I'll fetch Gavin something besides gruel unless you tell me otherwise. He is much better than I have seen him.'

She nodded before realising he could not see her with his back to them. 'Yes, that would be fine, but not much. If he eats a lot, he will likely just throw it up.'

She did not hear the door close when Gavin asked, 'What is under your cape?'

'My nightclothes,' she replied without considering.

He scowled. 'You wandered around in your nightclothes? With Duncan? In his house? Even I, barbarian Scot that I am, know you should not do that. Jenna, if someone sees you, your reputation will be ruined.'

She gripped her cape tighter where it had fallen on to her shoulders and opened at the bosom when she gave Gavin water. 'I was already in nightclothes when he arrived. I certainly could not ask him to help me dress. So…' she tossed her head '…I wore this. Besides, everyone else is tucked up for the night.'

Gavin groaned. 'I doan know what pains me more, Jenna, love, your *naïveté* or my wound.'

Contrition gripped her immediately. 'Oh, Gavin, what I wear is of no importance compared to your health. Let me see your shoulder.'

He gripped her wrist and held it tightly. 'Jenna, be careful.'

She forced a smile. 'I always am, Gavin.'

He shook his head, exasperation knotting his brows. 'Duncan is not the man for you.'

Her pulse jumped. Surely her attraction to Duncan was not so obvious. She was barely aware of it herself.

'Do not talk nonsense.' It was an effort to keep her tone light.

'Jenna, I know ye. I can see the sparkle in your eyes.' His hold intensified. 'Duncan has secrets, Jen. Secrets that make him a hard man. And he has The Cause. He will not give it up for a woman—any woman.'

Her chest hurt with the effort to keep from naysaying him. He knew Duncan better than she. She did not know her cousin's rescuer at all. She just desired him. Even in her innocence, she knew the difference.

She had to change the subject. 'As you say, Gavin. Now, how is your wound? I asked you once before and you changed the subject. I will not let you do so again.'

He released her. She pulled her hand close and massaged her wrist under cover of her cape.

'My wound is very well indeed, Jenna.' He angled away, but the pallet did not give him much space.

'It might be much improved,' she said drily. 'But I still want to see it.'

He rolled back so she could get to the dressing. Gently, knowing that, no matter how careful she was, it was still going to hurt, Jenna undid the covering. The wound was red, but did not radiate heat and it smelled clean. She sighed with relief.

'I believe you are on the mend,' she said, redoing the bandage. 'Someone has given you excellent care.'

'Duncan.' His voice was only a little breathless from the pain. 'He is a good sawbones.'

'Again, down to practice,' Duncan answered from behind them.

Jenna jumped. She had been so focused on Gavin that she had not heard Duncan return. 'What did you bring?'

He smiled at her. 'Bread and warm milk. He can dunk the bread and eat it without trouble.'

'Baby's food,' Gavin groused. 'I'll not be eating it.'

Jenna scowled at her difficult cousin. 'You always were a poor patient, Gavin.'

Duncan laughed. 'I also brought some beef broth with shredded pieces of meat.'

'Ah, I should have known not to fash myself when you are bringing the food.' Gavin sounded much happier as he tried to sit up.

'Not so fast.' Jenna leaned forward to put her shoulder behind his back.

'Just so,' Duncan said, setting his tray down. 'You must eat the milk and bread before I will give you the treat.'

'Humph!' Gavin's indignant response was mirrored in the look he gave them both.

For the first time since Gavin had shown up at her stillroom door, Jenna felt nearly light hearted. The teasing and camaraderie between these two was balm to her tired spirit. Comforted, she kept silent and watched the byplay between the men as Gavin ate.

'Ach, that was much better,' Gavin said after the last bite. 'Now, if you will leave me—' he winked at Jenna '—I might even get some sleep.'

She eased from behind him, knowing he was doing well and was safe. Her heart felt at ease.

She followed Duncan from the room and silently through the halls back to her bedchamber. She slipped into her room and turned to beckon him inside. He looked askance at her. She motioned again and this time he entered.

'What?' he asked, his tone brusque.

Seeing his reaction, she realised he must think she was a wanton. But that had been the furthest thing from her mind when she had asked him in. 'Not what you seem to think,' she said, indignation setting red flags in her pale cheeks.

He quirked one black brow. 'No?'

She shook her head even as she became aware of the situation. His shirt was open at the throat, showing curling brown and bronze hairs. A lock of burnished gold hair fell over his left eye. He was no longer the impeccably turned-out dandy. He was a man after a long day who looked as though he was ready for his bed.

Bed.

She darted a look at her borrowed bed, then back at him. There was a speculative glint in his eyes as he watched her. The heat of indignation that pinked her cheeks turned to the fire of another emotion. She stepped back from him, suddenly feeling the need for distance from this very attractive man.

She gripped her cape tighter around her neck.

'Don't strangle yourself,' he murmured.

Chagrin brought a smile to her lips. 'Not like this. Not when I have something important to say to you.'

Now it was his turn to look uncomfortable. He moved closer to the door. 'Such as?'

'I told you I would like to help you.' She had thought much about this even before tonight. 'I still want to.'

'Help with Gavin? That would be hard when you live some place else. Besides, he is in good hands and safe.'

She nearly stamped her foot in frustration. 'I want to help you smuggle men out. I told you that earlier. I can help care for their wounds before they go.' Her voice fell to a whisper. 'I do not want anyone else to be caught and sent back to prison or hanged.'

Stillness settled over him like a disguise. She could not read anything in his body or his face. Unease crept over her as the minutes passed and he said nothing.

'You are Bloody Ayre's daughter.'

His bald statement hurt. She had thought he would immediately accept her help. But now she wondered why she had thought so, given who she was.

She considered carefully. 'I realise you do not know me well and that you care nothing for my father and certainly do not trust him. I understand, although I wish it were different. And I am English, but also half-Scottish.' She took a deep breath. 'Most importantly, I am a healer and knowing that men who only fought for something they believed right are being hunted like animals and killed outright or hanged and quartered as traitors turns my stomach.'

She shuddered and the words died on her tongue as the image she had just described formed in her mind. All she could see was Gavin. Moisture blurred her vision.

She turned away, not wanting this strong man to see her weakness. 'When you decide, please let me…know.' She was proud that her voice only shook a little.

His hand stroked the back of her head. 'Jenna? Miss de Warre?'

She kept her back to him, knowing that if she allowed his kindness to get past her barriers, she would fling herself into his arms and cry for all the men who had died in this senseless battle. If only kings and princes would think of their people instead of their power.

Slowly his hand moved to the nape of her neck; even

through the collar of the cape she wore she could feel the strength of his touch. He was a man who shouldered other people's burdens.

'I am sorry my anger brought you to this.' He spoke quietly, yet she sensed his sincerity. 'I did not know you felt this passionately about what is going on. I thought you cared only for Gavin.'

She gulped down a sob and lifted her head, determined to meet him strength for strength. 'I am a healer, Lord Byrne. If I did not care for people, I would do something else.'

He sighed and his fingers moved higher. 'Look at me.'

Wariness made her hesitate before shifting to face him. His palm cupped the side of her neck just below the ear. She had never thought such a touch would be erotic, yet she found her blood pounding even as she fought back the sadness of moments before.

She saw something in his eyes that hinted at what she was beginning to recognise as desire. Her response to him intensified.

'If you are of a similar mind tomorrow, let me know and I will think seriously about letting you help. With your reputation around here and the fact that you often travel at odd hours, your help could be indispensable.'

She nodded, her throat too tight to speak. Unaccountably, she wanted him to kiss her. She wondered if it would feel differently now that she knew him better than it had when he had been a rogue she admired and—yes—hero-worshipped, but really knew nothing about.

As though he read her thoughts, his head lowered. His eyes darkened, a question in them. She answered by lifting her mouth to his.

His lips met hers as his fingers sifted into the thick

folds of her hair. She felt a pin slide out as her curls tumbled down. He pulled her closer with only a slight pressure. Her need bade her respond.

His mouth moved softly over hers as his fingers massaged her nape. She shivered as though caught in an ague, but she knew what she felt was nothing like an illness unless desire could be such. She wanted this man for all the reasons that made him who he was.

She pressed to him. Layers of clothing separated them, but her breasts tingled and her nipples hardened. Her stomach tightened and delight radiated out and down. She opened her mouth for his tongue.

He nipped her bottom lip. He slipped his tongue in and out. He slanted his mouth over hers and moved against her.

Dizzy with reaction, Jenna reached for him, letting go of her cape. It fell from her. Cold licked along her back and down her legs, only to be engulfed by the fire his lovemaking created.

His hands travelled over her, ranging down her shoulders and over her back. His fingers massaged as he explored. He stopped where her waist swelled into her hips and lifted his head from hers.

She saw the question his eyes asked. Did she dare? Did she let this moment continue? She was a maiden. She swallowed back her acquiescence and stepped away. He let her go.

'Tomorrow,' he said, his voice a harsh sound in the quiet of the room. Behind them a log popped. He left.

Jenna gulped in great lungfuls of air while heat and need and desire roared through her. Her entire body ached with the feelings he had evoked. She finally understood why women gave themselves to men regardless of the consequences.

A little longer and nothing would have mattered but his body covering hers, his hands exploring her, his maleness moving inside her.

Chapter Nine

The next morning, dressed in her evening clothes from last night, Jenna joined the other guests for nuncheon. She had overslept, exhausted from her emotions. Her dreams had been disturbing and unsatisfactory.

She still throbbed with sexual awareness, but pushed it down as she sat beside Mrs Kingston. She felt safer sitting next to the reverend's wife than being next to the man who had aroused her to true passion for the first time in her life. Not that his previous kisses had not aroused her, but nothing compared to last night. It made her wish for more.

Hopefully, they would be able to leave today, for she feared her resolve would not last if there was a repeat of Lord Byrne's lovemaking. She was too attracted to him. She also respected and liked him too much to resist him when everything he did made her aware that she was a woman to his man. That he was secretly The Ferguson intensified everything.

'How did you sleep, Miss de Warre?' Captain Lord Seller intruded on her thoughts.

Jolted from her amorous musings, Jenna stared at him. Did he know? Had they been caught out? Surely not, or he would have arrested them in the king's name last night, not needle her this morning. She was overreacting.

She pleated the heavy satin of her skirts under the cover of the linen napkin. 'Very well, thank you, Captain. And you?' Thankfully there was no tremor or huskiness in her voice. She even sounded calm and poised.

His eyes narrowed. 'Considering that I am used to sleeping in strange beds, I never anticipated not sleeping well.' He looked around the table, catching the eye of each person as though he interrogated them.

'I am glad to hear that, Johnathan,' Lord Byrne said, his voice hearty. 'Mother does her best to see that anyone staying with us is treated as family and not as a temporary guest.'

The tension broke and small talk started back up. Jenna felt her shoulders relax even though her fingers still fiddled with her gown. She made herself stop.

She glanced at her host. He watched her as a hound would a fox. There was a gleam of speculation in his hazel eyes, and she felt herself blush. She looked away, only to see Captain Seller studying her with the same intensity. She felt trapped.

No longer hungry, she rose. 'Please excuse me. I must find Papa and see if we are able to leave today.'

Mrs McNabb stood. 'Viscount Ayre has ridden out with your coachman and several of our grooms to try to remove the tree from the road. He thinks that once that is done, it will be a matter of mere hours before you may leave. He should be back soon.'

'Oh.' Jenna nearly sat back down, but knew she was

too agitated to be still. 'Then, with your leave, madam, I will take a walk outside.'

'Of course.' Mrs McNabb resumed her seat and began speaking with Mrs Kingston. From the lively tone, it seemed the two women had much in common.

Jenna made a brief curtsy and left without looking directly at anyone else. With luck and strong backs, they would be gone from here soon.

But first, she had to find a discreet way to tell Lord Byrne that she still wanted to help. She knew it would be dangerous, but she also knew that, after seeing Gavin's condition, she would risk much to help these men. Now she just had to convince her host that she understood what she volunteered for and wished to do it.

Her host. Lord Byrne. Surely he could be Duncan to her now, after what had transpired between them. The urge to speak his name out loud, to see how it felt on her tongue, was impossible to resist.

Once in the frost and snow-dressed gardens, she made sure no one was in sight. 'Duncan,' she said softly, relishing the movement of his name over her tongue and lips. 'Duncan.'

'No longer Lord Byrne?'

His question startled her. She had not seen him coming behind her. She whirled. 'Ah, Lord Byrne.'

His look was predatory. 'Duncan, I think.'

Her smile faltered. She felt vulnerable having been caught whispering his given name like a lovesick schoolgirl. 'Lord Byrne.' She straightened her shoulders, thankful for the heavy black cape that had provided her cover and protection in many circumstances through this prolonged visit. 'My host.'

'Ah, yes. That, too.'

Was he alluding to what had happened between them last night? He moved closer until she felt as though the air around her was being squeezed away. It became difficult to take deep breaths.

She knew he could—they could—do nothing here in the open. Anyone might see them. She was safe from any amorous advances he might want to make. She thought she was grateful for that, but perhaps not…

She changed the subject, hoping to ease the sensual net he seemed to so easily snare her with. She made herself stand her ground against his forwards movement. 'I still want to help.'

He stopped his momentum. 'Ah.' His hands went behind his back and a different persona engulfed him, harder, edgier. 'I see.' He glanced around. His attention came back to her. 'Fortunately, no one was around when you said that.'

She blanched. 'I… Oh, dear. I am not used to subterfuge.'

'That is abundantly obvious. You will have to become adept at it if you are to help.' His tone was hard and left her in no doubt that he would not suffer her to err again. 'Too much is at stake.'

She nodded, wondering if she would be a handicap and a danger to him and the men he rescued instead of the help she longed to be. 'I know, really I do. I will be more careful—'

'But you want to help,' he finished for her, his mouth twisted into wry resignation. 'Sometimes the best intentions do not give good results.'

She hung her head, remembering the patients who did not get better no matter what she did. Regret and sadness pierced her. 'I know.'

'Being a healer, I am sure you do.'

She looked at him. He had understood exactly what she had not said. It seemed there was a connection between them. Did he sense it as she did? She doubted it. He was a man who lived his life on the edge of destruction. He had to understand people and read their motives if he was to survive. It had nothing to do with her.

'Will you still consider my offer?'

'I would be a fool not to. A couple is less suspicious than a single man. There is always great need for healing.'

'Jenna?' Viscount Ayre's call caught her attention. 'Where are you?'

She gave Duncan one last look and turned in the direction the viscount's words came from. 'I am here, Papa.' She glanced back. Her host was gone.

Her father came around a yew hedge, clapping his gloved fingers together for warmth. 'Walking in this weather? I am surprised you are not trussed up like a goose in front of the fire.'

She laughed. 'Oh, Papa. You know how difficult it is for me to sit quietly when there are things to do or see.'

His smile radiated love. 'Yes, I do. You are like your mother in that regard.' His eyes lost their sharpness for a moment, and she knew he remembered his wife. Then he snapped back to the present. 'The road is clear. We will be leaving as soon as everyone is gathered.'

'And not a moment too soon,' she said without thinking what impression her words might create. Seeing his questioning look, she added, 'I am ready to be home. I have tinctures to make and drying herbs to crush and put into containers. It may be winter, but my work never ends.'

He offered her his arm. 'Yes, you always find something to do.'

Together they headed inside.

A week later, Jenna stood in her stillroom, looking out the frosted window at the snow falling. Soon it would be dark. The room was cold in spite of the fire she had been burning all day. It was the stone walls. They never warmed. In the summer they kept everything cool, but summers were short here. Winters seemed interminable.

Or perhaps it was her mood. She had not heard from Duncan, Lord Byrne—The Ferguson. He must have decided not to accept her help. She was too inexperienced and a hazard. She could not blame him for that choice, even if she ached to help.

Nor could she go and visit Gavin. She could pay a call during the day, but would not be able to see Gavin then. It would be too obvious and someone might easily see. Nor could she pay an evening visit. She could only hope that if Gavin turned worse, Duncan would get word to her. She had to be content with that.

She turned from the window, frustration and pent-up energy taking their toll. It was not as though she did not have plenty to do. Tinctures took large amounts of time to make. And grinding up herbs until they were a fine powder was tedious business and hard on her wrists. She could occupy more than a week doing just those two things. Not to mention her daily rounds of the neighbourhood and the calls she was requested to make.

She supposed she could make the social calls that other ladies of her rank considered necessary. She had tried when they first moved here, but her heart was not in social exchanges. She needed to help others. It was air and food to her.

She lit a brace of candles on her work table to offset the gathering dusk. A knock on the outside door made her drop the smoking taper she had used. It landed harmlessly on the oak table where she rubbed it out with her thumb.

Thankfully someone needed her care. She did not think she could stand to remain cooped up all evening after being indoors all day.

She cracked open the heavy door. A man stood bent over and covered in patched garments. A knit cap covered his head and came low on his forehead. His breath created puffs of cloud in the air.

'Mistress?' The word slurred. 'Can ye help?'

She had never seen him before. She peered closer. Or had she? 'Look at me.'

He did and a sly smile showed blackened teeth. A fringe of black hair framed glinting hazel eyes. 'I listened to what you said. Satisfied?' he asked in a firm, deep voice.

She suppressed a giggle caused by nervous anticipation and the relief of knowing who her strange visitor was. Instantly, she knew she needed to play along with his parody. He would not come here at this time of day in disguise if he were not about to embark on a rescue.

'Yes. What can I do for you?' She opened the door wider and motioned him in. He shuffled past her, true to his part, even to the smell. Stale tobacco smoke and sweat entered with him.

He held his mitten-covered hands to the fire so the wool steamed. 'That feels good. There are days I wonder how the poor survive.'

'With difficulty in weather like this,' Jenna said tartly.

He turned to face her. 'I imagine those on your father's property fare better than many.'

'We try.' She shrugged. 'Are you sure you should speak out of character, even in here? There might be someone listening.' Even as she said the words, she knew she was poking at him because of how he had censured her for being careless.

'And is there danger of being overheard?'

'Likely not.' She locked both doors. 'But better safe than sorry.'

'You are learning.'

'I am trying very hard to do so.'

'I know and I would not be so hard on you if it did not matter so much. Particularly with Seller and his army combing the neighbourhood.' He yanked off his cap and scratched his scalp. 'Thing itches like the devil.'

She smiled. 'Seller is out and about, you were saying.'

He grunted. 'He is always out and about. He is as determined to catch and stop me as I am to escape him and succeed. I spent too long setting this smuggling route up to leave just because of him. And Bering doesn't help matters. He is starting to snoop around.' He pulled the hat back on his head. 'Perhaps you can help me there.'

Wariness tightened her hold on the key she still held. 'Just exactly what do you mean?'

He slanted her a calculating look. 'Probably something you will refuse to do.'

'Such as try to occupy his time?'

'Yes.'

'I do not want to do that. And I seriously doubt that I could, even if I wanted to. Which I do not,' she added for emphasis.

'I thought not, but it did not hurt to ask.'

It did not hurt you, she thought. If he cared anything for her, he would not have asked her to do that. She would never ask him to play up to another woman, no matter what the cause. But he made no secret that his purpose in life was to save Jacobites. Everything else was a distant second.

Just as well, she told herself, ignoring the emptiness in her stomach. She was still Bloody Ayre's daughter.

She turned away from him to hide the unhappiness she knew was in her expression. She was too inexperienced for a man like him, no matter that he had kissed her and wanted to make love to her. She knew too well that the act of love was not the same as the emotional commitment of love. Not to men.

When she thought her expression was bland, she turned back to him. 'What else can I help with?'

He watched her carefully. ''Tis dangerous.'

Impatience made her short. 'We have had this discussion. It always is.'

His face darkened. 'I have a wagon outside with hopsacking piled in the bed. I need to get a man from the Whore's Eye to a boat before the moon sets tonight.'

'Why do you need me?' Even though she had begged him to help, she found herself being contrary. She knew it was because he had hurt her.

He let out a gust of air. 'If you don't want to help, just say so, Miss de Warre, but then don't come another day and ask me to risk everyone by letting you help when you don't really want to. This is not a game I am playing.'

Irritation flared at his plain speaking, but she knew he was right. Either she helped with no expectation of his caring for her or she stayed out of everything. It was not as though she did not have enough to do with her own life.

She set the brace of candles carefully on her work table and faced him. 'You are right. I am being contrary. What do you need me to do?'

He continued to study her while the fire crackled behind him and the scent of his clothes—nothing like his personal muskiness—filled the room. 'I need you to be the old woman to my old man. The Eye bought a pig from a local farmer and we are transporting it.'

'Why at night?'

'This is when we have the time. We spent the day gathering rocks to make a wall to protect our little plot of land from people riding willy-nilly over it and destroying the vegetables we will grow in the spring and summer.' He ran his fingers through his hair. 'This is extra income for us.'

'Yet we can afford a wagon?'

'Borrowed from the farmer who sold the pig to the Whore's Eye.' He ran his fingers through his hair, not noticing the lamp black that stained his hands. 'We are picking up rags from the Eye.'

'Why don't the other workers keep the rags?'

He groaned. 'Why do you ask so many questions?'

She cocked a hip and planted a fist there. 'Because the Excise men and any soldiers who stop us will ask. If that happens, am I to let you do all the speaking?'

'It would be best. You are new to this disguise. I use it all the time.'

'All right. But what am I to wear?'

'Your clothes are here.'

For the first time she noticed the tattered bag he had let drop to the floor. Her nose wrinkled. The old woman's things would be as smelly as his. But she had asked for this. She was not going to complain.

'Best you change here rather than your bedchamber,' he said as she headed to the door with the baggage. 'If a servant sees you after you have put those things on, they will recognise you and wonder what you are doing.'

She stopped in the act of unlocking the door to the inside hallway. He was right. She turned back and scanned the room. There was no privacy. Anywhere.

Watching her, he began to smile. 'You may change here near the fire, and I will turn my back.' When she did not move, he added, 'My word as a gentleman that I will not look—no matter how great the provocation might be.'

Her eyes widened. He teased her by saying he was tempted to see her unrobe. He did not really…and yet… Perhaps he did. A memory of his kiss in the bedchamber in his house set her pulse racing.

She told herself not to be silly. No matter what he *said*, he was here to get her help in smuggling someone out. That was their purpose this night.

She turned her back to him and the disturbing glint in his eyes and pondered how to get undressed. Normally Lizzie helped her, what with stays and pins and tabs.

She wore a bodice that was closed in the back by hooks and eyes. She could not get out of it without help. She looked over her shoulder to see him still watching her.

'Is there a bodice in there? By itself?' He nodded. 'Please hand it to me.'

He dug through and brought out a roughspun grey wool top. Jenna took it, ignoring the smell as best she could. Luckily it fastened in the front with a tie. She pulled it on over her own bodice. Today she wore stays. They would remain since she couldn't reach behind herself and undo the lacing. Nor was she going to ask him to help her. The act was too intimate.

Next was her skirt. This time she turned around and pointedly looked at The Ferguson. 'Now is the time for you to put your back to me.'

He grinned. Even with blackened teeth, his smile was charming enough to make the breath catch in her throat. She frowned as he pivoted on his heel until he faced away.

She undid her skirt and let it fall to the floor. She did not have hoops on, not liking the width they provided. When wearing them, she invariably knocked something over and that was the last thing she needed to do here.

She knelt and rummaged through the bag until she found the skirt. It was a heavy brown wool. She pulled it up and over her hips and fastened it at the waist. She kept her own quilted petticoat on underneath for the warmth. Surely no one would look under her skirts and see that she wore an expensive garment.

When she was dressed, the coarse wool made her skin itch everywhere her own garments did not cover. 'I am clothed.' She scratched her arm where the wool rubbed and hoped it was not bugs instead.

He turned back to her, his gaze running over. 'Bend over more. You are too straight.'

'I was afraid of that.' She spread her hands out helplessly. 'My… I cannot bend.'

For a moment he looked puzzled. 'Ah, your stays.'

She flushed. 'You are very familiar with feminine undergarments.'

He gave her a roguish grin. 'It always helps to know as much as one can.' He moved toward her. 'We will have to take them off.'

'But I cannot do it by myself.' She backed up.

'I know.' He stopped a foot from her. 'That is why I am going to unlace you. Turn around.'

Natural modesty made her pale, then flame. Her attraction to him, so recently acknowledged and awakened, flared. She felt hot, then cold, then her stomach tightened until she thought it would knot into cramps. But it did not. It felt—exciting was the only description she could think of.

Still, she tried to thwart him. 'Are you sure I cannot just lean forward? With all these clothes and the capes needed to stay warm…I could also cover my shoulders with a blanket. No one would be the wiser.'

His rakish grin increased. 'You could. But what if we are stopped and you have to get down? No, 'tis always best to perfect your disguise. Then, if something happens, you don't have to worry about it.'

'But I pulled the bodice on over mine. If we are to get the stays off, I will have to undress.'

His look turned quizzical. 'Yes, that is how it will have to be.' He spoke slowly as though speaking to a dull child. 'But it isn't something we can avoid.'

'But…' She knew she was being stubborn and to no good end. He was right if she was going to have the stays removed. She sighed, knowing she was defeated, and nodded.

'Turn around,' he said again. 'I will do my best to be quick. And it will speed things up if you take the two bodices off yourself.'

'Such consideration,' she muttered to herself as she followed orders.

She was thankful he did not attempt to help her. The anticipation of him undoing her stays was quite enough. If he also touched her to help her undress, it would be like priming a pistol before shooting it. She was beginning to realise that around him her ardour was like a combustible material just waiting for the spark that would make it explode.

He chuckled. 'I do try to take others' comfort and pleasure into consideration.'

Mortification intensified her reaction. She had not meant for him to hear her. And his answer. Even to her inexperienced ear, he sounded provocative. It opened up possibilities she was not sure she fully understood.

Unable to speak, she pulled at the tabs and ties, keeping the top portion of her costume in place. Her fingers shook.

'Are you cold, love?' His deep voice moved over her like warm fur. 'Let me help.'

With hands that seemed to linger everywhere, he helped her push the blouse off. Goosebumps rose on her arms as the cold air hit her. Her chemise provided no warmth or cover from his gaze. It was made from fine, gossamer muslin.

His sharp intake of breath turned her face and chest to a fiery red. Even though he stood behind her, she knew he could see her breasts. The peaks, mounded above her stays and visible through the material, ached. She resisted the urge to cover herself with her hands.

He started unlacing her stays. Was it her imagination or did his lips graze her shoulder? It could not be. Then the stays fell away. She caught them before they tumbled into the fire. Her breasts bounced free and out of her chemise.

He groaned. 'Best you cover yourself, Miss de Warre. I only have so much self-control and it is sorely pressed at this moment.'

'What?' She twisted around as her hands automatically went to cover her bosom. He looked as though he was in extreme pain. Her healer's instinct made her reach to feel his forehead, revealing one breast. 'Are you hurt? Is there something I can do?'

The rakish look left his countenance. Stark hunger stared at her. She realised belatedly that he had no wound. His gasp had been caused by something entirely different.

'You can let me make love to you.' The bald statement seemed to come from him without his volition.

She backed up and he caught her arm. Sparks travelled her entire body. With a jolt of painful awareness, she realised that she wanted nothing more than for him to make love to her.

'Don't back into the fire.' His muttered words were nearly slurred. 'I would prefer to ignite you with passion, not fire.'

Molten warmth settled in her abdomen. Her nipples hardened. Her breathing became short and did not seem to give her enough air. Her lips parted.

His gaze moved from her exposed breast to meet her look. 'Is your nipple hard because you desire me or because of the cold?' His voice was deep and harsh as though he fought each word.

'I do not know,' she whispered, caught by his need, responding to him. 'Both?'

His laugh was not from amusement, but from some more primal emotion. His hands moved up her arms to cup the base of her neck. His thumbs rubbed gently along her collarbone. The roughness of his skin was like fine gravel along her flesh, making his caress even more intense. She closed her eyes and her head fell back to give him better access.

'Ah, Jenna, do you know what you are doing?'

She felt his question as warm air on her exposed neck instants before his lips joined his hands. She gasped as his mouth coursed over her neck and upper chest. His tongue traced a flicking line from the hollow of her collarbone to the top of her exposed breast, then stopped. Intuitively she knew he waited for her to tell him to go lower.

She could not. The maiden was too entrenched in her.

'I…I cannot…' She trailed off, mortification mixing with desire so she no longer knew what she wanted.

He released her and stepped away. 'We move too fast.'

She stared at him, wanting him even as she denied them both. 'Yes.'

'I understand.' But his voice was harsh and pained. His gaze lingered on her still-exposed bosom. 'Best you dress quickly before I forget that I have never forced a woman.'

She nodded, still emotionally confused.

He grimaced. 'I forgot poor James. He is in the wagon, waiting for us. In the delight of making love to you, I forgot the poor man.'

'What? Someone is outside in the cold?' Concern for the man overcame her embarrassment as nothing else could. 'Then I must dress and we must go.'

She scrambled into the rough clothes, pulling the tattered cape on and a blanket over that. She pulled a heavy knit cap over her hair.

Duncan used the small shovel near the fireplace to get soot in which he rubbed his hands, before then rubbing his hands down the exposed tresses of her red locks. She grumbled, but said nothing. Like the lamp blacking he used on his blond hair, this was as much a part of her disguise as the rags.

'Ugh,' she said when he stepped back. 'That will take some work to get out.'

He grinned. 'Be glad I did not set it in with lard.'

She shuddered at the thought. 'I suppose I must be grateful for small favours. But we must hurry. Your friend must be near to frozen.' She glanced back at him from the door. 'Why did he not knock?'

He looked at her as though she were a simpleton. 'He is hiding.'

'Oh. He is the one you are smuggling out.'

He nodded.

'Will I meet him?' She opened the door and glanced around to see that no one was about.

'I think it better if you don't. That way, if anything happens, you will not be able to identify him.'

A jab of pain that he still did not trust her made her stumble. His strong hand caught her elbow and kept her on her feet. Even knowing he considered her a possible risk, his touch sent shock waves to her core.

She knew that if she answered her voice would shake and then she might say more than she should. She said nothing.

Chapter Ten

Jenna noticed a ramshackle wagon and donkey close to the door. The back bed was filled with hay. A pig lay in a cage situated in the middle of the wagon's bed. The fugitive must be under the hay. Hopefully he was warm enough.

Jenna marched over and started clambering on to the seat. She had one foot up when Duncan's hands closed about her waist and he lifted her high. Her stomach plummeted and the breath left her lungs in a whoosh. He deposited her on the hard wooden seat.

Still, she said nothing. He released her and she nearly toppled into the wagon at the loss of warmth and support. Immediately, she chided herself. She was becoming too attached to him.

She focused on the black night. The only light came from a few windows in the castle where candles glowed as servants went about their evening chores. And even those were distant from them as she had specified her stillroom be built in the back of the castle away from the bustle of daily routine. She liked quiet and privacy. They had stood her in good stead these last weeks.

The wagon shifted as Duncan climbed in. She thought it moved again after he was seated, as though the man they smuggled had adjusted his position. But she could not be sure. It must be very difficult for a man fleeing for his life to be still and allow his fate to be completely in the hands of another person. She would have a hard time doing such.

With a flick of the reins, Duncan urged the donkey into motion. She put the other thoughts aside to concentrate on what they were doing. She had to be a poor labourer if they were stopped.

The wagon rocked over ruts and grass as Duncan guided it to the gravel road. Hopefully, no one in the castle would look out and see them. But if someone did and mentioned it, she would explain it as someone coming for a remedy.

Neither of them spoke as they made their way to the dirt road that would lead them to the coast. Curiosity ate at Jenna, but she bit her tongue. If he did not want her seeing the man they transported, he would not tell her what his plan was. He had told her what they would say if stopped and that was enough.

She had time to ponder what had happened between them.

She had nearly let him make love to her. She was a lady, a woman who should have never allowed a man to take such liberties with her. Was she a wanton? Was she one of the women one heard about who could not get enough of a man's touch? Surely not.

She chewed her lip and stared at nothing while her hands pleated the coarse material of her skirt. Worry was not new to her. But usually she focused on others. Her life was too good for her to spend much time wishing for something else. Yet now, she was afraid.

She did not think she was a harlot who had not yet found her calling. No. She thought it was much worse than that.

She cast a surreptitious look at the man who had nearly seduced her. All he needed to do was touch her, and she ignited into flames of passion that should shame her, but only excited her to want more. Even more disturbing than that knowledge was the realisation that no other man did this to her. No other man had ever come close.

At twenty-five she had had suitors. One or two had even stolen a kiss, but their lips had left her mildly disgusted and wanting no more of what they offered.

Her nails ripped through the open weave of her skirt and she quickly pulled them out and smoothed the material across her thighs. She sensed his attention on her, and she did her best not to look at him. But it was hard.

Harder than she had thought possible, because she finally realised why he made her senses explode. It was knowledge she was not sure she wanted. But she was too honest with herself to refuse to acknowledge it.

She loved him.

There, she had thought it. He shifted and for a moment she feared she had said the words out loud.

She looked at him. His face was in shadows; for all she could tell, he looked at the road they travelled, not at her. Disappointment was a bitter pill, just one of many she feared she would be swallowing in the future.

She loved him and he desired her. She had seen more than enough results from that type of unequal sharing. They were in every town and village, the by-blows from illicit love affairs. And now she was in danger of succumbing to this exciting, sensual man who delighted in his ability to entice her to paradise with only his lips and hands.

She shivered and told herself it was the cold night air, not her desire for him or her dread of what she would allow him to do to her. But how long could she fool herself?

What a coil. He was everything she was not. Being in love with him felt like a betrayal of Papa and all Papa held right.

Worse than that was knowing that Duncan, The Ferguson, Lord Byrne desired her, but did not love her. She cast a glance at him, wishing she could see his face, perhaps know what he thought. 'Twas for the best. Even if they could find happiness together, it would be short lived. He existed on the precipice of disaster. Life with him would be intolerable.

The road hardened as frost replaced mud.

Neither of them spoke and Jenna was thankful for that. She did not know what to say to him.

His leg brushed her thigh and she jumped, moving to the very outside edge of the seat. She felt him look at her. She looked back. It was nearly impossible to see his expression in the moonless night.

Hoofs pounding on the hard ground caught her attention. She was thankful for the reprieve from her response to him until she remembered the Jacobite hidden in the back.

She hunched into herself in imitation of some of the older women who spent their lives labouring on the land. Her shoulders shifted forward and her back rounded. She felt Duncan shifting beside her. They were two old people trying to eek a living from a hard life.

'You, there! Stop the wagon.'

The words were cultured and Jenna recognised the voice. She groaned silently as Lieutenant Bering came into sight. Behind him were ten soldiers. Their luck could not be worse. Surely he would recognise them, no matter how good the disguises.

Duncan halted the wagon, but said nothing. Under the cover of the night and the volumes of clothing they wore, his hand squeezed hers. She understood. Don't speak. She squeezed back.

Bering drew his horse up close and unshuttered a lantern. He shone the light on them. 'What are you doing and where are you going?'

Jenna's hackles rose at his imperiousness. If they were what they appeared, they had every right to be here. But poor people like the ones they impersonated would be intimidated by this. Bering could have them killed and no one would contest him.

'Me and me wife, sir, we be goin' to the Whore's Eye to collect rags. And deliver the pig.' Duncan's voice creaked and all hint of culture was gone. He could have been the peasant he portrayed. He jerked his head back to indicate the pig and hay covering the bed of the wagon.

Jenna felt as though she had stepped into a play even as her mind caught the word 'wife' and repeated it silently. He called her his wife. Would that she were.

The sheer temerity of the thought made her breath stop. Even now, when they might be skewered for no other reason than that they were here, she thought of him and how she wanted him.

'At this time of night?' Disdain and disgust laced

Bering's voice as he edged the horse to the back. He leant over and sniffed.

''Tis dark early, sir. We worked our bit of land first.' Duncan's voice now held subservience and he seemed to grovel, as though Bering's insulting remarks had belittled him.

'In the winter?' Bering lifted the lantern higher.

'Yessir.' Duncan slurred the words together. ''Tis all we have.'

'Peasants,' Bering said unpleasantly, his long nose wrinkling.

Jenna angled her face away from the yellow glare of the lantern. It was all she could do not to give Bering a set-down. Even though anger heated her, she knew they were in a very dangerous situation.

Bering urged his horse to the back of the wagon.

Fearful of having him out of her sight, Jenna twisted so she kept him in view. She noted that Duncan held the reins so the donkey did nothing.

Jenna swallowed her gasp of horror when Bering pulled his sword from the scabbard that hung from his waist. Her eyes widened and a whimper caught in her throat when he thrust the point into the hay. He pulled it out and plunged it into the musty hay again and again.

Jenna turned away, unable to watch. Any second she expected to hear a cry of pain. Blood would stain the hay and puddle on the wagon bed. Their passenger would be lucky to escape death.

If their lives would not be forfeit, she would have risen up and grabbed Bering's arm. But she could not. It would be a death sentence for Duncan. Better to survive today to help someone else. But her heart broke.

After what seemed an eternity, Bering stopped. Disappointment etched lines into his narrow face as he slipped the sword back into its scabbard. He drew away from the wagon and scowled at them. 'I should kill the pig, but I won't. Be on your way.'

Duncan bowed his head. 'Thank you, my lord sir.'

He took his time urging the donkey forward and Jenna's stomach did a series of somersaults in her anxiety. Sweat broke out on her forehead and palms in spite of the cold. She wanted to round on him and chatter until her nerves were eased, but knew she could not.

They had to get away and find a place to stop. She needed to help their passenger. But they had to get away first, she told herself over and over.

She craned around to look behind them. Bering's lantern light disappeared. She turned back. They continued on, neither speaking.

When she could stand no more, Jenna gripped Duncan's arm. 'We have to stop. James—the man in back—may be bleeding to death.'

Duncan did not look at her. 'Not now. 'Tis too dangerous.'

'But he might die before we reach the Whore's Eye.' Her fear mounted as the possibilities played out in her mind. 'If I get to him soon enough, I might be able to save him.'

'Relax, Jenna,' Duncan murmured. 'He is fine.'

Her fingers tightened on his arm. 'How can he be? Bering slashed the hay until it flew. Anyone hidden in it will be lucky to still live.'

'Shh,' he said. 'James is fine.'

'But—'

He cut her off. 'Because there is a false bottom under the pig.'

Her hand dropped from his arm. Her pulse, which had jumped until it pounded in her ears and her chest hurt, calmed. 'A false…'

'Yes. Now be quiet. We are almost there.'

Her anxiety fled, leaving her limp. It was all she could do to remain upright on the hard wooden bench. There was nothing more to be said.

They pulled to a stop in the cover of trees just before the Whore's Eye. 'Don't move,' he whispered before climbing down.

Jenna twisted to watch him. He prowled the area, a two-barrelled pistol in one hand. She bit her tongue to keep from speaking.

He returned to the wagon bed and shifted the hay so there was space around one side of the pig cage. With a knife he pulled from his right boot, he pried at a side panel below the area where the pig now stood. The wood came away.

The wagon rocked and Jenna saw a dark area the shape of a man move around. He slipped from the back and blended into the trees. Duncan came back and climbed on to the wagon bench.

She glared at him, willing him to tell her what was happening. He ignored her and drove them to the entrance of the Whore's Eye.

'Stay here while I go inside and tell the owner his pig and hay are here,' Duncan murmured.

Jenna said nothing, knowing there was nothing to say. Her nerves were calmer, but their danger was no less. Was the Jacobite waiting for them to return to him? What if they were stopped between here and wherever they were going?

She huddled into her rags, wishing it were not so cold. But this was winter.

While time passed, she thought about what had just happened. The more she thought, the angrier she got. He could have told her about the false bottom in the beginning. It would have saved her a lot of agony. It would have also been smart. What if her fear for their passenger had overcome her fear of being discovered? She could have given them away by just a word or a gasp.

Her head ached as her ire at Duncan increased. When he returned, she would tell him just how dangerous his arrogance had been. Not to mention the emotions he had made her endure.

He was back quickly with another man so she held her tongue. The two of them hauled the hay into the stable before dragging the caged pig into a pen where they released the fat animal. The other man helped Duncan return the cage to the back of the wagon. A pile of rags was added.

With a wave to his helper, Duncan climbed into the driver's seat and they headed out. 'Now, if Bering checks on us, our story is confirmed.' His voice barely rose above the noise of the wagon wheels and donkey hoofs.

'Are we going back for our passenger?' she asked through clenched teeth, willing herself not to lash out at him. Not yet.

'Of course.' He spoke as though to a child.

Jenna's jaw ached from holding it stiff. 'I only ask because that seems the logical thing to do, but then it would have been logical for you to tell me about the false bottom to the cage at the start.' Her voice was sweetly sarcastic. 'And you did not do that. Therefore, I was not sure you would think it logical to go back for our passenger. You might have meant him to make his way on foot from here.'

He said nothing. Flicking the reins, he urged the donkey back to the thicket of trees. A shadow emerged, but stayed still. Duncan got off the bench and went to the man.

Jenna, furious now, kept her back to them as they got into the wagon bed and the Jacobite was secreted once more. When Duncan joined her, she angled away so her shoulder was to him.

They started off with a jolt that rocked her against him. She pulled away, feeling as though a scalding brand had brushed her. This was not what she wanted, this response to him.

'We haven't time for this,' he finally said, his voice low and harsh.

'It seems we have not time for anything that might be called communication.' She knew her tone was accusing, but she was right. 'If we are to work together, we must talk to each other.'

'The less you know, the better for everyone—including you.' His voice brooked no argument.

She rounded on him. 'There are some things I should know. Like that false bottom.'

'I disagree.' He looked straight ahead.

She turned away. It galled to let him have the last words on this argument, but if he was not willing to admit he had been wrong, then there was nothing else to do. Thank goodness there were too many reasons why he was not for her.

If only her treacherous body agreed.

It was another half-hour before they reached the beginning of the salt marshes that lined the coast. Duncan halted the wagon, motioning for her to stay there. He prowled the area, a cocked pistol in one hand, a sword in the other.

Jenna was no stranger to violence, tending people who were hurt. She even carried a small pistol of her own. But watching him stalk the area, and knowing he was ready to kill anyone he found who should not be here, was unsettling. She knew he was dangerous. It was eye-opening to see just how much.

Thankfully the only light came from the stars. As it was, with only the tall grass and occasional trees, he was easy to see. If there were any soldiers patrolling this area, he would be a target.

She shivered from tension and pulled her rags tighter. She looked around, squinting into the dark, looking for the flicker of a lantern. Nothing.

He came back and laid the sword on the wagon seat. He kept the pistol in his right hand. Once again, he drew out his knife and wedged it between the pieces of wood in the bottom of the cage. Their passenger emerged.

This time the Jacobite hunched beside the wagon. He had been wounded and the trip had been difficult. Jenna studied him, wondering what type of man they rescued.

He was tall and gaunt with sunken eyes. Layers of clothing hung on him and he still shivered. He was sick. But she had not brought her medicines. Had not realised she needed to. Concern ate at her.

She moved to him. 'You are sick.'

He looked at her. 'Not so sick that I cannot make the voyage.' His voice was stronger than she had expected. There was determination in him.

Duncan stepped between them. 'The smugglers will

have brandy. That will help. We cannot linger here. This is too exposed. Hopefully, our luck will hold and the soldiers have already patrolled here.'

He led them into the sand. The Solway Firth was shallow here, with sand and mud that shifted with the tides. Ships did not come this far inland. The smugglers would be in a rowboat.

Jenna squinted in an effort to see where the sand ended and the water began. The dark cloaked the transition.

The Jacobite moved slowly over the shifting sands. His sharp intake of breath made Jenna wonder if he was capable of the difficult walk.

Duncan touched her shoulder and she looked at him. 'I want you to stay here. Get into the trees and brush and keep quiet.'

She frowned, her previous ire at him returning full force. 'I want—'

'I know you do, but as I keep telling you, the less you know, the better for everyone.' His hand tightened on her. 'I don't have time to argue with you. We have to walk until we meet the smugglers. They will come as far inland as they can, but that depends on what the tides have created.'

Jenna clenched her palms, but kept quiet. He was right about this. She stepped back and let them pass. Only when they were out of sight did she go to the small stand of stunted brush and grass. To be completely hidden she would have to squat or sit. She went to the wagon, noting for the first time that the grass grew as tall as the bed, and got some rags to ward off the cold ground. She had no idea how long her wait would be.

* * *

Jenna counted the stars when the clouds allowed. When the wind off the water blew the overcast away, it was light enough for her to see Duncan's footprints in the sand. Hopefully the tide would come in and wash them away before someone came this way.

A twig cracked and she jerked. Her pulse pounded. Then she saw a man's silhouette. Duncan was back.

She jumped up and rushed to him. 'Is he gone? Will he be all right?'

He put a finger to her lips to hush her. His head went from side to side. 'Has anyone come?'

She shook her head, his finger still against her mouth, making her begin to remember his lips against hers. What a strange time to start feeling amorous. Even stranger was the realisation that her concern for him had eroded her previous anger.

Instead of taking his finger away, his thumb rubbed against her bottom lip. 'He will make it. They had brandy and dried biscuit. That is more than he's had in a long time. And he is determined.' He smiled and his teeth glinted.

His thumb moved to the corner of her mouth and pulled her bottom lip taut. Pleasure formed where his flesh touched hers and flowed outward.

Feeling guilty, she said, 'I should have brought my medicinals. That is one of the reasons you recruited me.'

He smiled. 'One, yes. But I didn't tell you to bring them. Blame the lack on me.'

His magnanimous taking of the blame eroded more of her anger until her fury was only a memory that left behind an extra awareness of him. If only he had not been so gracious.

Blood still pumped through her body so that she was filled with heat and excitement. She found this illicit smuggling of Jacobites to be heady stuff, indeed.

She barely felt the cold that lay a dusting of frost on the bare limbs of the trees. But she was disturbingly aware of the man who stood so close that she would swear she could feel the heat of him.

'Another one gone,' Duncan said softly, his breath a white cloud.

She nodded. 'Hopefully to reach France safely.'

'We have done our part.'

'Yes. And soon it will be Gavin we put on a boat.' Her excitement intensified as she thought of her cousin finally escaping beyond Butcher Cumberland's reach. 'He will be ready to travel soon.'

'Aye, he will.' Duncan's free hand gripped her shoulder, his fingers pressing through the layers of her cape and clothing. They felt like white-hot irons. 'Will you stop helping me when he is gone?'

'Never.' The word left her mouth before she even thought about its implications. She responded to the emotions of the moment. Excitement and danger coursed through her body. But she meant it. 'No, Duncan, I will always help The Ferguson when he needs me.' Chagrin tinged her voice. 'And next time I will bring my medicinals.'

She heard his sharp intake of breath and felt his fingers tighten on her shoulder. Her stomach knotted as a sensation she was becoming all too familiar with flooded her body.

He turned her until inches separated their lips. He smelled of the cold night and the musk that was his own scent. Her toes curled in anticipation of something she had never experienced before, but sensed would change her world.

'Kiss me,' he ordered.

She shuddered with the suppressed passion he ignited in her. Standing on tiptoe, she pressed her mouth to his. Instinct bade her relax into him, opening so his tongue could slip between her teeth.

He licked, sipped and nipped her lips until they felt swollen and sensitised beyond all reason. She moaned and leaned into the strength of his body, knowing that if he let her shoulder go she would melt on to the cold ground like hot wax from a lit candle. She was aflame with need for him.

What would happen to her if he did more than this? She longed to find out.

He lifted his head and looked at her. 'Are you sure you want this?'

She nodded, not sure what he asked, but knowing she was too far gone in the moment and the excitement of the past hours. Danger was an aphrodisiac she did not need in order to respond to him, but it heightened her pleasure.

'Yes,' she whispered, twining her arms around his neck and pulling his mouth back to hers.

She felt as though drugged on laudanum, languorous yet tense, when he lifted her. She hung on to him as he carried her to the wagon. Even when he stood her on her feet, she continued to cling to him.

He laughed a rich, deep rumble. She longed to press her palm to his chest to feel the vibration of his delight against her skin. Too many clothes separated them.

She slipped her gloved hands between their bodies and under the cape he wore to fumble with the buttons of his coat, then his shirt. Frustration became a tight growl of irritation.

'My God,' he breathed, releasing her long enough to help her pull his shirt from his breeches. 'You are hot.'

Her laugh joined his as her hands slipped against his skin and her fingers found the hair on his chest and then a tight, hard nipple. She reveled at her boldness.

'I don't know what it is,' she murmured, rubbing her fingers along his flesh. 'But tonight it seems that part of me is aching to bursting and only you can help.'

''Tis the excitement of what we have done.' He reached low and pulled her skirts up.

She gasped and tensed, her curiosity and eagerness gone as the cold night slapped her thighs.

He stopped.

She closed her eyes and sought for words. 'I…I do not know what to say. What to do. I am sorry.'

He rested his forehead against hers, taking deep breaths that moved his chest against her breasts. 'You are right. This is not the time or the place. You drive me to distraction.'

He shifted away from her. She let him go. He turned and paced away. Came back to her.

He stared down at her. 'I am a bloody fool to want you, Jenna de Warre.'

'Why?' she asked, the word barely audible. Something had changed.

He groaned and ran his fingers through his hair. 'Your father killed mine.'

Jenna felt as though the air had been punched from her. 'My father killed yours?'

'Yes.'

She knew Papa had ordered the killing of many Scots, but… 'I am so sorry. I…' What could she say?

''Tis not your fault.' He paced away from her.

The cold night wind off the ocean whipped Jenna's cape into a frenzy. She knew she should be freezing, but her mind did not connect with her body. All she could do was stand here.

'No wonder you hate Papa.' She resisted the urge to reach out to Duncan. He did not want her touch or he would not have moved away. 'I am surprised you agreed to let me help you.'

He returned to stand close. 'I let you help because I thought you could provide me better cover—which you did. The search earlier would not have gone so easily if I had been a man by myself. There are too many smugglers here and the English know that.'

'Of course,' she managed to say around the lump forming in her throat. She meant nothing to him. She was merely a means to an end. But she could expect nothing else. Especially now.

'Is that why you moved here? Even though you must have known Papa was here.'

He nodded. 'Yes. 'Tis easier to use a system already in place. It would have taken me too long to establish connections between here and France. I needed them now.' He looked away, then back at her, as though what he wanted to say was difficult. 'I knew Viscount Ayre lived here, but it was an ideal location. Gavin told me about it.'

'My cousin?'

'Yes. He contacted me and we decided he should flee here. As you know, it was not swarming with English until Seller tracked Gavin here.'

'And now it is. And Papa.'

He looked down at her as though he read her mind in her face. Jenna wondered if he saw Papa in her features and if he hated her because of that. She dragged air into her tight chest and turned away from him.

'Shouldn't we be leaving? The longer we stay here, the greater our chances of being discovered.' More important to her was the need to get away from this man. He heated her blood even though she knew they were not for one another.

His hand caught her shoulder, searing through the material. She stopped, but said nothing. There was nothing she could say.

'I did not know Ayre had a daughter.'

His voice was barely a whisper, and she thought she misheard. Her pulse pounded in her ears, like the surf beating on the shore.

'You have made things very difficult for me, Jenna.'

She turned her head to see him. There was no moon, but the clouds were gone and the stars provided enough light for her to see the harsh line of his jaw. He was not happy.

'I am sorry, Duncan. If it will help you, I will not push myself at you to help.' They were some of the hardest words she had ever said. The urge to be with him and to help the desperate men he smuggled was strong.

His Adam's apple worked as though he swallowed something unpleasant. 'No, Jenna, I want your help. The men I rescue need you.'

'Ahh...' She trailed off and turned to face the wagon, unable to watch him any longer. 'I will do what you need.'

His hand fell away, and she moved like a rabbit pursued by hounds. Better to get on the wagon and get away from here and him.

He followed her, climbing on to the driver's side of the bench. He urged the donkey forward without looking at her again.

Jenna knew she was foolish beyond belief to want more from him. Their differences had been great before he had told her what Papa had done. Now a chasm separated them.

Chapter Eleven

Jenna gazed out as their coach carried her father and her to Lord Byrne's ball. She had not seen him since they had smuggled the Jacobite out and Duncan had told her what her father had done.

Everything was changed. Duncan had not called afterwards, and she had not felt comfortable visiting his mother or even coming to see Gavin. She chided herself for neglecting her beloved cousin, but her nerves would not allow her to come here.

She had nearly claimed illness tonight, but her father had been eager. She had known that if she did not come, he would send his regrets as well. And he had made no secret of the fact that he was interested in Duncan's mother. Another tangled web. Jenna shuddered to think what would happen if her father and Evelyn McNabb decided they cared for each other.

She was jolted from her pondering by the sound of gravel under the wheels. The carriage rocked to a halt.

Her pulse jumped. Even knowing she and Duncan were not meant to be together, she wanted to see him.

Try as she might, her heart dictated her emotions. She was in love with him.

The carriage door opened, and one of Duncan's footmen stood to help her descend. She took his hand. Her father followed.

Frost covered the ground, making it sparkle like a carpet of diamonds in the light from the hunting box's windows. There must be a thousand candles lit.

'Very impressive,' her father said, having exited behind her. His voice broke her melancholy thoughts. 'Shall we go and enjoy ourselves?'

She managed to smile, wondering what tonight would bring. Everything was changed now. 'Yes, we must.'

The hoops of her formal gown billowed around her as they made their way up the steps to the entrance. The doors were opened before they had a chance to knock, and the butler bowed them inside.

The parquet floor shone as brilliantly in the artificial light as it did when the full force of the sun was upon it. Hunting weapons and armour decorated the entrance hall walls. Handel's music drifted to them.

Another footman, dressed in Lord Byrne's colours of green and gold, took her cloak. Another took her father's greatcoat, hat and cane.

The viscount handed over their invitation, and they were led to the back of the house where the music became louder and mingled with the sound of voices. They passed through double doors and into a room thronged with their neighbors and the officers of the English military billeted around the countryside. It was a phantasmagoria of colour and shape and sound.

Jenna paused and surveyed the room. She took a deep breath to quell her nerves and felt her father's arm stiffen where her gloved fingers still rested. Even though he had wanted to come, she sensed he was as uncomfortable as she. For different reasons. They did not go out in company much, and she thought they had made a mistake to come to such a well-attended ball. But she had not thought everyone in the county would be here. Duncan and his mother were new to the area, after all.

Fortunately, they were late arriving and the reception line had been done away with. She needed time to gain her composure before being exposed to Duncan's charms. The last thing she wished to do was allude to what had happened between them. Nor did she want to simper at him like a lovesick miss.

Minutes later she was thankful for the time. He stood amongst a group of fluttering women, many of whom she recognised as being unmarried. No wonder there was such attendance. She should have realised there would be.

Lord Byrne was a most eligible gentleman. Every unmarried woman in the county would have her sights set on him and every matchmaking mama would be supporting her daughter's attempt.

A young woman with *de rigueur* black hair said something to him that made him laugh. Even over the music and the conversation, Jenna thought she could hear his rich baritone.

'Miss de Warre, how nice to see you here.'

For a moment she did not place the voice and turned uncomprehending eyes on the speaker. 'Ah, Captain Lord Seller, I did not see you approach.'

His smile held a hint of pique as he bowed. 'My apologies for sneaking up on you. I would never inten-tionally do anything to frighten you.'

She returned his bow with a curtsy and forced a smile. 'You look quite handsome tonight. A uniform is ever attractive.'

'Or frightening, depending on your persuasion.'

Her gaze sharpened. Did he mean something by that? He had never mentioned in word or deed that he had recognised her at the Whore's Eye that night. Perhaps he had not. She had worn her cape's hood over her hair. She had to behave as though he had not.

'Oh, la, it would never be frightening, sir. We all know you are here to protect us from scoundrels.'

'Scottish scoundrels,' drawled a familiar voice.

Jenna's heart started a heavy thumping that made her feel light-headed. She licked suddenly dry lips before turning to Lord Byrne. Duncan. Her co-conspirator. The man she loved.

'Lord Byrne,' she murmured, her throat tight with emotion. She hoped he did not hear the breathlessness she felt.

'Miss de Warre.'

He bowed and took her hand from where she unconsciously held it at the base of her throat. He turned it so her palm was up and kissed her wrist. Even through the fine cotton of her glove she felt the heat generated by his mouth. And when he looked up at her from heavy-lidded eyes, she felt as though he touched the most inner part of her.

Fully clothed, with no part of them actually touching, it was as though he made love to her. All the sensations that she had drowned in just days ago flooded over her. A flush mounted from the low cut of her stomacher to her cheeks.

He released her. She stepped back and he stepped

forward. Her embarrassment intensified. He brushed her cheek with one knuckle, his gaze holding her.

'You are beautiful when you blush,' he murmured.

His words moved over her like a caress. She thought her knees would fold.

'I see I am *de trop*.' Seller's dry tone cut between them. 'Excuse me.'

She cast a grateful look at the English soldier. Much as he made her uncomfortable, she had to be glad he had released her from Duncan's spell. She was making a fool of herself.

Jenna stepped away from Duncan. Seller made them a curt bow and left, but not without an ironic look that went from one of them to the other.

Duncan gave her a wicked grin. 'He is very astute.'

She trembled so much the ostrich feather in her powdered hair fluttered against her forehead. 'Or we are very obvious.'

He shrugged. 'Perhaps, but no one else seemed to notice.'

She glanced around. 'I think you are mistaken, my lord. Many women are sending me venomous looks.'

His smile widened. 'I am a novelty to them. Soon they will weary of the sight.'

'I very much doubt that.' She flicked open her gilt fan and started cooling herself. It was mercilessly hot. With the candles, the crowd and her response to this man, she was burning.

He drew her free hand to his arm. 'Will you honour me with a dance?'

Unease stole over her. This was very heady stuff. 'Even after what Papa did?'

His fine mouth thinned and his sparkling eyes

seemed to dim. 'I find myself doing things my mind tells me not to. It seems you are a potent elixir.' He shrugged. 'Unfortunately.'

His last word negated everything he said before it. Her emotions were an up-and-down rush, elation followed by despair. She forced a smile. 'Then perhaps I should refuse your request.'

He sighed and reached up as though to run his fingers through his hair, stopping just in time. ''Twould be better for both of us if you did, but I hope you will not.'

Her smile softened. He was as confused as she. 'I will accept if you will protect me from the claws afterwards.' She attempted lightness when she felt the opposite.

'Unto the ends of the earth.'

There was an intensity in his words that shocked her. She stumbled and only caught herself because he held her firmly against him. Too honest by far, she asked, 'Are you flirting with me, my lord?'

His countenance took on a hunger she could not mis-interpret. 'After what has transpired between us, I am not flirting.'

She dropped her gaze and increased the movement of her fan. 'You are bold.'

'I am entranced.'

They reached the area set aside for dancing before she had to answer. She did not know what to say. She had agonised that he would ignore her completely. Now she worried that what he spoke would lead them into something they would both regret. She had never been on such a course as the two of them were embarked upon. Regardless of what lay between them, she wanted to be with him.

They took their place amongst the other couples. He

bowed as she curtsied. She darted a glance at him, only to see his simmering gaze on her. Her blush intensified.

The orchestra secreted behind a screen began to play a minuet. It was a stately dance, not rambunctious like a country one. Normally when she participated, she felt regal and calm. With him she felt anything but.

When she joined hands with another man, it was as always—nothing. When her fingers brushed Duncan's, it was a conflagration. Even meeting his eyes when others were between them created a yearning that made her chest hurt.

She had never expected love to be this mix of ecstasy and uncertainty, pain and pleasure. If only she could sink into the pleasure he gave her instead of worrying about the rift that should keep them apart. He had made it plain that he could never forgive what her father had done.

She missed a step, stumbled and hastily caught herself. The man she was beside glanced at her out of the corner of his eye. She smiled brightly at him, wishing she could turn and flee this situation.

Never had a dance been more difficult.

The last note of music faded into the air and the other couples drifted off. Jenna watched Duncan.

His eyes held hers and it was as though no one else existed. She gulped in air, wondering if her stays were too tight and that was why she felt light-headed. When he moved toward her, she stepped toward him, the sway of her hoops and the swish of her satin petticoat mimicking her motion.

His gaze dropped to her lips and Jenna trembled.

He bowed. 'Would you like some refreshment?'

She nodded, afraid to speak for fear her voice would reveal how she felt—sensual and desirable and in love. She found herself staring at the little black heart patch at the corner of his mouth. She wanted his lips on her.

With a gulp, she started fanning herself.

He held his arm to her. She rested the tips of her fingers lightly on him. Warm tendrils of awareness stroked up her arm. The rational part of her mind told her that her reaction to him was dangerous. No man should have this effect on a woman.

He led her to another room where refreshments were laid out. Footmen stood ready to help. Others carried out empty platters and bowls that were quickly replaced by filled ones. Guests milled about or sat on chairs and settees.

Duncan situated her in a small alcove partly concealed by a screen. She whisked her fan back and forth so quickly the sound of air moving was audible. She had to control her reaction to him.

'I hope this helps you cool down.' His voice penetrated her thoughts.

She took the cup of punch and drank greedily, having let the fan fall from the ribbon around her wrist. The chill liquid helped her dry throat. 'Thank you.'

He smiled. 'I am sorry the rooms are so hot.' He waved an arm, the silver embroidery on the turquoise satin catching the light and winking. ''Tis all the people and candles. Mother invited everyone within several hours' distance.'

Jenna sat the empty cup on the floor. ''Tis a crush.'

'Yes, but Mother is happy.'

'I understand perfectly. 'Tis always nice when one

has worked so hard to make a party perfect to have everyone show up and enjoy themselves.'

He put one foot on the settee beside her, his inner thigh closing her in, and leaned forward. 'Are you enjoying yourself?'

Her hard-won composure fled. Musk and bergamot filled her senses. If she turned slightly, her chin would touch the inside of his thigh. It was a battle to focus on what he said and not on what she felt.

He raised one golden brow when she did not answer. 'Are you feeling unwell?'

She closed her eyes and licked dry lips. He was not doing this to seduce her. Her reaction was her own. 'No, I am fine.'

A wicked glint made his eyes look like golden topaz. 'Are you enjoying yourself?'

She realised he had asked that before. She chided herself into composure. 'Of course, my lord. Why would I not?'

He shrugged. One arm propped across his knee, he leaned into her. His free hand touched the ostrich feather that framed her face. His finger traced the ornament to her cheek and stopped.

'Will you meet me in the portrait gallery?' His voice was deep and husky, barely audible.

Jenna's eyes widened in reaction to his touch and to his words. 'Now?'

He skimmed the line of her cheek to her chin. 'After we part. After the next dance.'

Her blood pounded. Did she want to meet him? Could she bear not to? What could he say to her? They had no future together.

'Yes,' she breathed before her better sense could convince her to refuse.

'Make sure no one notices you leaving.' He stared intently at her, as though he thought her not listening. 'We are not married.'

The blood pounded in her ears so loudly she thought she misheard him. 'Married?'

Tenderness softened the harsh angles of need in his face. 'Meet me, Jenna.'

All she could do was nod.

He placed his foot back on the floor and Jenna's sense of enclosure lessened, but it was no comfort. She felt safe when he was close.

She stood and put her fingers on his extended arm. 'Where are you taking me?'

'Not to your parent. He will notice when you leave him.'

'I am his only chick.' And Papa worried about her.

They re-entered the ballroom. She scanned the crowd of people, her attention caught by a laugh she recognised. Turning away from Duncan, she saw her father. He was with Duncan's mother, Mrs McNabb, and he was smiling and laughing at what she said.

'How unlike Papa,' she murmured, even though happiness at his enjoyment was like a ray of sunshine. She looked back at Duncan to say so, only he frowned.

'It seems your father and my mother are entertaining one another.'

'You do not seem overjoyed by that.'

His frown intensified. He glanced at her and back to them. 'No, I am not. And you know why. But never mind them.'

She felt a shudder run through his body as though he

shook himself free of some restraint. Unease flowed from him to her. His reaction did not bode well for them.

He brought her hand to his lips, breaking her apprehension. 'I will leave you here, Jenna. And hope to see you soon.'

She gazed at him, wondering why he sought her out when his father's death was so fresh to him that even now he could not stand to see his mother speaking with her father. His face held no hint of his feelings, other than the heat in his eyes as he looked at her. His body was once more relaxed.

She made a brief curtsy to him. 'Soon.'

It was an effort not to watch him walk away from her. Everything about him intrigued her. He excited her more than anything she had ever encountered. She turned away, knowing she loved him.

Nothing would keep her from their rendezvous.

Not even Seller, when he accosted her. 'Miss de Warre.' He stepped in her path and made an elegant leg, the gold braid on his uniform sparkling in the candlelight.

She stopped and curtsied. 'Captain Lord Seller.'

'A word of warning only, madam.'

Had he seen her with Duncan in the alcove, that intimate pose and her stammering reaction? Blood suffused her cheeks. 'What about, sir?'

His smile was innocence incarnate. But he ruined it with a frown. 'I have heard from many of the villagers and crofters that you travel about the countryside with only a groom and sometimes not even that. They say your errands of mercy have you about at all hours.'

She nodded, wondering where he was going with this. Would he mention the Whore's Eye now?

'I feel it my responsibility as an officer of his Majesty's army and a guest in your home to warn you. There are Jacobites in this area. They are desperate men and will stop at nothing to reach freedom.' He paused, watching her as a cat might a mouse. She hoped her face held only polite inquiry. 'I would be glad to accompany you.'

Her heart thudded heavily. The last thing she needed or wanted was his company. She managed to smile. 'Thank you, sir, but I am accustomed to going when and where I need to. I am sure you are too busy to be at my beck and call.'

His eyes narrowed as though he sensed what she did not say. 'These men are dangerous. One of them particularly so.'

'Really?' She realised the music had stopped. She was supposed to meet Duncan.

'Yes. He is called The Ferguson. He is a criminal wanted for treason to the Crown.'

The fingers gripping her fan tensed. She made herself take a breath before speaking for fear she would blurt words that would reveal something. When her pulse felt only slightly fast, she spoke. 'I have not heard anything about such a man. And, surely, with my errands I would have heard something.'

'Perhaps not.' He looked as though he doubted her, but his tone was light.

She shrugged, resisting the urge to fiddle with her fan. 'If I do hear anything, I will be sure to tell you.' She smiled her most friendly smile at him and hoped it was enough.

'Of course.' His smile was as false as hers.

'I see a neighbour, sir. If you will excuse me.' She slipped around him, the wide skirts of her gown brushing his stocking-clad leg. She resisted the urge to lift her skirts away.

He made her a curt bow as she left.

Jenna felt his gaze boring into her back, making her spine tingle with unease. She refused to look behind, but she did go behind a group of people and kept walking until she was in the entrance area. No one was about, not even the butler since everyone was here and no one was leaving yet. Now to remember her way.

Up the stairs, down halls, around corners—it seemed ages before she finally entered the double doors leading to the picture gallery. In the winter months or when it rained, people would come here to walk and talk. She came for a romantic tryst.

He stood by one of the windows, gazing out at the night-shrouded garden. At the sound of her footsteps on the wooden floor, he turned.

She did not pause or even think before rushing to him.

'Ah, Jenna,' he said, taking her hands in his. 'I had begun to think you had changed your mind. That you had more will power than I.'

She sighed and raised his hand to kiss his palm, her heart thundering. She did not know where they were going, but she was willing to go wherever he led. 'Never.' She looked up at him. 'Seller stopped me.'

Stillness fell over him. 'And?'

'He warned me about The Ferguson.' She could not take the fierceness in his eyes and turned away.

'He was trying to see if you know anything.'

She nodded. 'I did not tell him anything.'

She hoped he believed her. It would be unbearable to have got this close to him and to have him doubt her now, after all they had been through. After what he had told her about her father.

'I know you did not. We had best be more careful of him than before. I had planned to take you to visit Gavin while everyone else continues dancing.'

She shivered. This large room was not warm. ''Twould be too dangerous.'

He nodded. 'He is mending nicely and getting impatient. I had hoped that talking to you would ease some of his jitteriness. But I don't think we should risk it.'

She sighed. 'I worry about him constantly.'

He freed his hands from hers and gently stroked her cheek. 'He is safe here.'

Without thinking, she leaned her face into his caress. Strangely, given what was between them, he made her feel safe and cherished. 'I know, Duncan, but that does not ease my need to see him. We are cousins, but he is like a brother to me.'

'And to me.' His eyes searched her face as though he looked for a sign of some sort.

Reacting to his unspoken communication, she asked, 'What is wrong?'

His hand fell away. 'I am wondering why I want you, even knowing who your father is.'

She stepped back, needing distance, hoping that not being so close would ease the pain his words caused. Perhaps, even ease her need for his touch. She forced coolness into her voice. 'I imagine what you think you feel is merely a reaction you would have for any woman who has shared the dangers with you that I have.'

'Do you truly believe that?' His voice was a breath of warmth on her skin.

She could not lie to him any more than she could deny what he made her feel. 'No.'

He reached for her. His lips brushed her hair and travelled to her exposed ear. His tongue rimmed her earlobe, sending darts of pleasure to her stomach.

She let out a shuddering breath and cast caution to the wind. No matter what stood between them, she would enjoy whatever he gave.

She lifted her face to his.

His mouth took hers in a kiss that teased and aroused. She opened for him.

His hands ranged over her back, up and down, pulling her tighter and tighter to him with each pass. Her breasts felt engorged by his ardour and crushed by her stomacher. When he pulled his mouth away and dropped it to her bosom, her head fell back to give him access.

He nipped and kissed and licked his way down her flesh to where her breasts surged above her stomacher. Her fingers clawed at his back.

He laughed low in his throat. 'You are magnificent.'

His words returned a semblance of sanity to her. Taking deep breaths, she pressed her palms to his chest. 'This is madness.'

He sobered, but his arms retained possession of her. 'Yes. 'Tis that and more.'

'With what lies between us, we should be avoiding one another.' She said the words sensibly even as her heart denied them.

'You are right, Jenna. We should.' His arms hardened. 'But I find that when I am near you, what I should rationally do—what I plan to do—takes flight. All I want is you and the past is merely a dark shadow.'

Unease skated down her spine. He wanted her, but even as he said that, he used powerful words to describe the past. 'Perhaps we should concentrate on finding a time for me to visit Gavin.' They were not the words she wanted to say, but they were safe.

He released her and moved away. He kept his attention focused on her. 'I cannot touch you and remember why I should not even speak to you.'

Desire, insidious and undeniable, curled through her like smoke in a cold room. 'When can I visit my cousin?'

'Come tomorrow afternoon. Call on my mother. She will know.' His voice was cool, all the passion of seconds before doused like it had never existed.

Jenna began to doubt her senses if he could turn off his ardour that easily. What chance was there for them? None.

'I will be here.'

'Good.' He held his arm out to her, his face telling her that they were finished here.

She settled the tips of her fingers on his coat. Awareness shot through her. She told herself to ignore her reaction.

There was nowhere for them to go with their passion.

Chapter Twelve

Jenna watched Lord Byrne's stable boy take Rosebud's reins. 'She is a gentle creature,' she assured the youth.

He smiled and patted the mare's neck.

Jenna, assured that Rosebud would receive every comfort, turned away and climbed the stairs to the front door. The butler opened the heavy portal before she knocked.

'Thank you,' she murmured, entering. She gave him her hat and riding crop.

He led her to the drawing room where Mrs McNabb sat. The older woman motioned Jenna to a chair.

'Miss de Warre, how nice of you to call.'

Jenna sat, suppressing her impatience to see Gavin. It was only polite to spend time with her hostess. 'Thank you for receiving me. And for last night. Papa and I enjoyed ourselves immensely.'

Mrs McNabb's hazel eyes lit up. 'I am so glad you were both able to come.' She fingered a fold in her heavy wool skirt. 'Viscount Ayre is very entertaining.'

Jenna smiled in pleasure. 'Thank you.'

It was only after she spoke that she remembered Duncan's father had been this woman's husband. Did Mrs McNabb know?

For a moment, sadness pulled the older woman's features down. 'It is too bad about the past.'

Jenna stiffened, not sure what to say.

'Do not fret, Miss de Warre. I know. For many years I allowed my anger and grief to rule me.' She spread her hands in acceptance. 'I was not even sure about moving here. But having met your father, I can forgive him. I believe he regrets what he did and would not do it today. That is all one can ask of someone.'

Relief and comfort spread through Jenna. 'You are a very generous person, Mrs McNabb. I do not believe everyone would be as forgiving.'

'I am afraid you are right.' She rose. 'Will you have tea with me, or are you too anxious to visit?'

She did not say Gavin's name, but Jenna knew who she meant. 'If you don't mind, I have not seen him for a while.'

'I understand. Please follow me.'

Jenna rose and trailed her hostess just as she had trailed Duncan what seemed an eternity ago. They quickly came to the kitchen.

Mrs McNabb stopped. 'I am sure you know your way from here.'

Jenna paused. 'Thank you so much for doing this.'

Duncan's mother shrugged. 'We do what we can.'

''Tis dangerous.'

'True, but this is my son's passion.' The smile she gave Jenna was tired. ''Tis better than many he could have.'

Jenna wanted to touch the other woman, to somehow convey her gratitude for all they risked. But she could not. She was not familiar enough with Mrs McNabb to do so.

Instead, she turned and made her way through the kitchen. The cook and a scullery maid watched her, but said nothing. She went through the pantry and behind the casks, just as Duncan had shown her.

She knocked softly on the hidden door before entering. She closed the door quietly. Gavin lay on the pallet.

'Wake up, sleepyhead,' she said softly.

He rubbed his eyes, using the arm attached to his healing shoulder. He did not even wince. Satisfaction was a warm feeling in her stomach.

'Oh, 'tis you.'

She smiled. 'Only me. How are you feeling?'

'Ready to be gone. Duncan told me to tell you to be ready on the first night of the new moon.' He continued to watch her as she sat on the stool beside his cot. 'What are you doing here? Come to wish me luck?'

Jenna froze, her right hand in the process of reaching to push the hair off Ian's brow. 'What are you talking about?'

His frown deepened. 'I'm talking about my escape. Don't tell me Duncan sent you to tell me it is being postponed—again.' He shifted, throwing the covers off. 'I will not put it off again.' He stood, his head nearly hitting the low stone wall before he ducked. 'Look at me. I am fine.'

Jenna watched him, but her mind was on what he said, not the fact that her cousin was strong enough for the journey. 'When are you going?'

'I told you, Jen. The first night of the new moon. A week from now. You are to be prepared for us. Duncan told me what a help you were to his cover.' He trailed off, worry replacing his frown.

'That makes sense,' she said, wondering when Duncan had intended to tell her.

Gavin knelt in front of her. 'He didn't tell you.'

She lifted her chin. 'No. Likely he forgot.'

Gavin shook his head. 'Duncan never forgets. He probably decided 'twould be easier for me to give you the information. He said you would likely visit today.'

'True.'

Gavin took her hand. 'Your fingers are like ice.'

She forced a smile. ''Tis not every day I am told to be prepared to help smuggle my beloved cousin out of England. In fact, 'tis a first.'

He gave her his lopsided grin. 'And hopefully the last.' He rubbed her hand until warmth came back. 'Jen, look at me. What is going on between you two?'

She widened her smile, feeling as though she was grimacing. 'Nothing. How can there be? We are worlds apart in everything.' She looked away from him. 'Smuggling Jacobites out of the country is not the safest of things to do.'

'True.' He held on to her hands when she tried to pull them free. 'And Duncan's life is devoted to doing just that. Do not be forgetting that.'

She sighed. 'How can I?'

Gavin shook her hand. 'You cannot. Ever.'

She grimaced and pulled her hand from his grip. 'I will not.'

'But…' He lifted one auburn brow.

'But what?' She dropped her gaze. She did not want him seeing the pain in her eyes.

'But there is more that you are not saying.' He leaned into her, forcing her to look at him.

'You are so domineering!' She smiled at him.

'And you know how to get around me if you really want to. You did it all the time when we were children.' He touched her shoulder. 'I'm thinking you want to tell me.'

She took a deep breath and let it out slowly. 'I am in love with him.'

Gavin groaned and leaned back on the cot so that his shoulders touched the wall. 'I was afraid of that, Jen. Even if he loves you back, 'tis a bad match.'

Exasperation fought with pain. 'I know that, Gavin, but knowing does not change anything.'

'I suppose not.' He scrubbed at his face with the heels of his hands. 'I'm sorry.'

The sympathy in Gavin's voice was nearly her undoing. He was her beloved cousin whom she'd grown up with. He was more a brother. But that did not make her comfortable crying on his shoulder. She was stronger than this.

'So am I, Gavin. But 'tis done.' Pulling her hands from his relaxed clasp, she stood. 'Tell Duncan I will be ready on the first night of the new moon.'

He grinned, but she could tell it was forced. 'I think 'twould be best if you weren't. The less you see of that devil, the better you will be.'

'Likely you are right.' She shook her head. 'But I told him I would help him. More importantly, I would walk on coals to be with you when you leave. Now, enough. Go back to sleep.'

When she entered the kitchen minutes later, everyone was gone. She debated whether to say goodbye to her hostess and decided against it. She did not feel cheerful and capable of discussing the weather and her neighbours.

A week later, Jenna huddled into her rags. Her hair was a black, snarly mess hanging down her back. The wagon bench was a hard slab that made her muscles ache. Wind tossed the branches of the trees where she and Duncan had left Gavin so they could deliver to the Whore's Eye the pig that was their disguise.

Light from the Whore's Eye spilled into the dark night, sparkling on the mist that filled the cold air. Soon it would rain.

Jenna sighed. A miserable night to say goodbye to her only cousin. Thankfully, Gavin would be safe after this. That thought kept her hunkered down in the cold and wet.

Duncan emerged from the kitchen with another man. A woman walked with them. The two men went to the back of the wagon and got the pig. The woman stopped beside Jenna.

'I know who you are,' Nelly's strongly accented voice said.

Jenna looked down at her, wishing there was more light to see the other woman's expression. But there was not. 'I trust you not to betray me.'

'Why shouldn't I?' Nelly grasped the shawl covering her head as the wind tried to rip it away.

Jenna thought she heard anger in her voice. 'Because you would betray *him* with me.'

Nelly shifted. The clouds drifted. It seemed that for a moment Jenna could see the other woman's features. They were twisted. Jenna shivered. Why did this woman think she was a threat?

'I won't let you have him.' Flat and plain, yet so softly spoken that the men could not hear.

Jenna's unease intensified. 'He is not mine.'

'We are ready,' Duncan's voice intruded.

Nelly edged away, holding her skirts from the mud underfoot. She went to Duncan. 'Be careful.' Her voice was warmer than Jenna had ever heard it.

Duncan waved at the woman. 'I always am. Take care of yourself, Nelly.'

The man who had helped Duncan with the pig took Nelly's elbow and led her back to the kitchen door. They disappeared inside, but Jenna knew the woman watched from the window.

Duncan flicked the reins and the creak and rattle of the wagon was a relief after the tension of her meeting with Nelly. The donkey plodded back to the trees where Gavin hid.

Jenna debated whether she should tell Duncan what Nelly had said. It sounded melodramatic now.

Duncan did not want her. Or he wanted her, but he would never love her. Her father stood between them. Nelly had nothing to fear from her.

Duncan pulled into the trees so that the sides of the wagon scrapped the trunks. Gavin emerged, a darker shadow in the night, and clambered into the back. The wagon rocked as Jenna twisted around to watch her cousin. She smiled at him, even though she knew he could not see it. 'Twas like black ink under the trees.

Duncan handed her the reins and got into the wagon bed to secure Gavin in the secret compartment under the pig cage. Gavin was a big man and he barely fitted. She could hear both men grumble and mutter, but neither raised his voice. They were too close to the Whore's Eye to take the chance that sound might travel.

Minutes later, Duncan climbed back aboard. He flicked the reins, and the donkey pulling the wagon lumbered forward. The animal's pace was steady, but not fast. It would be some time before they reached the beach.

Cold knifed through Jenna's outer rags and heavier clothing beneath. Her palms slicked from nerves. They had a way to go still. Anything could happen.

Jenna scanned the area behind them for any movement and strained to hear any sound. Better to be forewarned about other travellers than to be taken unawares.

Duncan's thigh brushed hers and she jumped. He stared straight ahead. If she had thought there was any remote possibility that Nelly's jealousy was founded, she knew now that there was none. He acted as though nothing had happened while her leg burned with sensation.

No, she was no threat to Nelly. There was no sense in telling Duncan what the other woman had said.

They lumbered through the dark. She pitied Gavin his cramped quarters, but he had to be warmer than they were. The rain had started and the dirt road they travelled was becoming a quagmire. She hoped a wheel would not get stuck in the mud.

A chill breeze caught the hood of her threadbare cape just as the wagon lurched. Duncan urged the donkey on, but the wagon stayed put.

She heard him exhale in irritation.

They both climbed down. Her feet pulled free from the mud. They got to the right rear wheel, which was a foot deep in the muck. Exhaustion slumped Jenna's shoulders.

Duncan ran his fingers through his loose hair.

They were so close and now this.

Duncan put his shoulder to the back of the wagon and pushed. Nothing. 'Go urge the donkey forwards when I push.'

Jenna nodded, knowing it would be nearly impossible to co-ordinate their efforts without shouting. And they dare not make any more noise then necessary. So far they had been lucky and not run into any English troops. But they all knew the army patrolled the coast every night for smugglers.

She grabbed the donkey's harness and urged the animal forwards. As she did so, she felt the vibration of Duncan's push from behind. Nothing.

Duncan joined her and put his lips to her ear again. His breath was warm and tickled. If only they were somewhere else.

'I am going to release Gavin. Maybe the two of us can get the wheel loose.'

She nodded. The rain came down. Soon, if her freezing hands and feet were any indicators, it would turn to snow. It was a miserable night to be out in, even if they had been in a covered carriage with hot bricks. Which they were not.

But it was a new moon and it was past time for Gavin to leave. They had to make do with what they were given.

Even as she pondered their situation, Duncan turned and made his way to the wagon bed. She felt him climb inside and heard the noise of his activity. Gavin clambered out of the tiny area. She saw him stretch, a dark outline against the black night.

Then both men were on the ground. The wagon rocked as they put their shoulders to the stuck wheel. She urged the donkey to pull. A plop and sucking noise told her the wheel was coming unglued.

But did they dare continue to use it?

Minutes later, Duncan and Gavin stood beside her.

'We got the wheel out, but chances are good it will get stuck again. We're less than a mile from the coast.' Duncan looked at each of them. 'I think we should walk.'

Gavin asked, 'Will we get there in time?'

Duncan squinted at the sky, judging the time by the stars. 'We should. We can be there in twenty to thirty minutes by foot.'

Jenna gathered her skirts up, the heavy wool and cotton made heavier by the rain. 'Then we had best start.'

Duncan caught her arm and leaned into her. 'I don't suppose you would stay here with the animal?'

She shook her head vehemently, afraid that if she spoke she would shout. She had come too far to quit now. This was the last she would see of her beloved cousin.

Gavin bent and got a handful of mud which he rubbed through his hair. Jenna shuddered, but knew it was wise. There were not too many redheads in this area. He would stand out. As it was, his clothes would give him away if they encountered someone. He was dressed too well.

Duncan went back to the wagon and rummaged under the driver's seat. When he returned to them, he held a two-barrelled pistol and a knife. Jenna's sense of disquiet increased. She had known they were in danger, but seeing him armed brought it home with a punch.

They had not planned for any of this. But they had to make this work. Hopefully the weather would keep the English from being so thorough.

They struck out without talking. Jenna was the only one unarmed, as Gavin had brought his own set of pistols. She led the donkey that they had unhitched from the wagon.

Gavin would go through the Solway Firth to the Isle of Man and from there to France. Duncan said this was better and why he had picked this location. 'Twas longer, but less well patrolled by the English. And more people around here were sympathetic to the Jacobites.

But the Firth was dangerous with its shifting sands and shallow waters. Birds and shellfish populated the area. In some areas trees grew nearly to the water's edge—where they would go.

The closer they came to the Firth, the more she smelled the sea. Even the rain seemed to lessen. This close to water, the threat of snow eased.

After what seemed an eternity in the wet, cold night, Jenna thought she saw the glint of starlight on moving water. She even began to think she heard the sound of waves hitting the beach.

They paused at a clump of scrub brush and trees stunted by the wind off the water. They tethered the donkey in a group of trees and marsh grass.

They would cross the sand to where the smugglers would pull up their rowboat. Normally the men brought illegal whisky from Scotland. Tonight they would take a Scot to safety.

With no lantern to light their way, they had to trust in Duncan's knowledge of the flats, which shifted constantly. Jenna shuddered as she stepped on to the sand and her foot sank several inches down. The tide was out now, but when it shifted it could rise as much as twelve feet in two hours.

Duncan prowled the area first before motioning

Gavin and Jenna on. Gavin went first and Jenna followed. Both men held their pistols ready.

Chills moved over her.

They had a schedule to meet and could not dally long to make sure the way they trod was safe. The tide waited for no one, and they had timed themselves to arrive minutes before the smugglers would be rowing into the cove. The less time spent here, the safer for everyone.

They reached the rendezvous area, and Jenna could see the boat pulled on to the soft sand and mud. Several men hunkered around it.

Duncan approached the smugglers and Jenna heard the faint rumble of voices. Gavin stayed with her, scanning the sea in front of them and the flats behind them.

Duncan returned. 'They leave as soon as you are aboard.'

Gavin stiffened. 'Thank you for everything, Duncan.'

'Do not thank me, my friend. You deserve this.'

Jenna watched the men shake hands and hug each other briefly. No sooner did Duncan release Gavin than she wrapped her arms around her cousin's neck. 'Take care of yourself, understand? You are better, but far from well and this will be a long, uncomfortable crossing.'

'Doan fash yourself.' His tone was light, but he held her tight. 'I will return, you know?'

She blinked to keep back the tears that threatened. 'When 'tis safe.'

He knuckled her chin in a mock-punch, a sign of affection he had used with her when they were children. 'Doan cry, Jen. Everything will be fine.'

She nodded and gulped back a sob. 'I know. 'Tis best this way. I will miss you.'

'And I you.' He squeezed her one last time and stepped away.

She threw her arms around his waist and hugged him tight. Even knowing this was the only chance he had to live, she ached to lose him. She thought she saw his teeth flash in a grin, but he said nothing.

She watched him approach the men. He got in the boat and the smugglers pushed the craft into the water. She heard the soft dip and splash of oars.

Relief that he would soon be safe warred with the misery of his loss. France was a long way. She had never been out of England. But she would visit him.

When the boat was no longer visible, she turned from the shore. Duncan stood behind her, and she nearly collided with him.

She gave him a wan smile and trudged on. The sand sucked at her feet, seeming to want to pull her into its damp embrace.

'Careful…' Duncan's whisper penetrated her melancholy '…let me lead the way.'

She slowed enough for him to reach her. His hand gripped her shoulder, and even through the layers of rags it was as though he branded her.

Her pulse jumped in response to him. It was an unwelcome response. She loved him and knew he did not feel the same for her.

He leaned into her. 'You will feel better when you are rested.'

She nodded, knowing he was right. 'Yes, but I will miss him sorely.'

'As will I.'

His hold on her lowered to her elbow. Firmer and stronger than she, he helped her over the shifting sands. The wind picked up and the lapping sound of the waves increased.

'The tide is coming in,' Duncan said. 'We must hurry.'

She picked up her pace, slightly breathless from the exercise. Or that is what she told herself. She had to resist the sensations he always evoked in her.

Her legs felt like wooden pegs when they finally reached the tethered donkey. The stalwart animal neighed at the sight of them. Jenna's heart softened.

'This little beast has worked hard for us tonight. I hope he gets a reward.' She patted the animal's neck.

'He will soon be in my stable, making my blue-blood stock feel insulted.' Duncan chuckled as he untied the animal.

Before Jenna realised what he was about, his hands gripped her waist and hoisted her to the donkey's bare back. Heat spread from where he still clasped her.

'You are not wearing stays again.' He voice was husky.

She shook her head before remembering it would be hard for him to see her in the dark. The stars hid behind clouds. 'No, I am not.'

His hands fell away, and she grabbed the donkey's mane to keep from tumbling off. Duncan moved in front of the little animal and led him back the way they had come.

Jenna watched the darker shadow of his shoulders swinging easily. His long strides ate up the ground faster than her shorter steps would have. She wanted to say something, but held back. They were not safe yet.

Lulled by the rocking of the donkey's gait, she dropped into a semi-slumber. The clouds blew away, and the starlight rimmed Duncan's lamp-blacked hair in shades of grey. Before she realised it, they were beside the wagon.

He returned to her before she could slide off the animal's back. Keeping his face turned up to her, he gripped her waist and lowered her so her body slid along his. The skirts of her peasant clothing rucked up her legs and tendrils of cold crept up her thighs.

Neither spoke.

His lips found hers. His arms circled her waist. Her fingers combed through his hair. She clung to him, dazed and aroused and hungry for something only he could provide.

When he pulled away, she opened her eyes. His face was a dark shadow in the night. It was impossible to see his expression.

'Ah, Jenna.' His voice was a husky rasp.

Feeling breathless, she said nothing. Better not to speak when 'twas obvious he regretted their kiss before it was even over. She was not used to rejection. She felt used and hurt.

He pulled her back into the warmth of his embrace. His body pressed to hers. The sense of hurt eased.

'I did not intend for this to happen.'

Indignation came to her rescue. She pushed at his chest in a futile attempt to escape. 'Then why did you kiss me?'

One of his hands rubbed up and down her back, leaving a trail of heat that contrasted sharply with the cold air. 'Because I couldn't help myself.' He groaned. 'Bloody Ayre's daughter. If I told anyone this, they wouldn't believe me.'

Holding herself stiffly, wishing his moving hand did not feel so good, she said, 'What would you tell them? That I am easy to seduce, and you have decided not to?'

Even as the accusation left her lips, her face flamed. She was never this outspoken. At least not about this.

'I wish that were what I would say.' The hand rubbing her back shifted to her face. He cupped her chin, his rough thumb rubbing her kiss-swollen bottom lip. 'I never thought myself a fool about women. And never would have thought I would say this to the daughter of my enemy. A woman who should be my enemy.'

Her eyes widened as pleasure coursed from his moving thumb to her stomach. Not even the cold night air penetrated the haze of desire and hope his actions and words created.

'What are you trying to say?' Her voice caught.

Hope, so intense and so sweet, swelled her chest. If only he cared for her. But, as he said, they were enemies. Or should be.

'Jenna, Jenna.'

The donkey shifted and Jenna, so intent on what Duncan was doing, started. She giggled nervously. They were in the middle of the marsh land near the coast. They had just helped Gavin be smuggled to France. They had committed treason to the Crown.

And she cared nothing for that. Her entire focus was on the man holding her and what he might be getting ready to say.

'We are fools,' she muttered.

'Aye,' Duncan said softly. His lips met hers in a fleeting kiss before going to her eyes and the tip of her nose. 'Aye, we are that.' He lifted his head. 'Look at me, Jenna.'

She opened her eyes and gazed at him, wishing she could see his expression. She had to be satisfied with the tenderness in his voice.

'Marry me, Jenna.'

Chapter Thirteen

Days later, Jenna caught herself wandering to the window for the third time in less than an hour. The winter sun cast watery light on the ground. Even in this weather, the estate workers were about their business. Just as Jenna should be about hers.

But she could not settle down to anything.

She had told Duncan she would marry him. How could she have not when she loved him so? He had promised to call on Papa in three days, to give her time to change her mind. She never would and had told him so.

He had delivered her home after Gavin's escape. She had not heard from him or seen him since.

Had he changed his mind? Was the three days really for him and not her? Worry ate at her like a canker.

She had never intended to wed and leave Papa alone. Yet, she had given her word to a man who was the enemy of everything her papa stood for and believed in. She loved Duncan more than was wise.

She sighed and rubbed her palms along her apron.

When she had told Papa that Duncan wanted to marry her and did he mind, Papa had been happy for her. He had told her the worst thing she could do to him was to deny herself the joy Duncan would give her—if she truly loved Duncan. And she did.

She turned away, intending to return to the batch of dried herbs she was bit by bit crushing. Movement outside caught her eye. She paused and adjusted her spectacles to better see.

A lone man on a roan horse moved across the courtyard in the direction of the front door. He wore his tricorn hat pulled low. A voluminous greatcoat shrouded him from neck to thigh, but did nothing to conceal his elegant and muscular seat on the horse.

Duncan. At last.

Jenna realised she was smiling as though all her wishes had just come true. Perhaps they had.

Everything else forgotten, she hurried out of her still-room and to the entry way. Papa should be in his study waiting for this visit. Her heart pounded in rhythm to her footsteps.

She managed to slow down just as the side hallway she traversed met up with the main hallway to the entrance. A lady did not act like a hoyden and rush up to the man who was calling to ask for her hand in matrimony. No matter that she was deliriously happy and wanted to throw herself into Duncan's arms.

Calming herself outwardly, she smoothed down her muslin apron and lifted her chin, making sure her smile did not go from one side of her face to the other. Her goal was to look serene and pleased to see him, not ecstatic and beyond control. Once she felt semi-assured of her success, she stepped forward.

'Lord Byrne.' She extended her hand just as he handed his tricorn and greatcoat to the butler.

'Ah, Miss de Warre.' Duncan gave her a conspiratorial smile and advanced to her. He took her hand, pausing to look into her eyes before putting his lips to her fingers.

Shivers danced up her arm and down her spine. Her smile broke loose. 'Papa is ready,' she murmured.

'Then I shan't keep him waiting.'

He released her and Jenna stepped back. Her pulse pounded, and anticipation had her twisting her fingers in the sturdy white muslin of her apron. Belatedly, she realised she had rushed out here in her working clothes. She had not even thought to dress appropriately for Duncan's call.

Dismay dimmed her eyes. She had wanted to look her best for this occasion, and she had allowed her worry and preoccupation to keep her from that. She should have dressed when she arose. But she had worried that working in the stillroom would soil her gown.

She sighed.

He smiled at her. 'You are beautiful,' he said softly.

Happiness engulfed her. It was as though he knew exactly what she was thinking. He always gave her what she needed. She hoped she did the same for him.

'Thank you,' she murmured. More than ever she wanted to throw herself into his arms.

'And I want to hold you and more,' he said softly so only she heard. In a louder voice he added, 'But I must meet with Lord Ayre.'

'If you will follow me, my lord,' Burke's cracked voice intervened. 'I have told his lordship you are here, and he will see you now.'

Duncan swept her a bow before turning on his heel.

She watched his proud, straight back disappear down the hall that led to Papa's study. The excited little girl in her wanted to follow and listen through the door, but the adult woman knew that was not the thing to do. She contented herself with pacing the foyer.

'Miss?' Burke's voice stopped her in her tracks.

She gave him a sheepish grin, thankful he was the one who had found her giving into her impulses. He had been with them since he was a footman, and she had not yet been conceived.

'Ah, I am on tenterhooks.'

He unbent enough to return her smile. 'I understand, miss. It should not be long.'

She nodded, sure he was right. There was not that much to discuss. Her dowry was ample and uncomplicated. It was the things that couldn't be spoken of that would have taken time. But there was no need for Papa to know what Duncan did. Better for all that Papa not know, and for Duncan to continue accepting that Papa was sorry for what he had done.

Duncan seemed to have come to terms with Papa's actions in the first Jacobite rising. Otherwise, why would he have proposed? He would not.

Jenna contented herself by moving into the saloon and pacing the carpet there. Burke would tell Duncan where to find her. She prowled past the richly brocaded chairs of dark oak so fashionable a hundred years before, continuing to the small slit windows and then back to the fireplace with its granite mantel.

Her mother's picture, done shortly before her death in childbirth, took place of honour above the fireplace. Papa would spend lengths of time staring at it. He had loved her beyond all else.

Jenna fervently hoped her marriage to Duncan would be as blessed with mutual love. Surely it would, otherwise he would not have proposed to her.

She heard the door close and spun around, her reverie forgotten in anticipation. Duncan smiled at her. She flew to him. He opened his arms, and she melted into his warmth and strength.

''Tis done,' he said, his lips on her hair.

She felt the warmth of his breath move strands of her hair. 'And we have Papa's blessing.'

He nodded, his chin rubbing her temple. 'Yes. But you never expected anything else.'

She shifted to look up at him. 'Never. Papa would never refuse when he knows we love each other.'

For a second only, she thought his eyes clouded. Then they were hazel and blazing and she knew she had to be mistaken.

'Your parents' marriage was a love match, was it not?'

'Yes.' She angled her head to the fireplace. 'That is Mama's portrait. Papa will not allow it to be moved. He spends time in here every day. It is as though through it he maintains contact with her.'

'Very touching.' He released her and went to get a closer look.

She frowned. Had he sounded sarcastic? Sardonic? Surely not. There was nothing in Papa's continued love for Mama to cause such emotions.

Jenna watched Duncan as he paused in front of the painting, aching at the sense of emptiness his moving away had left her with. Love was heady. It was also frightening that one person had the power to make her world spin with delight or plummet with uncertainty.

Shaking away the flare of doubt, she went to him. 'That was just before she died.'

He looked at her. 'You have the look of her.'

Jenna smiled. 'So does Gavin. 'Tis our Scottish blood.'

Duncan's eyes narrowed, but he said nothing.

She put a hand on his arm. 'Did I say something wrong?'

For long moments he looked at her. Then shook his head. 'Nothing I do not already know.'

She shivered. ''Tis cold in here despite the fire. 'Tis the stone walls.'

Like the sun breaking from the clouds, he smiled at her. 'I know how to warm you.'

Pleasure rolled over her. Everything was fine. She grinned at him. 'Yes, you do.'

'But first,' he said, reaching into the finely embroidered pocket of his outer jacket, 'I have something for you.'

Jenna smiled, thinking it was a betrothal trinket.

He pulled out a small velvet box and flicked it open. Inside rested a marquise-cut ruby surrounded by diamonds. The ring was breathtaking.

She gasped. ''Tis beautiful.'

He lifted it from the satin-lined case. 'I am glad you like it. It is our family engagement ring.'

'Surely your mother should be wearing it.'

He smiled at her and reached for her hand. 'It goes to the new bride.'

He slipped the ring on to the third finger of her left hand. Love filled her heart to bursting. He bent down and kissed her hand where his ring now settled.

She went into his embrace. His mouth claimed hers. His arms slipped around her waist and pulled her to him.

She molded herself to him, her fingers burrowing into the thick waves of his hair. She revelled in the roughness of his tongue against hers and the satin feel of his hair slipping through her fingers. He was heat and desire to her.

'Ahem…'

Papa. Jenna started and jumped, trying to put distance—even an inch—between her and Duncan. Duncan held her close, allowing her only to shift enough to face Papa. Her side pressed to Duncan's with no space. Her face flamed.

'Papa, I did not hear you.'

Papa looked from her to Duncan and back, a slight lifting at one corner of his mouth. 'That was abundantly obvious.'

'Sir,' Duncan said, making a modified bow, still gripping Jenna to him. He looked down at her and back to Papa. 'We were solidifying our commitment.'

Papa's smile grew. 'I thought as much. Next time you might lock the door first.'

Jenna's mortification grew. It was disconcerting enough to be caught by Papa in her lover's arms. It was more so to have Papa, of all people, tell them how to make love without being discovered.

Duncan gave her a conspiratorial glance. 'Next time we will, sir.' He raised her hand, which he had continued to hold through this, and kissed her palm. 'I must be going, Jenna. I will call tomorrow.'

Her flush intensified until she thought her face must look like a torch. Afraid she would stammer and say the wrong things, so great was her embarrassment, she said nothing. She just smiled like an imbecile or a woman smitten with a man.

Duncan bowed to Papa and left, the door closing quietly behind him. Papa remained where he was, watching her.

'You love him a great deal,' Papa finally said.

She nodded. Words would not describe what she felt for Duncan. She loved him enough to leave Papa.

Papa strode across the room and wrapped his arms around her. 'I want you to be sure, Jenna. You are giving yourself into that man's hands for the rest of your life. That is not something to do lightly.' He paused as though giving her time to consider. 'And you have not known him long.'

She sighed. 'I am sure, Papa.' And, in spite of her doubts about Duncan's feelings toward Papa, she was sure.

'Then I am glad you found someone to love like that.' His deep voice rumbled in her ear. 'I would have given him everything for giving that gift to you.'

'Oh, Papa.' Tears of love and gratitude choked Jenna.

Papa stroked her hair, something he had done when she was very young. 'I hope he cares half as much for you.'

She nodded, her cheek rubbing against one of the buttons on Papa's coat. There was a rough edge on the metal and Jenna felt her skin break. She pulled away and reached to the spot. Her fingertips came away bloody.

'Oh, dear.' She reached through the slit in her skirt to the pocket tied around her waist and pulled out a handkerchief. She wiped the blood away.

Papa touched her cheek lightly. 'I am sorry, Jen. I must remember to tell my valet to replace these buttons or sand this one down.'

'Do not worry, Papa. 'Tis a small scratch. Nothing

more.' She dabbed once more at the cut. 'By tomorrow it will be nothing but a red welt. The day after it will be gone.'

Papa leaned forward and kissed her gently on the forehead. 'You are a brave and optimistic woman. Just like your mother.' He stepped back. 'He is lucky to get you. I hope he realises that,' Papa ended fiercely.

Jenna smiled, even though Papa's intensity made her uneasy. He was normally the most mild of men. For a brief moment, she saw the man who could have ordered the killing of so many. She pushed the picture away firmly. That was the past. This was now, and Duncan was her future.

'Everything will be perfect, Papa. My only worry is leaving you alone.'

His smile belied the brief glimpse of sadness in his eyes. 'I won't lie to you, child. I will miss you greatly, but I am glad you found someone to love. Your happiness means more to me than not having you around.' He stepped away and put his hands to the fire. 'Besides, you will just be down the road. Likely we will see each other every day.'

She knew him well enough to understand that he wanted to put any possible sorrow behind them and focus only on the good of her coming marriage. She could give him that.

'At least once every day, Papa.' She grinned as it dawned on her what to say. 'After all, my stillroom is here. For a while at least, I must come here to concoct my potions.'

He chuckled. 'I see you are still my Jenna.'

'Always.'

* * *

A week later, Jenna found herself in Duncan's home, having tea with her future mother-in-law. 'Thank you,' she said, taking the cup and saucer. She set it on a japanned table nearby in order to accept a plate of cakes.

'I am so glad you came,' Mrs McNabb said. 'Ever since Duncan told me, I have wanted to spend time with you.'

Jenna smiled, thankful Duncan's mother welcomed her. 'I am glad to be here, Mrs McNabb.'

'Please, Jenna—if I may call you that—we will soon be related. My name is Evelyn.' She sipped her tea. 'I was named for my English grandmother.'

Acceptance stole over Jenna. 'I would like very much to call you Evelyn.'

'Good. We have much in common, you and I.' Evelyn McNabb set her tea down. 'We are both Scot and English. More importantly, we are women caught in a man's war.' She sighed.

Discomfort moved over Jenna. She shifted in her previously comfortable chair. But she owed this woman honesty in so far as she was able. 'Are you speaking of the Jacobite rebellion?'

The older woman nodded. 'It has torn families apart and made men do things they have later regretted.' Sadness made her eyes, so like her son's, darken.

Jenna pushed down the discomfort coursing through her. She met Evelyn McNabb's implication openly. 'Are you speaking of my father?'

'And others.' She leaned forward. 'My son as well.'

Jenna stared at her, no longer sure what to think. She said nothing.

'Duncan was emotionally scarred by his father's

death.' Evelyn bit her bottom lip, her normal composure seeming to desert her. 'I hope his marriage to you will heal him once and for all.'

Jenna resisted the urge to take the other woman's hands in hers. Evelyn McNabb was not sick and did not need healing, no matter that she looked as wounded as she claimed her son to be.

Better to continue dealing with her openly. 'I hope so too. You know Papa's background. So does Duncan. He does not like it, but he has asked me to marry him. I hope—I believe—he would not do that unless he is able to accept and forgive Papa. Hopefully that forgiveness will help Duncan heal from the death of his father.'

The older woman winced before regaining what composure she had before. 'Bluntly spoken, but with no wish to hurt. I thank you, Jenna, for that.'

Jenna realised her mention of Duncan's father's death was tactless. Her heart ached for the pain she had inadvertently caused. 'I am sorry for being so blunt. I did not think.' She scowled. 'Not unusual for me, I am afraid.'

'No, do not apologise. 'Tis long past time Duncan and I moved on.' She watched Jenna as though searching for something she did not see. Jenna met her look without subterfuge. After several minutes, Evelyn sighed. 'Let us talk of something different. Do you have a dress for your marriage?'

More than willing to accommodate her, Jenna replied, 'No. I have been through everything in my wardrobe and nothing seems special enough.'

Evelyn laughed, a lovely tinkling sound. 'I am so glad you feel your wedding to be special. I was afraid it was a marriage of convenience at first. It all happened so quickly. But now I see 'tis not.'

Anticipation lent Jenna enthusiasm. 'No, 'tis far from convenient.'

Evelyn sat back in her chair and studied Jenna like an artist might examine the person she was thinking of painting. 'I might have just the thing. 'Tis a length of Spitalfields silk I bought before we arrived here. 'Tis quite fashionable, yet simple and elegant. I think it would look well on you.'

'Really?' Desire to look her best made Jenna eager. 'Are you sure? You bought it for yourself. I would not feel right about taking it.'

Evelyn laughed again. 'My dear, if you want it—and let us reserve judgement until you see it—then it is yours. You have brought a sparkle back to Duncan that has been missing for longer than I can remember. I would give you much more than my length of silk!'

Delight filled Jenna. Not only had she found a love she had never thought possible, but she had gained a mother. Evelyn would never replace her own mama, but she would go far in filling the void left after her mother's death.

'In fact…' Evelyn rose and pulled the bell by the fireplace '…I shall have the silk brought here. You can decide now; if it is right, I shall have my own modiste fashion your wedding gown.' She paused in the act of ringing the bell. 'That is, if you would like that.'

She gave Jenna such a sweet look that Jenna smiled back. 'Please.'

Within minutes the butler had found Evelyn's maid, who now stood before them, the length of silk spilling over her arms. The fine material was like a ray of sunshine on a warm summer's day. Embroidered flowers in shades of cream, crimson and pale pink spread across the silk in the semblance of a garden, and bees cavorted amongst the rich colours.

''Tis beautiful,' Jenna breathed, hardly daring to believe this beautiful length of cloth was to be hers. She turned to Evelyn. 'But surely, seeing it again, you do not want to give it away. 'Tis breathtaking.'

Evelyn waved the maid away. 'Monette, see that the silk is properly packed.' When they were alone again, she leaned forward and rested her fingers on Jenna's arm. 'My dear, that piece of silk is no lovelier than you. 'Tis the perfect colour for your complexion. You will be a beautiful bride.'

Jenna blushed at the praise. 'You are much too generous.'

Evelyn shook her head. 'No, I am not.'

Discomfort at the continued praise had Jenna fingering the ruby-and-diamond engagement ring Duncan had given her only a week before. She never took it off.

'What is that?' Evelyn asked. 'Ah, the family ring.'

Jenna's flush deepened. 'Thank you, Evelyn, for allowing him to give it to me.'

Evelyn smiled. 'Thank you for accepting it.'

The door opened and both women looked away from the ring. Duncan entered, moving with the sensual, predatory grace of a lion.

'Duncan,' his mother said, 'join us. There is some tea left and biscuits.'

He kissed his mother's hand before turning to Jenna. 'I see you are wearing the ring.' Heat flared in his eyes, turning them to amber.

She smiled, suddenly self-conscious. But she answered truthfully, 'I never take it off.'

Satisfaction eased the harsh angles of his face. 'I am glad.'

'Duncan,' his mother interrupted, 'Jenna is going to wear the Spitalfields silk I purchased before we came here. You remember the piece.'

He sank into one of the nearby chairs. 'The one you said was too beautiful to ruin by cutting it into pieces for a ball gown?'

'Oh, no,' Jenna said, looking from him to his mother. 'Now I know you should not give me the silk.'

'Shush, my dear girl.' Evelyn frowned at her son. 'That was for me. 'Tis perfect for Jenna. She will wear it on your wedding day.'

Duncan's heavy lids shadowed the expression in his eyes. He looked at Jenna. 'You will be a beautiful bride.'

'Yes,' his mother continued. 'It will go perfectly with her colouring. It will even complement the family engagement ring.'

Duncan smiled and stood. He bowed to both of them. 'I must be off.'

'But you just arrived,' his mother said, surprise lifting her voice.

He shrugged. 'I have remembered something I need to do before I meet with my secretary.' He took Jenna's hand from where it rested in her lap and raised it to his lips. His eyes stared into hers. 'Until later.'

Sparks of pleasure danced along her skin. Their wedding could not be soon enough for her.

Chapter Fourteen

Nerves held Jenna in their grip.

The beautiful golden cream silk had made up into the most elegant and flattering gown she had ever owned. The cream satin stomacher was embroidered with gold threads that complimented the more vibrant colours of the gown. Material fell from her shoulders in heavy folds, and expensive Brussels lace cascaded from her elbows where the three-quarter sleeves ended.

'You are beautiful,' Lizzie said. 'I have never seen you glow like this.'

Jenna's full-throated laugh broke loose. 'I have never felt beautiful before. Nor have I ever been this happy.'

She pirouetted to the only chair in the room that would accommodate the large hoops of the skirt and sank on to the seat. Her lacing was so tight she could not bend, and Lizzie had to slip the matching shoes on to her feet. Yet, even that inconvenience, which another day would have irritated her, only amused Jenna.

This was her wedding day to the man she loved. A man she also admired. A man who felt the same for her. Nothing could mar this occasion. Nothing.

A knock on the door brought her to her feet. 'Jenna, love, are you ready?' Papa's dear voice came from the other side.

Lizzie let him in and Jenna twirled around in sheer exuberance. 'I am more ready than I have ever been for anything in my life.'

She rushed to him and threw her arms around him. 'Do not worry, dearest Papa. I shall visit you so often you will doubt I have moved out.'

He patted her shoulder. 'I am not worried about seeing you, child. I only hope this marriage is what you truly want, and that you are not blinded by Lord Byrne's attractions. There are not many women who could resist him, I am thinking.'

If Papa only knew the whole of it. Jenna went on tiptoe and kissed his cheek. 'I know the man I am marrying. I would not so happily give myself into his care otherwise.'

'Just so, just so.' He continued to pat her shoulder as though he did not realise he did so.

Jenna stepped away. 'Is the nuncheon ready? And the winter greenery still fresh? And is Reverend Kingston here?'

Papa laughed. 'Everything is as you wished. Nothing will mar your morning.'

Nearly bursting with happiness and excitement and love for both the man who would be giving her away, and the man who would be taking her into his care, Jenna tripped down the hallway beside Papa. Not even the cold emanating from the stone walls could penetrate her cloud of glory.

They were to be married in the castle's small chapel, attended only by family and Mrs Kingston. Afterwards everyone in the neighbouring area was invited to nuncheon. Then she and Duncan would return to his hunting lodge and really celebrate their union.

She and Papa paused at the doorway to the chapel.

Jenna started trembling. She felt Papa take a deep breath. She smiled up at him, surprised to see a sheen of moisture in his brown eyes.

'I love you very much, Jenna. I hope you are happy with Duncan.' He hugged her close for a moment.

'Oh, Papa.'

Then they started forward. She smiled at Duncan's mother who stood in the front alongside Mrs Kingston. The Reverend Kingston beamed. If only Gavin were here, everything would be perfect. But he was safely in France. She could not be so selfish as to begrudge him that.

But she forgot everyone else when she saw her groom. Duncan stood straight and tall, watching her come to him.

For the first time since she had met him as Lord Byrne, he was sombrely dressed. His clothing was all black satin with silver thread embroidered along the hem of the coat and waistcoat. Diamond buckles secured his breeches at the knees and glittered in the light from a multitude of candles.

The scent of fir and pine filled the small space. Jenna knew she would always associate those smells with this moment. Happiness overwhelmed her.

Papa stopped beside Duncan and transferred her hand from his arm to Duncan's. Warmth flowed from that contact and expanded Jenna's thudding chest until she thought her heart would burst. She and Duncan turned to face Reverend Kingston.

The ceremony started.

* * *

What seemed a blink of time later, Jenna once more turned to look at Duncan as he slipped a rose-gold wedding band on her finger. It was a simple piece of jewellery, but to her it was a work of art and a symbol of a lifetime of love and commitment.

From the seriousness of Duncan's expression, she knew he felt the same way. Even when the ring stuck at her first knuckle and he had to push it on, she knew the band would never leave her finger, just as their love would never wane.

'You may kiss the bride—' the Reverend Kingston's voice washed over Jenna '—and seal your vows to one another.'

She looked up at Duncan, expectation parting her lips.

Duncan dipped his head and his lips touched hers. She forgot everything in the need he ignited in her. She went on tiptoe and pressed her mouth to his. His arms went around her and he pulled her close. Jenna went willingly.

'Enough or you will put us all to the blush.' Viscount Ayre's fine baritone finally intruded on the kiss.

Knowing she was rosy with pleasure and desire, she was still reluctant to step away from her husband. Duncan loved her.

Duncan stepped away, breaking their embrace.

Jenna smiled up at him. He was so handsome and so passionate. She loved him with all her being, but, more importantly, she respected him and thought him the bravest of men. Her life could not be more perfect than it was at this moment.

When he held his arm to escort her from the chapel, she laid her fingers lightly on his sleeve instead of throwing herself into his embrace. She told herself she could wait to be held by him. He was hers now, to have and to hold, just as she was his. They had time.

Duncan's mother beamed at them as they stopped for her kiss and hug. 'You are such a beautiful bride, Jenna. I am so pleased to have you in the family.'

Jenna's heart swelled. 'Your welcome means a lot to me.' She returned the embrace.

Beside her Duncan and her father shook hands. 'Welcome to our family, Duncan.' The viscount took Duncan's hand at the same time he clapped him on the back. 'I look forward to getting to know you better.'

Jenna watched her new husband. His smile was fixed and he did not return her father's enthusiasm. A tiny part of her pleasure died. She had hoped that by marrying her Duncan would be able to put aside the viscount's act during the Jacobite uprising. It seemed she had been too optimistic.

Still, surely, at some point Duncan's love for her would enable him to forgive her father. She had to believe that. She pushed the unhappiness from her mind when the Reverend and Mrs Kingston moved to offer their congratulations.

Soon they were all in the draughty ballroom of the castle where trencher tables and benches had been set up. People from all over the countryside, rich and poor, had been invited to celebrate this day. Jenna wanted to share her happiness with the world.

Their guests poured in.

The viscount stood. 'Attention, everyone!' Quiet filled the room. 'I present a toast to the couple! May they have a long and happy marriage blessed with children and prosperity.'

Tears filled Jenna's eyes.

Duncan rose. 'A toast to my bride. A woman of unusual courage and compassion.'

The room blurred, and it was all Jenna could do not to sniffle into her napkin. She would remember this moment for the rest of her life.

Applause and noise broke over the crowd. Bawdy comments combined with sincere wishes. People drank down the ample ale and ate the plentiful food. Jenna was so happy she could not eat and needed no drink to lift her mood higher.

All she wanted was to fill her mind with Duncan's image. If only he smiled instead of scowling into nothingness.

Finally he turned to her and raised one brow. 'I know a patch has not slipped, for I did not put any on.'

She reached a fingertip to the corner of his sensual mouth where he usually wore a small velvet star. Knowing they were on a dais raised above a hundred or more revellers kept her from tracing his lip as she longed to do.

'I never tire of looking at you.'

Warmth lit his eyes. 'Thank you, wife.'

Pleasure warmed her. 'So formal? Am I to call you husband now?' she teased.

He bowed his head. 'That is what I am to you.'

'Husband, lover, friend,' she whispered so only he could hear.

He studied her a moment more. 'Best we mingle.' He waved a hand nonchalantly. 'They are here to meet us and wish us well, after all.'

He was as impatient to be on their way as she was, she told herself, and they could not leave until they had personally thanked as many of their guests as they could. Duncan helped her to her feet and they made their separate ways into the group.

Jenna saw Jane James, her baby at her breast. A sudden longing propelled Jenna to the mother.

The woman saw her and rose to meet her, making a small dip. 'My lady.' Her gaze fell to the ground.

For a second Jenna wondered who Jane spoke to. Then she realised it was she. She had not married Duncan for his title and wealth. She had married a man who also had a title. Until now, she had not stopped to consider herself as Lady Byrne.

'I am still the woman who delivered your child,' she finally said, realising she spoke truly. 'And he looks bonny.'

Jane turned scarlet with pride. 'He is that, indeed, your ladyship. And he grows stronger every day.'

Jenna peered at the full round face and put a finger in the baby's chubby fist. 'Very strong indeed. Soon he will be in the fields with his father.'

Jane's husband laughed, every inch the proud father. 'Too soon for the liking of my wife. She dotes on him.'

Their happiness at the child radiated from them. Envy and longing engulfed Jenna. She had thought only fleetingly of children before, knowing they would be one of the outcomes of her union with Duncan and looking forward to that phase of their life when it arrived. Now, she longed for a small bundle of joy to hold to her heart, a creature she and Duncan had created together and would raise and love together.

'May I hold him?' Her voice was tentative as it never had been before when requesting to cuddle a newborn.

Before it had been a pleasure, but also part of her

calling as a healer to hold a child and examine him for anything amiss. Now this new life seemed so much more.

She took the babe and held him to her chest. He turned to her breast as though seeking milk. She gave him her finger, which he promptly began suckling. His little tugs sent tendrils of emotion all the way to Jenna's core. Everything that made a woman a mother rose in her.

She looked up and searched for Duncan, wanting to share this discovery with him.

As though he felt her gaze on him, he turned from the man he spoke to. Without her spectacles for near-sightedness, she could see him well enough. He met her eyes, then his own flicked down to the child she held. Longing as sharp and painful as a sword thrust passed across his face. Then nothing.

Her emotions were too volatile. She was seeing things where nothing existed. It was because she was so happy and she feared to lose the source of her happiness—Duncan.

Jenna gently pulled her finger from the babe's mouth and handed him to his mother. 'You are blessed, Jane. I am more grateful than I can tell that I was able to help deliver this child.'

'Oh, no, my lady,' the mother babbled. ''Tis I who am for ever in your debt.'

Jenna smiled at the woman, then moved to the next guest even as an ache of emptiness filled her chest where the babe had lain. But soon she and Duncan would have children of their own. Their life together would be rich with love.

Several hours later she and Duncan met up at the great doors that led from the room as though they had planned the rendezvous. Warmth filled her at how well they understood each other.

Everyone still enjoyed the hospitality.

Viscount Ayre and Evelyn joined them. Jenna noticed the older couple exchanged looks more than was normal. Was something happening here?

'Let me help you change into your travelling outfit,' Mrs McNabb said.

Jenna smiled at the woman who was now her mother by marriage and wondered if there would soon be an announcement of another tie to bind them. 'Thank you. Lizzie will be there, but I will be glad of your help.'

As she turned, Jenna could not help but notice that once more Duncan's features were devoid of emotion as her father talked to him. An ache she had not realised she had grew in her. Her stomach twisted, and she told herself it was from not eating in her excitement.

Because her skirts were so wide, she had to follow the older woman up the stairs that had been built several hundred years ago and not remodelled to accommodate the current feminine fashions. 'Twas just as well.

Her room seemed different with her personal belongings packed and ready to go to Duncan's estate. The trunk with her trousseau was already gone. Her travelling outfit, which was a new riding habit, lay on her bed. On the bed that used to be hers.

Soon she would be in Duncan's bed. Shivers of delight coursed down her spine and twisted deep in her abdomen. Embarrassment at her brazen thoughts made her glance at her mother-in-law. Evelyn seemed unaware that Jenna blushed from desire for her son.

'What a lovely shade of green your habit is.' Evelyn

turned to Jenna. 'I am very glad you accepted my son's proposal, Jenna.'

Warmth at the other woman's welcome welled up in Jenna. 'Thank you for making me feel so much a part of your family.'

Evelyn laughed. 'You are family. I would be a poor mother indeed—and a foolish one—if I spurned you. You will be good for Duncan.'

'And he for me.' Jenna glanced around, looking for her maid. 'Oh, dear, Lizzie must still be in the ballroom.'

'Do not worry, my dear. I am not so feeble that I cannot help you out of this dress.' When Jenna was down to her stays and chemise, Evelyn asked, 'Shall I loosen your stays? I am sure they are prodigiously uncomfortable.'

'Yes, please.' Jenna sighed with relief as she took her first deep breath since being laced many hours before. 'My habit has more room.'

Quickly, they dressed her. Jenna settled a little feathered tricorn hat, a feminine version of the man's accessory, at a rakish angle and studied herself critically in the mirror.

'You are lovely, Jenna.' Evelyn's voice was solemn. 'Duncan will be dazzled.'

Jenna stood and turned to look at Duncan's mother. 'I appreciate all your compliments, really I do, but I begin to wonder if there is more behind them.' She meant to keep her tone light, but to her discomfort she sounded worried.

The older woman looked away, then looked back at Jenna. Her normally clear hazel eyes, so like her son's, were dark. 'I still worry about how Duncan will go on with your father.'

'So do I.' It was a relief to tell someone of her worry. 'I know Duncan is still angry about what happened between our fathers.' She lowered her voice. 'I hope to help him deal with how he feels. Particularly as I know it impacts on his relations with Papa.'

Evelyn's face lit. 'Viscount Ayre. He is a good man. A sweet man.' Then her eyes clouded as though with troublesome thoughts. ''Tis hard to believe he… But then, in youth, we do many things we would never do later in life. We learn compassion with age, my dear.'

Jenna's eyes filled. It seemed she was to cry the entire day. An attribute she did not normally lay claim to. It was frustrating.

'Thank you so much for forgiving Papa.' The urge to throw herself into the other woman's arms—an offer that had not been made—and cry about her worry over Duncan and her father nearly overwhelmed Jenna. 'I know he is miserable because of what he did, and that if given the same order today he would disobey.'

'I know he would.' The older woman's voice was soft, but hard with resolution. 'I only hope Duncan comes to realise that.'

'Surely he will,' Jenna said, her optimism and happiness at her wedding and her groom reasserting themselves. 'He must, for Papa is now his papa.'

'I sincerely hope so.' But Evelyn sounded uncertain.

It took all Jenna's hope and enthusiasm to push her new mother-in-law's doubts aside as she descended the stairs one more time and took her new husband's extended arm.

Jenna stepped out into the overcast afternoon, expecting to see Duncan's carriage. 'Why is Rosebud here?' She turned to her new husband. 'And your gelding? I thought we were taking your coach.'

Duncan looked down at her in such a way that she blushed. 'I thought it would be faster this way.'

Her heart skipped. 'Faster?'

'The sooner we get home, the sooner I can introduce you to the servants as their new mistress. And we can…retire.'

Heat suffused Jenna from her head to the tips of her toes. 'Of course.'

Any disappointment she felt at not having the chance to be private in the coach disappeared. Duncan wanted to hurry things so they could be alone as a wedded couple. That was exactly what she wanted.

He moved aside so a groom could boost her on to the side saddle. She glanced at Duncan, wondering why he had not done the job. But he was mounting his horse and turned away from her.

Settling himself, he said, 'Mother is going into Carlisle for several days.'

'Oh.' She had hoped Evelyn would give them some time alone, but she had not known her mother-in-law was going to Carlisle. 'I hope she enjoys herself.'

She arranged her skirts over her legs and flicked the reins to urge Rosebud into a canter. To her disappointment the groom also mounted a horse and settled in behind them. There would be no intimate conversation on this ride.

She glanced at Duncan who winked at her. Her blush intensified. Thankfully, a damp breeze blew her hair and tugged at her hat, cooling her.

After what seemed a long time later to her, they reined in at the entrance to Duncan's hunting lodge. The groom had passed them fifteen minutes before to announce their arrival.

Exhaustion slumped Jenna's shoulders as she saw Duncan's servants lined up in the overcast light waiting to be introduced to her. She knew this was how a new bride was welcomed to her husband's home.

Knowing this was part of her duty, Jenna smiled and held out her hand to the steward. Soon she and Duncan would be alone.

Chapter Fifteen

Hours later, Jenna entered the suite of rooms that was now her private area in her new home. Even though it was winter and the sun was down, her bedchamber and boudoir were filled with light from the roaring fire and many candles. The furniture was covered in straw-coloured silk. The large bed had a canopy and a set of mahogany steps. A settee nestled in the alcove formed by the window.

She crossed to the paned glass and looked out at the knot garden below. Shadows chased across the shrubbery. She looked up at the full moon and sparkling stars. It was a beautiful winter evening.

The sound of the connecting door opening thrust everything else from her thoughts. Duncan was here. She twisted around, her pulse jumping.

He stood in the doorway, his hair dishevelled as though he had run his fingers through it. Strands fell across his brow in golden waves. His white shirt was open at the neck, curling hairs stark against the pale background. He still wore his black breeches and white stockings, but his feet were in slippers.

His gaze met hers and then lowered. She blushed from the collar of her riding jacket to her cheeks.

'Where is your maid?' His voice was harsh and raw.

She licked dry lips. 'Lizzie is still home—at Papa's—packing the rest of my belongings.'

He nodded and stepped into the room, closing the door behind him. 'Then I will play maid.'

She watched him approach.

Her breath caught as he stopped inches from her. Musk and patchouli scented the air. A dusting of beard darkened his jaw.

His head lowered. His mouth took hers. His arms pulled her tight and his fingers pressed into the small of her back, holding her flush to him.

Desire moved through her like a flash flood. Her tongue danced with his. Her fingers kneaded the muscles through his shirt, her nails digging into him.

Need, sharp and insistent, spiralled from her abdomen.

His palms ranged up and down the ridges of her back, stroking her and making her arch against him. Her breasts rubbed his chest and her nipples hardened into aching nubs of pleasure.

He nipped her lips gently before nibbling down the side of her jaw until his hot breath tickled her earlobe. He bit lightly. She jumped, only to subside into his strength, her head leaning back to give him better access.

He ran his tongue down her throat while one hand undid the top button of her jacket. Then another.

His fingers found her bosom. The rough skin of his thumb caught on the delicate linen of her blouse as he massaged her swollen breast.

His mouth followed.

Warm and moist, his lips closed over her nipple and he pulled. She moaned as sensation knifed to her core.

He sucked again and she pushed into him, wanting more. Her head spun as her body responded to him.

'Ah, Jenna…Jenna,' he murmured against her. 'You don't know how I have longed to do this.'

She held his head to her bosom, tears of happiness forming in her eyes. 'Or how I have wanted you to do this.' Her voice was breathy.

He lifted his head and smiled at her, promising her everything. With steady fingers, he undid the buttons of her blouse, then slid the jacket and blouse off together. She stood before him in her stays, chemise and skirt and petticoats.

He skimmed his hands down her sides and hips and lower. Deftly he undid the fastening of her skirt and pushed it down. Then her petticoats. The heavy materials mounded on the floor.

Her chemise did not reach her knees. Her black stockings, secured by black garters, rose above her riding boots. His smile turned wicked as he looked her over.

'You are perfect,' he murmured. 'Sit in the chair and let me pull your boots off.'

Trembling and alternately hot, then cold, Jenna did as he directed. She lifted her right leg and he took the boot in his hands and pulled. Then her left.

He went to his knees and stroked up her legs, smoothing her stockings where they had bunched. She licked dry lips, marvelling at how sensual his attention made her feel.

The fire was to their left and the flames cast half of his face in shadow. He was the devil incarnate, tempting beyond her ability to resist.

Gently, and slowly, he spread her legs. Embarrassment made Jenna tighten her thighs in an effort to keep him from opening them.

'Jenna,' he said softly, his voice thick and heavy, 'open for me.'

She shook her head. 'I cannot. Please, Duncan…'

He slid his palms along her flanks, up and down, slowly and erotically. 'Yes, you can. I won't hurt you.' His full lips parted and his teeth showed. 'I promise.'

His hands shifted from her outer thighs to the inner. She allowed him to open her. His gaze lowered and his smile turned slumberous. He inched forward until he was between her legs, then squatted down.

She could not watch him.

His fingers trailed along her flesh, advancing and re-treating. His breath was hot on her exposed softness.

She gasped when he touched her.

He explored her like a master musician would a new instrument. Then he slipped inside.

She shuddered and her hands fisted. She gasped as he stroked her. At his urging she spread her thighs wider. Then his tongue touched her and she slid down the chair. Heat suffused her.

She heard him chuckle and felt his breath waft over her. She had never felt anything like this. She had never thought anything like this existed.

Embarrassment made her shut her eyes, but pleasure kept her from telling him to stop. Sensation washed over her as he sucked and licked.

He played her like a master.

Her gasps turned to whimpers. She dug her nails into the chair. Something was just beyond her reach.

He stopped.

Her chest fell.

She opened her eyes to see him towering above her. In one swift, liquid move, he picked her up. She clutched his shoulders.

He laid her on the bed and stared down at her. His gaze moved from her face to her bosom and lower. 'I am going to make love to you all night, Jenna.'

She gazed up at him and smiled. 'If 'tis like what you have been doing, then I am eager for you.' The bold words were out before she considered them.

He smiled, a gleam in his eyes that kindled her desire. He ran his palms over her chemise-covered breasts, pushing the thin muslin down and easing her bosom over the stays. He bent and took one nipple in his mouth. His hand fondled the other.

Just as she arched to push her breast deeper, his hand left and skimmed her stomach. He caught the hem of her chemise and rucked it up.

Passion, hot and naked, stared at her from his face. She reached for him.

He caught her hands and held them, kissing each one. 'I have too many clothes on,' he muttered, his voice like thick brandy.

She nodded as he set her hands on her stomach.

With quick, efficient movement, he stripped off his shirt and breeches and smallclothes. He did not stop until he was naked.

Jenna took a deep breath, awed by his masculine magnificence. Broad shoulders, well muscled, tapered into lean hips and strong thighs. His calves were everything they should be. And his loins.

She looked her fill. She had seen many men during

her healing, but none had been prepared to make love to her. He was huge. She gulped.

He joined her on the bed, lying lengthwise beside her. She turned into his kiss.

His tongue teased her mouth open and she sighed. She felt his fingers on her back just before her stays eased. He pulled them from between their bodies. Then he eased her chemise over her head. He left her stockings on.

He looked at her. 'You are the most erotic woman. Some day I will have you painted like this and I will hang the portrait above my bed.' He smiled slow and sensual. 'I will gaze at it just before coming in and making love to you all night. It will prepare me.'

She stared at him, mesmerised by what he said. 'How…strange.'

He chuckled, his chest vibrating against hers. Her breasts jiggled and her nipples hardened. He kissed her again.

She wound her arms around his neck and surrendered to sensation. He stroked her, nuzzled her, nipped her and licked her—everywhere. His fingers explored every inch of her. When he slipped them inside her, she moaned.

'Duncan…' Need laid heavy on her.

'Soon,' he murmured, shifting her. 'Soon.' He rose above her and looked down at her. His thighs inched hers open.

She stared at him, knowing what was to come.

'Wrap your legs around me,' he said, the words barely audible. 'Tight.'

She did and he slid into her.

She gasped at the quick pain of his penetration and her body tensed. The sting was gone as quickly as it had come. Still, she did not move, not knowing what to expect.

He groaned and held still. 'Ah, Jenna. I have dreamt of this every night.'

Nearly delirious with desire, she wrapped herself around him, trying for more. With a chuckle he moved so that her pleasure mounted until all she could do was to hold him and urge him to go faster.

She exploded, her moans joining with his gasping breaths.

He stiffened. 'Ah, Jenna…'

Exhausted, she clung to him. He lifted his mouth from hers and gazed down at her, the only light from the moonshine spilling in through the windows.

He tenderly kissed her lips and then her nose. She forgot everything else and smiled at him, wishing they could stay like this for ever.

Jenna roused, cold penetrating the covers. The room was dark, the fire out.

She remembered everything.

She reached for Duncan, but he was gone. She sat up and searched the room. He stood by the window, looking out.

Warmth and love filled her. She stood and wrapped a cover around her nakedness, then went to him and wrapped an arm around his waist. He put an arm around her shoulders. She leaned into his strength.

'What are you doing?' she asked.

He continued to stare outside. 'Thinking.'

There was a tenseness to his body and a darkness to his voice that made her nervous. 'What about?'

'Us.'

Her mouth suddenly dry, she could not speak.

'We might have conceived a child tonight.' He spoke quietly, but there was a fierceness that made his words as clear as though he had shouted them.

She had not thought of that. His lovemaking had been so thorough and so intense that she had thought of nothing but what he did to her body. 'Yes, would that not be wonderful?'

For long minutes he said nothing. Her stomach tightened in apprehension. He should have agreed with her.

'I don't know,' he finally said. 'It would be Bloody Ayre's grandchild.'

Chapter Sixteen

Weeks later, Jenna sat in her favourite chair with a screen between her and the heat of the roaring fire. She always took comfort in being warm here. Duncan's hunting lodge was never freezing as de Warre Castle so often was.

Across from her sat Duncan's mother and her father. The viscount had come to call and then he and Duncan's mama had asked to speak with her and Duncan privately. Looking at them, she began to think her father had not come to visit her.

Evelyn had a glow about her that had not been there earlier in the day. Her father had a look of happiness and contentment that Jenna could not remember ever seeing.

But where was Duncan?

When she had sent the message to him about the meeting, he had been in the library, settling estate accounts. Or that was the story. She knew he had been looking over the maps. He had said another Jacobite fugitive was heading this way.

The butler entered with tea and cakes.

Duncan still did not arrive.

Jenna served the refreshments and handed Evelyn hers. 'Duncan should be here soon. He was in the library, finishing up the accounts.'

Evelyn's happiness dimmed. 'He will be here when he is finished.'

Viscount Ayre took his tea. 'I probably should have spoken to him privately.' He gave Duncan's mother an adoring look. 'But we thought it better to speak to both of you at the same time.'

Jenna's suspicions firmed. She glanced from one to the other. Each was slightly turned to the other. She smiled even as growing worry made her stomach knot. Her husband would not like this.

The door opened and Duncan strode into the room. 'Mama.' He made his parent a curt bow, his gaze going from her to the viscount. 'Lord Ayre.' He frowned as he sat in the chair beside Jenna's.

'Duncan,' his mother began, 'we have some happy news for you.'

Her father managed to tear his gaze from Duncan's mother to look at Jenna. 'My dear, I hope you won't mind.'

Jenna smiled, happiness for them overcoming her own apprehension at what Duncan would say. 'If 'tis what you want, Papa.'

'We don't even know what they want to discuss.' Duncan's cold tones cut across everyone else's voices. 'Let them speak.'

Jenna bristled at his order. Their marriage was a happy one and he had no right to deny their parents the same. She turned to him. 'Are you blind?'

His frown intensified. 'Unfortunately, no.' His attention returned to his mother. 'Go on.'

Evelyn's pleasure dimmed more. 'I know this will be hard on you, Duncan. That is why we wanted to tell you and Jenna together. Hoping your own happiness would help you understand.' She turned to Viscount Ayre.

'Yes,' he said, answering Evelyn's unspoken plea, 'we plan to get married. A simple affair, since 'tis not the first for either of us.' He kept his gaze on Duncan. 'We know this will be hard for you, but, as Evelyn said, we also hope that your own union will ease your dislike of ours.'

A muscle in Duncan's jaw twitched. His eyes narrowed. Jenna knew it took supreme self-control for him not to jump up and stalk the room. She was surprised he did not immediately lambast them.

He studied first one, then the other, settling on his parent. 'How can you do this?'

His mother met his condemnation with her chin high in spite of the sadness in her eyes. 'Because we love each other, Duncan. Surely you understand.' She gave Jenna a fond look. 'You married Jenna for love, even though she is Julian's daughter.'

Duncan's sharp intake of breath told her that his mother's words had struck home.

'That is different.' Duncan's voice was flat. 'She did not order the murdering.' Jenna flinched and looked up in time to see Duncan stare at her father. 'He did.'

Jenna released her breath with a sigh and folded down in her chair, then angled so her husband could not see her face. No matter that she tried hard to keep her expression blank, she doubted that she was totally successful.

'Yes, Duncan, I did.' Her father's voice was low and firm, but anguish ran through it like a dark stain. 'And I can never forgive myself for that. My only excuse is that I was young and eager for advancement. And I believed in the Hanoverian king. I thought—and still do—that he is better for us than the Young Pretender.' He took a deep breath, his eyes glittering as though he held back tears. 'That is small enough excuse, I know. I can never undo the horror I caused, even if I flay myself for the rest of my life.'

Evelyn rested her hand on the viscount's, whose fingers curled around hers as though she were his lifeline. 'Julian has suffered enough. I have suffered enough.' She looked at her son. 'We make each other happy. For the first time in over twenty years we have found peace and pleasure. You may not like that we have found it with one another. At first neither of us did either. But that is how it has happened. We would be fools to turn our backs on it.'

'Then be fools, dammit!'

Jenna jerked at Duncan's harsh, anger-wrenched words. But she said nothing.

'We tried.' Her father sounded tired now. Fighting Duncan's fury was taking its toll.

'Yes, we did,' Evelyn said softly, still holding the viscount's hand. 'But misery is not a state either of us likes. Please, Duncan, try to understand. Try to forgive. Please, for everyone's sake, let your hatred go.'

Jenna's breath caught at the heartfelt plea.

Duncan spoke through clenched teeth. 'I cannot stop you from this folly—no, this betrayal. But I don't have to condone it or accept it.'

He stood abruptly, his chair toppling backwards. Jenna jumped up, desperately wanting to do something to stop this horror, but knowing there was nothing she could do. Just as there was nothing she could do but watch him stalk from the room, the door slamming behind him in the force of his fury.

She sank back into her chair. It was all she could do not to cry at the disappointment and hurt on her father's and Evelyn's faces. 'I am so sorry.'

Duncan's mother sat stiffly, her lips trembling. 'I knew this would be hard on him, but I had hoped…'

'With your marriage.' Her father's voice was firm, but his eyes held hurt.

Jenna nodded, trying to keep the sob from her voice. 'I know. I know. I am—' She stopped herself. She had said it before. Her sorrow meant nothing and changed nothing. 'I was afraid this would happen.'

Evelyn searched Jenna's face. 'But he loves you. He wanted to marry you. I saw him court you. Surely I wasn't mistaken. He's my son.' She drew to a halting stop. 'I would swear he loves you.'

Viscount Ayre stood. 'It seems we overestimated the healing his love for you would bring.'

There was nothing Jenna could say.

Evelyn rose, her fingers clasped around the viscount's. Her features firmed. 'We will still marry. I am more sorry than I can say that Duncan cannot—will not—give up his anger. He was young when it happened and we were away. I had hoped that would also help.' She sighed. 'I was wrong.'

Jenna got to her feet. 'I wish there was something I could do.' She spread her hands briefly before bringing them back to her sides.

Her father shook his head and moved to her. He kissed her on the forehead. 'I know, my dear. But you cannot. Only Duncan can heal himself.'

She nodded. 'I know.' She whispered the words, knowing how true they were.

Evelyn rose to see the viscount out. She lightly

touched Jenna's cheek. 'I am more glad than I can say to have you for my daughter, Jenna. You make my son happy. As your father does me, and I hope I do him. We must hope that in time Duncan will understand, accept and forgive.' She straightened. 'But we are not waiting for his blessing. We have been sad too long.' She glanced at her fiancé. 'And we are no longer young. We want to find happiness in our later years.'

Viscount Ayre's arm slipped around Evelyn's waist and a smile of such contentment moved over his face that Jenna thought she would cry from the joy she felt for them. They deserved this second chance.

'You have my blessing.'

Long after her father left, Jenna sat in her bedchamber, the door to Duncan's room locked, as was the entrance from the hall. She needed to be alone. Tears tracked down her cheeks.

She took a hiccupping breath and wrapped her arms around her middle. How could she tell him about her condition? There would never be a good time to let him know he had a child coming. Their child. Bloody Ayre's grandchild.

It was as he had feared on their wedding night. He would not welcome any grandchild of Bloody Ayre— even one of his making.

Jenna roused to banging.

She shivered and realised the fire was long gone out. Her neck hurt from curling into a ball on the chair. Her back hurt from the slouched position. Her eyes felt gritty.

The banging continued. She roused herself enough to realise the noise came from the door to Duncan's suite.

For long minutes she thought about ignoring him. Then outrage flared inside her. How dare he treat their parents as he had and try to destroy their chance for happiness? No matter how great his personal pain over his father's death, their parents deserved better than what Duncan had delivered.

She surged to her feet and stormed to the connecting door. She unlocked it and flung it open.

He stood framed in the entrance. His golden eyes were framed in dark circles. His tawny hair was coming out of the queue as though he had been running his fingers through it.

The white lawn shirt he had worn earlier was unbuttoned at the neck and tawny hairs curled around the edges of the fine muslin. His black satin dressing gown, embroidered on each side with a golden lion stretched to pounce, looked rumpled, as though he'd slept in it. But he still wore his breeches and white silk stockings. His feet were in slippers.

It was as though he had planned to retire and then decided to come to her instead. A *frisson* of anticipation skimmed up her spine.

The scent of musk, patchouli and liquor came from him. 'Don't lock your door to me.'

Her eyes widened in surprise. That was the last thing she expected him to say. For precious seconds, it disrupted her chain of thought and blunted her anger. Then emotions swamped her.

'How dare you presume to order me!' She stomped her foot. 'I will do as I wish. You are the one who has gone beyond the bounds of acceptability.'

He strode into her room. 'This is my house. I can—and will—do what I want.'

She stood her ground. 'This is my house too, and you were awful to our parents.'

His eyes took on a hooded darkness. 'You will not lock your door to me again.'

Those words again. 'Then the next time our parents tell us they intend to marry, do not act like an unfeeling monster.'

He edged forward as a predator following its prey might do. 'I felt plenty. That is why I was so angry.'

Jenna shook her head in exasperation. 'Then next time, try to understand how they feel. Do not take your anger out on them. If they love each other, then so be it.'

'I will do exactly as I please.' He reached for her.

The first touch was fuelled with his hurt and fury over what their parents intended to do. The second torched them both.

Jenna struggled to consciousness, a nagging sense of unease clouding her mind. Her eyelids felt leaden, and her entire body felt as though it might sink into nothingness.

The last thing she remembered was making love with Duncan. She realised that, even though he made love to her, he was torn in two.

Duncan had married her. He made love to her. He cared for her.

He had never told her he loved her.

After what happened yesterday with their parents, she began to wonder if he did. He desired her. Her sore and satiated body told her that.

She had nearly told him about their baby. But something had warned her not to.

At some point, her body would tell him. She wished it did not have to be that way.

Chapter Seventeen

The next day, longing for distraction, Jenna sat down to nuncheon, wondering where she should relocate her stillroom to. Duncan's estate had many empty rooms, but not many with direct access to the outside like her old room at de Warre Castle.

The breakfast room door opened and she looked up, hoping it was Duncan. It was Captain Lord Seller.

Ever the gracious hostess, or trying to be, Jenna smiled at him. 'I did not know you were expected. I am sorry Duncan is out.' She waved her hand in the direction of another chair. 'Please join me.'

Captain Seller bowed. 'I am not expected. I was in the area and thought I would call on my old friend.' He returned her smile. 'I told the butler not to announce me. I hope that was all right.'

Her smile began to feel forced. ''Twould have been nice to know you were here before you came through the doors, but never mind.' Unease made Jenna's already temperamental stomach churn. She rubbed it under cover of the table cloth and her napkin. 'I do not know when he will return.'

'Ah.' Seller took the seat she had indicated.

'I hope 'tis not important.' She forced herself to take a bite of the poached egg in front of her.

Seller reached for the platter of ham since there was no footman to serve him. Jenna had ordered the dishes set informally.

'Nothing that cannot wait.' He helped himself to several pieces. 'He is supposed to have very good maps of the beach area. I want to look at them.'

Her arm stopped in the act of spooning another portion of egg. Belatedly, she brought the food to her mouth. 'Oh.'

His expression turned bland. 'And what of yourself, Lady Byrne? Are you still helping the sick at all hours of the day and night?'

She met his non-committal look with one of her own. 'I do what needs to be done, Captain. If that means I am about at strange hours, then so be it.'

The butler entered and made his way to her. 'My lady, there is a man here who wishes to speak to you.' He glanced at the Captain and back to her. 'He says it is urgent.'

Not wanting to receive anyone where Seller would be privy to the conversation, Jenna set her napkin aside and rose. 'Please show him into the salon.'

'Yes, my lady.' The butler left.

'Ah,' Seller said, 'you have still another assignation. If one did not know you are the local healer, one would think something else was afoot.'

Jenna stopped and turned back to him. 'And just what would one think, Captain?'

He met her glare without flinching. 'That you have convenient excuses to be about the countryside at all hours.'

Her jaw clenched at his implication even as tension crept into her shoulders. 'How interesting,' she said, willing her voice to stay cool. He knew nothing, no matter what he might insinuate.

She pivoted and left the room, focused on moving slowly and casually. She was not about to rush away as though he had upset her and thus give him fuel for his conjectures.

Entering the salon, she saw her caller was Jacob Smith. He was a big, burly man who was the local blacksmith. His wife, Anna, was expecting, but not this soon.

He barrelled toward her. 'Mistress…my lady, Anna is at her time.'

She frowned. 'Are you sure? I thought she had a month or more.'

Worry creased his brow, and his fingers folded and pulled his hat. 'Yes, my lady. She sent me.'

Worry for the woman replaced the unease Seller had created. Anna Smith had already birthed two stillborns. This did not bode well. 'Give me a few minutes, Jacob, to collect my things.'

He nodded. 'I will be outside.'

She did not reply, but hurried from the room.

Six hours later, Jenna rocked back on her heels and forced her fear for Anna Smith to the background. Better to show a serene face if she could not smile.

Anna lay in a large bed set in an alcove that backed to the wall that separated the living quarters from her husband's workshop. Sweat beaded the woman's forehead and upper lip. Her face was as pale as the sheets.

Jacob held his wife's hand, his thumb rubbing back

and forth, back and forth. His gaze moved from Anna to Jenna.

Jenna rolled her shoulders. 'I am going to use oil and rub Anna's belly to ease some of her pain. Do you want to stay?' Most husbands left when the birth was near or when it got too difficult emotionally.

Jacob met her look stoically. 'I will stay.'

Anna gasped and her body buckled as another spasm rocked her. Her fingers turned white, she had clutched her husband's hand so tightly. Jenna looked away to give them a moment of privacy.

She stood and went to her bag where she drew out a vial of clove, sage, rose and sweet almond oil. Behind her, the couple murmured to each other. Her heart ached for them. They wanted children so badly. At this point, she feared another stillbirth, or, worse, something happening to Anna.

Tucking a strand of hair behind her ear, Jenna returned. Jacob gave her a scared look, but he said nothing. She made herself smile at him as she laid the vial down before folding the sheet to expose Anna's distended belly. She removed the hot compress that she had soaked in a pot of marigold to help ease Anna's pains. Ripples moved across the taut skin as the babe struggled for birth.

Jenna poured oil on to her palms and settled herself on her knees, as Jacob shifted to give her room. With strong fingers and sure strokes, she started massaging.

Jenna got into a rhythm while Jacob dabbed his wife's forehead. The heat from the fire made the room hot and stuffy. The only sounds were Anna's groans and Jacob's nearly inaudible mumbles of assurance.

A sharp, loud rap on the outside door made Jenna

start. She cast a questioning look at Jacob. He shook his head. Before he could speak, the door banged open.

'Jenna!' Duncan's rich baritone was raised in fury.

She craned her neck to see behind. He stood, feet planted shoulder width apart, his greatcoat unbuttoned. His riding crop flicked against his right thigh as his gloved hand moved back and forth.

'Close the door, Duncan,' she said calmly and firmly. The last thing she needed was him upsetting this couple with his anger. 'You are letting the warmth out.'

To her surprise, he did as she ordered. She turned back to her patient. Another spasm ripped across Anna's belly and the woman whimpered.

'The babe is breach,' Jenna said softly, not wanting to increase the couple's anxiety, but unwilling to let them remain ignorant.

Jacob looked up from his wife's agonised face. His brown eyes were desolate. 'Can you turn him?'

Jenna shrugged, her tight shoulders protesting the movement and it was all she could do to keep from wincing. 'I can try, Jacob. This is what happened before.'

He nodded. 'I know.'

Anna's blue eyes were glazed over with exhaustion and pain, and Jenna hoped she had not understood what was being discussed.

'Here,' Duncan said, handing Jenna a clean cloth, a bar of lye soap and setting down a bucket of hot water.

She angled to him. 'Thank you.' She washed and dried her hands thoroughly. 'How did you know?'

He gave her a tight smile. 'The battlefield.'

Of course. Like he had known how to care for Gavin.

She focused on what she was doing. Gently and firmly she manipulated the unborn child. When Anna gasped or whimpered, Jenna gritted her teeth and continued. She had to turn the baby or she stood a good chance of losing both. Before, she had always managed to turn the unborn child, only to have the babe born with the umbilical cord wound around its neck. She took a deep breath, pushed that thought away and continued.

She sensed Duncan beside her and wondered why he stayed. Most men wanted nothing to do with this aspect of life. She had always considered Jacob the exception. But she was too tired to try to make conversation with her husband.

'Ah!' She smiled at Jacob, who looked at her with his face creased in worry. 'The babe is turned. Now…'

'Thank you, my lady,' Jacob said, knowing how hard she had worked to reach this point.

'You are very skilled,' Duncan murmured. 'I knew you must be good, but I had not realised how much.'

In spite of her focus on what she was doing, Jenna found herself flushing with pleasure.

'She is a miracle worker,' Jacob avowed.

Jenna felt the babe's head crown. 'Push, Anna. Push. He is almost here.'

The mother grunted, her breath coming in short, rapid puffs.

'That's my girl,' Jacob crooned, smoothing back his wife's sweat soaked hair. ''Twill soon be over.'

The baby slid out and Jenna caught him. Duncan slipped a warm, clean cloth to her. In the light from the fire and candles, Jenna caught her lower lip. The umbilical cord was wrapped around the child's neck—just as the other two. Her heart tripped.

With skill and fear, she freed the babe. His lips were blue and his eyes closed.

'No!' Determination and fear filled her equally. She stuck her fingers in his mouth and swabbed out the mucus, then she put her lips over his and forced air into his lungs. She barely noticed that Duncan had taken the child from her arms and held him firmly so she could concentrate solely on giving life to the mite. She blew another lungful into the babe. And another. Nothing happened.

Despair moved slowly over her.

'Jenna.' Duncan's soft voice finally penetrated her concentration.

She ignored him, vowing to herself that this child would survive. She could not stand to lose another babe. Anna and Jacob deserved more. She deserved more.

She tried again, moisture filling her eyes.

'Jenna,' Duncan said. 'Jenna, his chest... He's breathing.'

She lifted her face from the child's. The boy's eyes popped open and he coughed. Then he cried. Tears slipped down her cheeks.

In a blur, she saw Duncan turn the babe over and gently pat his back. Then her husband cleaned the child of blood and birthing fluids before wrapping him securely and placing him on his mother's chest.

Jenna blinked to clear her vision. She watched her husband as he pulled away from the small family. His hazel eyes gleamed as though water filled them, and there was a tender curve to his finely molded lips that she had never seen before. She would have never thought him sentimental, but he made no effort to disguise how the situation moved him.

As though sensing her attention on him, he turned to her. Something ignited in the depth of his eyes. She was afraid her love for him and her emotional exhaustion now made her see an emotion in his face that was not there.

She rose and said to Jacob, 'Do not forget to give her nettle tea. She will need it to strengthen her for nursing.'

Jacob glanced at her, his face glowing. 'Yes, m'lady.'

She smiled at him.

Duncan's hand gripped her elbow before she realised he had come close, and he propelled her outside the cottage. It was a shock to her to see it was full night. No moon rode the heavens, but stars were pinpricks of light.

'You left no message.' His tone was harsh, at complete odds with the gentleness that had flowed from him just minutes before.

Exhaustion engulfed her. 'I did not think I needed to. It was nuncheon when I left.' She knuckled her low back. 'I did not expect to be this late.'

He glared at her, his fingers tightening. 'I know when you left, Jenna. Seller was happy to tell me.'

'He is a troublemaker.'

'He is suspicious.'

She rolled her shoulders. 'Of me?'

'Of everyone.' A satisfied smile curved his lips. 'But it will be some time before he harasses me about you.'

She paused her motion. 'What do you mean?'

'I showed him what happens when he threatens mine.'

Her eyebrows lifted. 'Yours?'

'Yes.' His tone brooked no argument. ''Tis time we were home.'

He manoeuvred her to Rosebud who stood patiently where she had been left hours before. Jenna had not brought a groom, too anxious to wait for one to get ready. She patted Rosebud's neck and crooned to her.

'She deserves a treat when we get home,' Duncan said, putting his hands on Jenna's waist.

Jenna turned startled eyes on him. 'What are you doing?'

'Lifting you into the saddle.'

'Thank you.'

She did not protest. The only thing keeping her going was her joy in delivering the baby safely and the mother surviving. If not for that, she would collapse.

She allowed him to lead the way home, grateful not to have to think about anything. All she wanted was hot tea and bed.

Jenna sat sprawled in a well-cushioned chair pulled close to the fire in her bedchamber. Her stays were off, and she wore a loose blouse and skirt with a shawl over her shoulders. Hot tea and crumpets sat on a tray beside her.

Her stomach growled, and she realised how hungry she was. She had gone all day without anything to eat. She had forgotten in the strain of delivering the baby.

A knock came from the door connecting her room to Duncan's. She paused in the act of picking up her tea cup. She needed him now.

'Come in.' She did nothing to hide her exhaustion.

He entered swiftly.

Her breath caught. He wore an exotic Banyan with palms and tropical birds embroidered in vibrant primary colours. Underneath the coat, his black breeches hugged the muscles of his calves. His shirt was open at the neck with curling amber hairs swirling around his exposed chest.

He advanced to her. 'You are exhausted, love.'

She smiled at him, but knew it was a weak effort. 'Yes. 'Twas difficult. I nearly lost them both.'

He moved around to her back. His strong fingers found her shoulders and dug into her tight muscles. She let her head fall forward to give him better access.

'You were magnificent.' He rubbed and kneaded, easing her stress.

As she relaxed, different pleasures developed from his touch. His warm flesh heated her skin through her blouse, and she found herself wanting something different from him.

'How did you know I needed this?' she mumbled into her chest.

He chuckled and dug deeper now that she was more relaxed. 'I saw you flinch when you shrugged your shoulders back at the cottage.'

'You did?' Surprise coloured her words.

His thumbs found the tight spot at the base of her neck. 'I am not unobservant.'

'No,' she agreed, hoping he would never stop. 'You could not be successful at what you do if you were.'

'And I wanted to help you.'

His hands fell away completely and the next minute he knelt before her. She stared at him, sensing this was important.

He studied her. 'I watched you when you thought you would lose the babe and mother. I think, at that time, you would have given your life to save theirs.' Sadness darkened his eyes before admiration lit them. 'That is a rare quality. Not many have it.'

Embarrassment added to the heat his massage had already created in her. 'I am not so noble.'

He shook his head. 'Don't deny what is so much a part

of you, Jenna.' He caught her hands. 'That is only one of the many things I admire about you. I knew I had married a healer and a woman with courage. I've since learned my wife is a tigress who I cannot stop thinking about.'

His praise made her uncomfortable. To her horror, she giggled. 'I am not used to someone saying such nice things about me.'

He kissed her fingers one at a time. 'Then people have been remiss.'

Desire curled up her arms and into her abdomen. He always made her feel this way. 'There is very little opportunity for people to discuss this. And why are you doing it?'

He lifted his head to stared into her eyes. His grip on her hands increased. 'Because I want you to know how I feel about you. Seeing you working so hard to save that baby and then cradling it to your chest…'

His head fell back and he stared at the ceiling. His chest rose and fell. 'You know this is not easy.'

'I know nothing of the kind, Duncan. I don't know what you want to say.' But she sensed that for him it was monumental.

His Adam's apple moved as though he swallowed something large and difficult. 'I want you to have my baby.'

The air left her in a whoosh. Something sweet and precious unfurled in her heart. 'But I thought you did not want Bloody Ayre's grandchild. That is why we have taken precautions since the first time.'

He nodded. 'You are right. But I have changed my mind. Seeing you tonight… 'Tis hard to explain. I have learned much from you and about you.' His mouth twisted. 'Women are stronger than men. As you and my mother have both shown.'

She sighed. 'Are you sure?'

He fell to one knee in front of her. 'Yes, love, I am sure. Please forgive me, Jenna, for denying us the opportunity to have everything life offers. What I did to us was wrong. My anger has been my constant companion. It was all I focused on ever since I realised it was what I felt.'

She looked down at him and marvelled that, even dishevelled as he was, he still made her pulse race. She freed one hand and smoothed the hair from his forehead.

He grabbed that hand and kissed her palm and then her wrist. Sensation chased up her arm. The urge to go to her knees in front of him nearly overwhelmed her.

'I love you,' he said so quietly she almost did not hear it. 'I want you to have our child.'

Still, uncertainty made her hesitate. This seemed such an abrupt change. And she was already pregnant with their child. 'Are you sure?'

'I love you so much, Jenna, that I am ready to go to your father tomorrow and tell him we will host his wedding to my mother.' He paused and took a deep breath. 'I love you so much that I want to have children with you—no matter who the grandfather is.' He stood up and pulled her with him. 'I promise to spend the rest of my life proving that to you.'

She went into his arms.

Jenna stretched, wondering why she felt so good. Then remembered. Her eyes popped open.

She was in Duncan's bed.

Raised on one elbow, he watched her. A lazy smile lit his eyes. 'Sleepyhead.'

She smiled at him, remembering there was something she had not told him. Their lovemaking the night before had been so intense and so prolonged that she had finally fallen into a deep sleep.

'Duncan…' She could not keep the tremble from her voice.

His brows knit. 'What is wrong, Jenna love?'

She smiled. 'Nothing is wrong, but—but there is something I have not told you.'

He drew back. 'What?'

Her stomach roiled. 'I need the chamber pot.'

His eyes widened in surprise, but he threw back the covers and rushed for the pot without question. He got it to her just in time.

Mortification turned Jenna scarlet from her hair to her stomach. She pushed strands of hair behind her ear and met his gaze over the rim of the full chamber pot.

'You are pregnant.' His quiet words filled the room.

She nodded.

He carefully set the container on the floor and pushed it under the bed. Then he jumped up and shouted, 'I am to be a father.' He reached for her and pulled her off the mattress and into his arms and swung her around.

Jenna braced her hands on his shoulders and laughed for joy. Everything would be fine.

Gasping for breath, she finally said, 'Enough, Duncan, or I cannot be responsible for what I do.'

He grinned at her seconds before catching her mouth with his. The kiss deepened until they tumbled on to the bed.

Her entire body flushed as his free hand stroked her belly and moved down. 'Duncan.'

His smile turned wicked. 'Jenna.'

'Are you not satiated?'

His eyes took on a golden glow. 'Never.'

'Never?'

'You are going to be the mother of my child. You are everything I want.' He stilled. 'And you are giving me a family.' He leant forward to gently kiss her. 'I love you, Jenna. I will never have enough of my body buried in yours. Never.'

She flushed until heat radiated from her. But she released his wrist and wrapped her arms around his neck. With a sigh of pleasure and joy, she welcomed him inside.

A long time later, Duncan slipped from the bed and stood naked, then stretched. Through passion-lowered lashes, Jenna enjoyed his maleness. His back was to her so she allowed her gaze to travel over the firm, sculpted muscles that defined his shoulders and rose from his spine. With a shiver of delight, she lingered on the rounded strength of his buttocks before lowering to his well-shaped thighs and calves. He was heart-stopping and breathtaking.

On bare feet, he padded across the thick carpet to the walnut wardrobe against one wall. He opened the door and fiddled with one of the drawers, leaning forwards to reach inside.

The curve of his rear and the strong muscles of his thighs and calves bulged as he twisted. She remembered how they felt when he had made love to her, hard and sleek as her fingers dug into them, urging him deeper. She sighed and wished he would come back to bed. She could not get enough of him, no matter how the realisation of her need made her blush.

Finally, he pulled something from the wardrobe and turned back to her. She registered a velvet box before her attention went lower. He wanted her as much as she wanted him.

Pleasure and satisfaction were twin flames of warmth in her heart. She flung back the covers to welcome him back, but though his gaze ranged over her exposed flesh, he held back.

His eyes met hers, and she saw the desire he did nothing to hide. 'Give me a moment, love. Then I will service you.'

Her cheeks burned at his description for their loving. 'Am I that greedy?'

He grinned and sat on the bed, rubbing one palm along her flank. 'Yes, but that's a good thing.' He released her and flipped open the box. 'For you.'

A golden citrine pendant carved in the likeness of a lion lay in the satin interior. Ruby eyes flashed.

''Tis beautiful.' She ran one finger along the smooth flank of the beast.

'Like you. A lioness who will protect those she loves at all cost.' He lifted it from the box. 'Sit up so I can fasten it.'

She did. His fingers were soft on her nape. Then the heavy jewel settled between her naked breasts, cool against her heated flesh.

He cupped the pendant in one hand, his knuckles brushing her skin. ''Tis perfect.'

She smiled at him. 'Thank you.'

'Wear it as a reminder of my love for you—and our unborn child.'

As his fingers wandered over her stomach and rested with his hand cupping the small mound that was the only evidence of their child, she sighed. 'Are you glad?'

He did not pretend to misunderstand. 'More than I can say, Jenna, my love.' His eyes clouded for a moment. 'My only regret is that I could not get past my hatred to realise how important you and a family with you are to me. I am sorry you felt you could not tell me sooner.'

She covered his hand with hers. ''Tis all right, Duncan. I love you.'

He caught her hand and raised it to his lips. 'I don't deserve you.' He kissed the tip of each of her fingers, going back to the fourth finger of her left hand.

The tears slipped from her eyes. 'Yes, you do, my love.'

He lay down beside her, one leg rubbing hers. Soon they joined again.

Jenna knew she would never have enough of this man.

Chapter Eighteen

Burke did not smile at her, but his old eyes twinkled as he announced her. 'Lady Byrne.'

Jenna did smile at him. She swept past the old retainer into her father's drawing room. 'Papa…' she moved to him '…I am sorry it has taken so long for me to return your visit.'

He took her outstretched hands and drew her to him, kissing her on the cheek. 'Jenna, child, do not fret. I miss you, but another man comes before me. As it should be.'

'Just as another woman comes before me.' She freed one hand and patted his arm.

'Ahem.'

Jenna twisted around. 'Oh, Captain Lord Seller, I had not realised you were here.'

He had been sitting in the tall-backed brown damask chair that was pulled close to the roaring fire. The large wings of the chair helped to keep heat focused on the occupant, but they also hid the person.

Seller stood with his back to the fireplace and gave

her a curt bow. 'Lady Byrne. I wish I were not here, so you and his lordship could visit privately.'

She inclined her head. 'Thank you, Captain.' She gave her father a fond glance. 'We do not see nearly as much of each other now as I would like.'

'Come, come,' the viscount said, his narrow cheeks tinged with red. 'Burke will bring refreshments. Neither of you came to expound on our relationship, Jenna.'

'True.'

She took another chair pulled close to the fire and held her hands to the warmth. The comfort of Duncan's modern hunting box had spoiled her to the discomforts of a stone castle in spring.

Captain Seller remained standing. 'I must be on my way, Lord Ayre.'

'Surely you can have a glass of wine to fortify you against the cold,' Papa said, ringing the bell for Burke.

Indecision flitted across Seller's harshly angled face. 'One glass, my lord, then I must be gone. As I told you, my informant says this is the night.'

Foreboding chilled Jenna's already cold flesh. Duncan was smuggling a Jacobite out tonight.

'Something special is happening tonight?' She hoped her voice sounded light and only mildly curious, as she would be about any activity going on.

Seller looked at her.

Burke entered with a silver tray. He set it on the table near Jenna. She might no longer live here, but to him she was the mistress of the house. The butler withdrew and Jenna busied herself with biscuits and the port for the men. It was all she could do not to ask Seller again.

Her father took the plate she handed him. 'Captain

Seller was just telling me he has heard a Jacobite is to be smuggled out this evening.'

Jenna's knuckles turned white where she held the tea-pot handle. 'Really?'

Seller frowned as though he had not wanted Viscount Ayre to say anything. 'Yes.' He drank down his port.

Jenna made herself take a sip of tea, not surprised that it had no flavour. 'How do you know? I would think whoever is doing it would not bandy about the information.'

He set his glass carefully down. He looked at the viscount, then back to Jenna. 'I suppose that, being his lordship's daughter, you are interested in catching the perpetrators.'

She did her best to look serious without looking dismayed. 'Of course, Captain. My father is a loyal follower of the Crown.'

'So you must be as well,' Seller finished. 'It stands to reason. As is your husband, but the fewer who know, the better.'

'He is my husband.'

Seller shrugged. 'Yes, but I am not as sure of him as I am of his lordship.' He indicated the viscount with a nod.

Jenna carefully set down her still full cup of tea. 'If you insist.'

'I must.'

Viscount Ayre stood. 'Let me refill your glass, Seller, while you tell us more.'

The Captain looked as though he might protest, but instead handed his empty glass to her father. 'Nelly at the Whore's Eye is my informant. She told me yesterday that another Jacobite will be smuggled out tonight.' He paused to take the now full glass from the viscount, then took a long drink. 'She says the man will be going with a group of smugglers who work between here and France.'

'My goodness.' Jenna did not have to feign surprise. That Nelly was betraying Duncan was a shock. A dangerous one. 'Has she been giving you information all along?'

Seller shook his head. 'No—that is the strange part. It was just recently that she sought me out. Before this we knew Jacobites were using this area to hide and flee to France from, but we never knew when.' He set down his empty glass. 'That is why my troops and I are out at all hours. As it is, we have not caught one.'

'Not for lack of trying,' Viscount Ayre said, sipping his port.

Jenna nodded, unable to speak while she absorbed Seller's words and their import. Nelly was not to be trusted. But worse than that, Duncan needed to know. Immediately.

Seller stood and bowed to the viscount. 'Thank you for your kind words, my lord. We knew there was smuggling going on, and I had decided the fugitives might be going with them, but now 'tis confirmed. She has even told me which cove they will be working out of tonight.'

Jenna hoped she still looked politely interested. Her face felt frozen. She wanted to jump up and run from the room, ordering her horse be brought around immediately. She looked at her father, who looked at her. She forced a smile and hoped it did not look sickly.

Her father stood. 'What if I join you, Captain Seller? It has been a long time since I went on a mission for the Crown, and I find myself intrigued by your plans for tonight.'

For a moment, Seller looked as though he would refuse. 'Thank you, Viscount Ayre. That is not necessary.'

'Oh, no, Seller, I want to go. 'Twill give me something to do. Make me feel like I continue to earn my title and this castle. All given to me by the King for service.'

Jenna doubted if Captain Seller heard the irony and sadness in her father's tone. Few people realised how truly sorry Papa was over what he had done as a young man.

Captain Seller bowed. 'If you insist.'

Jenna stood, thinking this was the time for her to escape. Every second was precious. 'I will leave you two to decide how to go about this evening.'

She moved to her father and stood on tiptoe to kiss him. She took his hands in hers and squeezed, trying to tell him without words how grateful she was to him for doing this. She knew he would do everything he could to stall Seller and to even make the Captain and his men miss the rendezvous.

'Take care, my dear.' The viscount squeezed her hands back. Turning to Seller, he said, 'Please excuse us, Captain. I want to see my only child to the door.'

Seller stood his ground, but the look on his face said he was impatient. He looked like a dog being held tightly on a leash when it wanted to rush forward.

The viscount took Jenna's arm and guided her to the front door and outside where they could speak without being overheard by Seller. 'This is a dangerous situation from the look on your face.'

Jenna nodded, finding it difficult to speak through the tightness in her chest. 'Oh, Papa, this is awful.'

He put a finger on her lips. 'Don't tell me anything. The less I know the better. I will do my best to delay him.'

She nodded again. Thankfully the groom brought Rosebud. Jenna used the servant's help to mount. Without a backward look, she urged the mare into a gallop.

Duncan was going out this afternoon. He had not planned on returning home until after the Jacobite was safely on the boat headed to France. She had to get home before he left or she might not be able to find him in time.

Over an hour later, Jenna acknowledged that Duncan was gone. None of the servants knew where he was. He could be anywhere. He had not told her his plans because they had decided if she was not participating, then the less she knew the better for everyone. How she regretted that choice now.

Neither of them had imagined that Nelly from the Whore's Eye would betray him. If only she had told him what Nelly had said the night they smuggled Gavin out. It seemed a lifetime ago.

The sun was going down and darkness turning the cold day to a very cold night. Plus there would be no moon.

Perfect for smugglers.

But it was too early.

Jenna put a protective hand over her stomach. She did not show yet. They had decided she was not to participate because she carried their babe. But as much as she wanted a child and would love that child, if Duncan was not with her to raise their baby, then her life would be empty.

She stood up. Even if it meant endangering their unborn child, she had to try to find Duncan before Seller and his troops did.

Still wearing the riding habit she had donned to visit Papa, a forest green, she grabbed a black cape. She would be nearly impossible to see in the approaching night.

Being early spring, the days were lengthening. It would be later in the night before Duncan and the Jacobite would make for the pickup location. She would go to the Whore's Eye and confront Nelly. The woman obviously knew where the rendezvous site was. If she could tell Captain Seller, then she *would* tell Jenna. Or else.

Jenna guided Rosebud in the direction of the Whore's Eye. Hopefully her father could delay Seller in his gathering of troops long enough for Jenna to get the same information from Nelly.

She kept Rosebud at a canter rather than a gallop. They had miles to go.

Dusk shaded the land. Clouds skimmed across the lavender-and-slate sky. Jenna shivered in her riding habit. It seemed she was always cold—except when she was with Duncan.

The smell and taste of salt air came with the ocean breeze. She was nearly at the tavern. From there it would be a short ride to the location. She hoped.

Time was precious.

Jenna slid from Rosebud's back and handed the reins to the stable boy. She did not care if someone saw her. But, more importantly, she doubted that any English soldiers would be here. They would all be with Seller.

Gripping her cape tightly to her neck, Jenna strode to the kitchen entrance. There was no sense in allowing all the customers see her tear into Nelly, either.

The warmth of the kitchen was like an enveloping

blanket after the brisk chill of her ride. Her glasses, which she had put on after getting off Rosebud so that she would be able to see Nelly clearly, fogged. Exasperated, she yanked them off and wiped them on her cape before putting them back on. She wanted to clearly see the other woman's features.

She glanced at the cook who held a butcher's knife in mid-air. 'Good evening.'

The cook just stared at her. The boy turning the spit gaped. Jenna continued to the door that led to the bar area.

Pushing open the heavy oak door, she slipped inside the smoky, dim hallway. Raucous laughter and yelling filled the space. Someone walked her way.

Jenna squinted in the dim light. A female. Nelly. Her pulse sped up in anticipation of the coming confrontation.

All her instincts to help and heal were buried under her rage at this woman who had put Duncan in harm's way. Not a shred of softness or compassion remained.

The other woman made to edge around her, not recognising Jenna, but Jenna reached out and grabbed a handful of the woman's blouse. 'Not so fast, Nelly.'

Jenna was glad of the anger that lent her strength when the other woman yanked away. Jenna kept her grip. Pulling with all her weight, Jenna dragged Nelly down the hall to the first door she came to past the kitchen. She shoved Nelly against the wood hard enough that Nelly dropped the empty beer mugs she carried.

Jenna pushed her face into Nelly's. 'What did you tell Seller?'

Nelly glared at her. 'Stupid woman. I'm not gonna tell you.'

Jenna reached down and turned the knob so the door

swung open, then pushed Nelly through. The serving woman stumbled backwards and landed on the floor. Jenna crouched on top of her.

'Yes, you are.'

Nelly spat at her.

Jenna, seeing the woman purse her lips, had shifted so the mucus went over her shoulder. 'You will tell me or I will have the magistrate arrest you.'

'Hah! And I will tell him all about you and your new husband.' Bravado put flags of colour in Nelly's round cheeks.

Jenna leaned into her. 'Go ahead, Nelly. You know who the magistrate is. Do you really think he will do anything about your information?'

'Seller will.'

Jenna wanted to punch the woman in the face. She wanted to strangle her, but knew in her heart she could not. 'He will not be here for ever, Nelly. But I will. My husband will. My father the magistrate will.' She let the words sink in. 'Do you want to leave this area and start anew? It might be a wise thing to do if you do not tell me where the pickup point is.'

Nelly wiggled, but Jenna's knees were on either side and she still held the woman's blouse. Nelly tried to buck Jenna off. Fed up and running out of time, Jenna slapped her.

'Stop it!' Jenna panted. 'I do not have time for this. Where is the pickup point?'

Nelly swung at Jenna. Jenna caught her wrist and twisted and twisted some more. Nelly groaned.

'Tell me, Nelly.' Jenna had never thought herself capable of violence. But Duncan was in danger. 'Tell me.'

'So that you can turn me over to your father the magistrate?' she spat.

Jenna held both of Nelly's wrists and studied the other woman. Nelly's pupils were large and her lips thin. With a start, Jenna realised Nelly was scared. Instantly, Jenna's innate compassion returned.

More gently than she would have thought possible, Jenna said, 'If you tell me, I will see to it that you get enough money to leave here and start over some place else. Enough money to be comfortable there.'

There was a long silence.

'Near Rockcliffe.' Nelly looked sullenly away. 'Get off me.'

Jenna rolled off Nelly and stood. 'I will see that you get the money by next week.'

Nelly got to her knees and up. 'Tomorrow. I need to be gone by tomorrow.'

Jenna frowned, not sure she could come up with that large an amount so quickly. Particularly given what was happening tonight.

'Tomorrow,' Nelly reiterated, 'or I'll find that captain and tell him about this.'

Jenna wondered if she could really trust this woman, but knew she had no choice. 'I will get you the money tomorrow. But if you double-cross me tonight, I will see to it that you are in the dungeon at de Warre Castle by tomorrow night.'

Nelly grunted, but said nothing.

Jenna did not wait to see what Nelly did. The woman would either tell Seller—provided she could find him— or not. Right now, Jenna had a rush against the captain and his troops. Hopefully, her father would be able to delay them enough.

* * *

Jenna and Rosebud reached the general area that Nelly had indicated. To the west, Jenna thought she could discern the gleam of starlight on water. Maybe not. But she did not see any moving figures or lantern light. Some of the tension that held her stiff in the saddle eased.

The wind picked up. She heard it sough through the beach grasses and a copse of trees that looked like mounded shadows. Her fingers fiddled with the reins.

Duncan might be there unless they were already headed for the site. Either way, it would be the best place to leave Rosebud. Everything else was flat except for rivulets and dunes in the sand.

She slid from the saddle. When the soldiers got here, they would search this area as it was the only place to offer concealment. She could not leave Rosebud here. Jenna had no choice.

She tied the reins to the saddle horn and gave the mare a light swat on the rump. Rosebud was trained to return home to de Warre castle. Jenna would have a long walk back, but there was no other option. If Rosebud were found by Seller, the man would know everything.

Jenna took a deep breath, gathering her determination about her like a cloak. She found a dead tree branch and started walking toward the firth, dragging the branch behind. It was the best she could do to get rid of her tracks. Hopefully, the rising wind would also help by shifting the sands.

It was difficult to walk on the giving and soft sand. Her calves ached before she got to the shore. The scents of sea and salt and marsh were strong. There were dry rivulets where the Firth had flooded and then withdrawn.

She stumbled and dropped the branch.

A shape loomed out of the ground not five feet from her. Her pulse jumped and she bit down on a scream. Wide eyed, her glasses having slipped off, she strained to see.

'Jenna!' Duncan's warm baritone whispered so softly that for a moment she thought she had imagined it. Then his arms were around her. 'What are you doing here, love?'

She clung to him. Her heart thundered. His chest rose and fell under her cheek.

She caught her breath. 'Nelly betrayed you.'

He held her at arm's length. 'What?'

Nodding vigorously, she repeated, 'Nelly betrayed you. She told Seller about tonight. He is on his way here right now.'

Duncan's grip tightened. 'But why?'

Jenna marvelled at his ignorance. 'Because she is jealous.' She hung her head. 'She told me when we smuggled out Gavin that she would not let me have you.' She looked back up at him, noting the strong lines of his face in the starlight. 'I ignored her because at the time I did not think you cared enough for me to overcome what Papa did. Then I forgot about her.' She sighed. 'This is my fault.'

He pulled her back into the warmth of his embrace. 'No. 'Tis mine for trusting her.'

'You could not know. She was loyal until we married.'

'She was loyal afterwards—for a time.'

'But where is the Jacobite?' Jenna pulled away enough to look around him. 'We must get out of here. Papa is trying to delay Seller, but they will be here soon.'

'Ayre?'

'Yes, Papa.' His surprise at hearing that her father would do such a thing irritated her. 'He loves me and he knows how it would hurt me to lose you. Of course Papa.'

'I changed the plans. The tide is coming in and ordinarily the smugglers would have ridden it in and picked up my man.' He set her to his side. 'For some reason, I decided to walk out and meet them before the tide came in. The water will cover our footprints.' He shook himself. 'My hunches again. They have saved my life more than once.'

'So all we have to do is escape.' Relief eased the tension in Jenna's shoulders.

'If it were that easy,' Duncan murmured. 'I see a bobbing light inshore. That is likely Seller and his troops.'

She squinted. 'Why are they announcing themselves like that?'

Duncan shrugged. 'Who knows, but I am glad they are.'

Jenna edged close until her hips touched his. 'But what are we to do? There is no cover.'

'Aye.' His voice was a breath against her ear. 'There is marsh grass to our left and slightly closer in. If we can make it there, we might be safe.'

Instead of speaking, she nodded.

He took her hand in his and urged her to bend over to make as small a shadow as possible. She hurried behind him, her thighs aching from the stooped position. But her pounding heart gave her energy.

All the while the light came closer, jerking up and down and to the side. Jenna could make out figures. Horses whickered. She was glad she had sent Rosebud home. Men talked.

The soldiers were not as quiet as she would have

thought they would be. She could hear her father's voice and knew he was trying to warn them.

She and Duncan reached the marsh grass. It was several feet tall in areas. They lay on their stomachs. The cold wet sand penetrated her clothing. If they made it through this, she would have to throw out her riding habit.

She nearly giggled at the inane thought. She was so scared, she was not thinking straight. If they made it through this, a ruined riding habit was a small price to pay.

'Are you sure this is where they are?' Viscount Ayre's voice came on the breeze. He spoke loudly.

'Shh, my lord,' Seller's irritated voice replied.

Jenna smiled. The viscount was doing everything he could, and Seller was obviously regretting he had brought him. If their danger had not been so acute, Jenna would have laughed. Now, she only hoped her father could keep the English soldiers from scouring the area.

'The tide will be in soon,' the viscount continued in his loud voice. 'This entire beach will be flooded then. Surely this cannot be the place.'

Fear twisted Jenna's stomach. In their need to find shelter, she had forgotten what Duncan had said about the tide. If Seller and his soldiers did not leave soon, she and Duncan would drown.

She edged closer to her husband. She needed the warmth and the feel of him more than ever. Duncan put an arm around her and held her tight.

The sea wind whistled through the grass, blunting some of the noise made by the soldiers. She shivered in spite of Duncan's warmth.

'I don't see anyone,' the viscount said. His voice

seemed too close for comfort. 'We should go back before the tide finishes coming in.'

'They have to be here,' Seller argued, annoyance colouring his words. 'That tavern wench told me he would be here. She would not lie.'

'Perhaps she sent you on a diversion.' Her father's tone was insinuating. 'She might have planned for you to be here while the Jacobite left from another beach.'

'I want to search the entire beach before we give up.' Seller's words were determined.

They would see their tracks leading here. She gripped Duncan's hand until her own turned numb. If only Nelly had not betrayed Duncan. Now they would be caught and hung for treason. Not even her father would be able to save them.

And her baby.

She pressed her face into the rags covering Duncan's chest. His grip increased.

She heard splashing and realised Seller and Papa were coming toward them. The smell of burning fat and rushes churned her stomach. Joined with her fear, it was nearly impossible to keep from doubling over in sickness. That would certainly reveal them.

Jenna put her sleeve to her nose, hoping to block the scent. She gulped down the bile.

'I wouldn't go too far,' Viscount Ayre said, sounding too close for comfort. 'When the tide comes in, this area floods quickly. Already the sand is moist from the incoming water.'

Jenna felt Duncan shift away from her. Cold replaced the warmth where he had been. With a start, she realised he had drawn his pistol.

Apprehension turned her fingers to icicles. Not even Duncan could hold an entire troop of soldiers at bay. Her papa would help and die trying.

Misery and anger mixed equally. If she survived, she wanted to make Nelly pay. But she had given her word to protect the woman and give her money. Right now, she felt like breaking it.

'I say, Seller…' Viscount Ayre's voice intruded on her thoughts '…what is that?'

'What?' Seller sounded impatient and his tone bordered on insolent.

'I see something toward the south.' The viscount's voice faded. Then the sounds of something falling in the water muffled the noise of the surf hitting the beach.

Jenna tensed. Had her father fallen in the rising sea water?

'What are you doing?' Seller sounded furious. 'I brought you along because you asked and because I thought you deserved to be here when I catch The Ferguson. But you are like a bumbling idiot.'

Cold and deadly, her father replied, 'You overstep yourself, Captain.'

'Not nearly as much as you, Viscount Ayre.'

The encroaching waves lapped at Jenna's boots. She realised she was lying in several inches of water. Jenna knew that soon she and Duncan would have to sit up, their heads above the marsh grass.

'We must get out of here.' The viscount's words were an order. 'There is no sense in drowning ourselves. The wench obviously lied to you, Seller.'

'Blast that serving wench.' Seller's voice boded no good for Nelly. 'When I get to the Whore's Eye, I will see that she learns the folly of making a dupe of me.'

They were leaving. Now if they only left in time.

Jenna strained to hear the splashing of the soldiers' boots. Their curses were loud in the night air.

The water was high enough that Jenna had to support herself on her elbows. Please, let the English soldiers go. She and Duncan had too much to live for.

If they survived tonight, she was going to insist that he stop smuggling Jacobites. He had a family now. Someone else could do this. He had done all he could. Now he needed to devote himself to her and their unborn child. She would demand that he do so.

The water inched up.

She strained to hear the soldiers. The splash and clop of horses' hoofs and the neighs of discontent the animals made as the water rose. She dared not look over the marsh grass to see.

Duncan shifted so that one elbow supported him and his pistol was in the opposite hand, above the water. They were running out of time.

The salty water lapped at Jenna's raised chin. Soon it would cover her nose. She shuddered.

Something brushed her hand. She jerked and fell into the water. Water rushed into her mouth. She resisted the urge to flap her arms. Instead, she flattened her hands to the sand, sinking inches down, and pushed up until her head was once more above the water. She was thankful for her leather gloves that kept the worst of the scratchy sand from her skin.

She spat the water out.

Duncan gently touched her shoulder. Comfort flowed from him—and courage. They had only a few minutes more.

When Jenna knew she had to sit up or drown,

Duncan took her arm and lifted her. She struggled to her feet, staying crouched. Her glasses were gone and her hair hung around her face. She had lost her hat long ago. She hurt everywhere.

She squinted ahead and turned her head from side to side. She did not see any light. But that did not mean they were safe. Seller might have ordered the lantern doused and they had not heard him.

Anything might happen.

Her teeth chattered and her back ached. Her stomach churned.

Duncan motioned for her to stay. She nodded, catching his free hand and squeezing. His skin was cold and clammy. Disguised as a labourer, he had worn wool gloves. They were gone.

To ease her back, she knelt. The water was to her neck, but 'twas easier than crouching.

With wide eyes she watched Duncan ease through the grass and prowl the immediate area. The sky was blanketed with clouds, threatening rain, so there was almost no starlight. She quickly lost sight of him.

He had not returned when she had to stand. Her clothing was soaked through, the heavy wool pulling her down. Her boots clung to her calves like clammy hands. The breeze was a slap in the face.

They needed to be away soon. She did not know how to swim, and even if she did, her clothing would drag her to the bottom. But she dared not move until Duncan returned.

She felt an eddy of small rivulets hit her hips and the sloshing sounds of someone labouring through the water. She hoped it was her husband.

Duncan appeared, still holding the pistol. He took

her hand and pulled her toward him. His lips to her ear, he whispered, 'I think we are safe.'

She nodded, thankful for the small amount of warmth his breath had given her. But when he pulled her with him, her skirts threatened to pull her down. Nearly sobbing from exhaustion, Jenna clung to his free arm. Duncan dared not lift her and encumber himself in case he had to fight.

They waded through the rising tide. Jenna laboured from the exertion. Duncan's chest rose and fell in a steady rhythm. Neither wasted energy speaking. They were not safe yet.

Gradually the water got shallower. Then Jenna could lift her feet out of the water with each step. Her skirts dragged behind her in the sand. Her boots squelched. She was miserable.

But Duncan was safe.

They reached the trees, and Duncan turned to her. 'Why did you risk yourself and the babe?' He tightened his grip on her. 'I told you not to do anything like that— ever. No matter what.'

She looked up at him. 'I had to. You know that, Duncan. Without you, what kind of life would the child and I have? The one you and your mother lived. Would you wish that on us? I had to warn you.'

He groaned and bent his head until his mouth found hers. He tasted of salt water and cold night. He tasted wonderful. She clung to him.

He released her lips and stared down at her. 'Don't ever do anything like this again.'

She shook her head sadly. 'I will do anything necessary to protect you.'

He released her and stalked away, his anger driving

him to rake his fingers through his hair. Returning to her, he said, 'You would risk our child again?'

She nodded. 'I told you, Duncan. You are more important to me than anything else in this world. I would do the same again if you were in danger.'

'Ah, Jenna. You are stubborn. No wonder I love you.' He grabbed her arms and stopped just short of shaking her. 'But you frustrate me to no end.'

She wanted to ask him to stop smuggling out Jacobites. Selfish as it was, it was the only way to protect him. But she knew better. It was his life. She bit her tongue.

'Ah, Jenna, love.' He crooned her name as he pulled her to him. 'This is my calling. This is what I do with my life. Did.' He sighed, the movement of his chest against her body strong. 'But you are my life now. You and our unborn child.'

She held her breath, afraid to hope.

He lifted her face. 'I love you more than anything, Jenna.' Sadness darkened his eyes for a moment. Then he smiled. 'I could not live with myself if harm came to you because of what I do.'

She watched him, the hope she had suppressed beginning to rise.

'I am going to stop, I am going to do something else with my life.'

Relief and love for this stubborn man suffused her. But she did not want him to be miserable for the rest of his life. 'Are you sure, Duncan?'

His lips twisted. 'Yes, Jenna. I value you more than anything else in the world.'

With a sigh, she stood on tiptoe and pressed her mouth to his. 'Thank you,' she whispered.

'I will find someone else to take my place. Someone with no ties to anyone here so that he cannot be betrayed by Nelly.' Bitterness tinged his words. 'How did you find out?'

She ached at his pain over the betrayal before smiling at the memory of her father's antics. 'Seller told Papa. But he won't do so again.'

Duncan chuckled. 'No, he won't.' He sobered. 'We would not be standing here without your father.'

'I know.' She hesitated, but had to know. 'Will you forgive him now?'

Duncan ran his fingers through his hair. 'Yes. He saved your life and our child's.'

'And yours,' she said softly.

'And mine.'

She reached up and stroked the wet hair from his brow. Exhaustion swept over Jenna, making her sway, as relief took all the energy from her body. She put a hand on his shoulder to steady herself.

He put his arms around her and bent to kiss her. One hand rested on the slight swell of her belly. 'I love you, Jenna McNabb, Lady Byrne.'

She sighed and gave herself up to his strength and his love. 'And I you.'

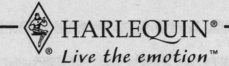

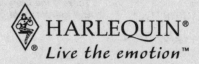

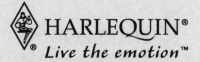

HARLEQUIN®
INTRIGUE®

BREATHTAKING ROMANTIC SUSPENSE

Shared dangers and passions lead to electrifying romance and heart-stopping suspense!

Every month, you'll meet six new heroes who are guaranteed to make your spine tingle and your pulse pound. With them you'll enter into the exciting world of Harlequin Intrigue— where your life is on the line and so is your heart!

THAT'S INTRIGUE— ROMANTIC SUSPENSE AT ITS BEST!

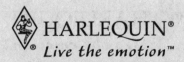

HARLEQUIN®
Live the emotion™

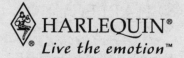

HARLEQUIN®
Presents

The world's bestselling romance series...
The series that brings you your favorite authors,
month after month:

Helen Bianchin...Emma Darcy
Lynne Graham...Penny Jordan
Miranda Lee...Sandra Marton
Anne Mather...Carole Mortimer
Susan Napier...Michelle Reid

and many more uniquely talented authors!

Wealthy, powerful, gorgeous men...
Women who have feelings just like your own...
The stories you love, set in exotic, glamorous locations...

HARLEQUIN®
Presents

Seduction and Passion Guaranteed!

HPDIR104